LESSONS IN OBEDIENCE

'And your knickers, please, Lucy.'

'But Mr Mortensen, I –'

'Now, please, Lucy,' I interrupted.

She hesitated another second, then hooked her fingers into the waistband and slipped them down her thighs. She stepped out of them and turned quickly, bundling them into a ball in her hand.

'Give those to me, please.'

'But Mr Mortensen, they –'

'Lucy, please do as you are told. Hand them to me.'

Her eyes darted down nervously as she dropped the incriminating little bundle into my hand. I opened them out fully and displayed the clear stain that so embarrassed her. I raised them to my nostrils to inhale her sweet scent while she stared at the ground, her cheeks a blazing bright crimson that spilled down her neck to her breasts.

LESSONS IN OBEDIENCE

Lucy Golden

This book is a work of fiction.
In real life, make sure you practise safe sex.

First published in 2000 by
Nexus
Thames Wharf Studios
Rainville Road
London W6 9HA

www.nexus-books.co.uk

Typeset by TW Typesetting, Plymouth, Devon

Printed and bound by
Cox & Wyman Ltd, Reading, Berks

ISBN 0 352 33550 5

To my Teacher

I would never have become the person that I am
if I had not received the education that I did.

I know how it was for me.
I hope it was like this for you.

1

Monday

She first appeared a little after three o'clock on a bright
warm afternoon in May, the fourth consecutive fine day in
what was turning into one of those glorious spells that
show winter finally to be behind us. My last work, a
tedious although well-paid piece on a new type of oil
filtration plant, was finally complete, and I could embark
on something new, something which looked to be both
more challenging and more interesting: the translation of a
recently discovered collection of Italian erotic poetry from
the late eighteenth century that just might have been the
work of Giovanni Casanova de Seingalt himself. I had
settled in my study with the French windows open on to
the lawn, welcoming some clean fresh air, and had spread
open the source, reference books and my notepad on my
desk when the doorbell rang.

I was irritated at the interruption, half minded to ignore
it, but finally stamped down the hall to discover a young
woman hovering nervously on my doorstep. She looked to
be barely twenty, a little over five foot six inches tall, of
slim build and with fair hair drawn back into a ponytail,
with some escaping straggles hanging round her quivering,
anxious face. Guessing that she had come to try to sell me
something that I neither needed nor wanted, I put on a
blackly unwelcoming expression.

'Mr Mortensen?' she asked. 'My name's Lucy Golden
and I'm David Palmer's fiancée. I wonder if I could speak
to you for a moment.'

The words flowed out as if rehearsed, and seeing the look of terror in her face did melt my animosity a little. I stood aside and gestured for her to come in but still she hesitated, fiddled with her bag and glanced over her shoulder for some support or perhaps salvation before she finally muttered thanks and stepped into the hall. I closed the heavy door behind her and showed her into my study, where she perched on the front edge of an armchair, still twisting the strap of her shoulder bag round her fingers.

David Palmer, the man who was apparently her fiancé, had been dealing with an insurance claim that I had made following a storm which had caused extensive damage to one attic room of my house and to a number of fine and rare books stored there. I had been most dissatisfied with the speed and efficiency with which the claim had been handled and when I expressed these views to Mr Palmer, his reaction was insolent indifference. Eventually I was so angered by the total lack of progress that I complained to Graham Worthing, the chairman. He was a man I happened to know through my particular area of study – late medieval and early Reformation erotica – but I had acted on the spur of the moment, and was ashamed of myself afterwards. I do not like using a personal friendship in this way.

I was told that the insurance company had reprimanded David Palmer and, after swiftly settling the claim, were considering further disciplinary action against the young man. Although I had nothing against him personally, and no doubt it was his youth and inexperience that had led him into these mistakes, I have to say that I did feel some action was necessary since he had clearly failed to behave or deal with the matter in a proper and professional manner. The young man's fiancée now sat shivering in my study, glancing intermittently up at me and round at the towering bookshelves which encircled her, while she tried to address her problem.

'Mr Mortensen, I am not here to apologise. I do understand that this has all gone rather wrong and I know that it is partly David's fault, but I just want to see if there is anything I can do to put it right. It looks as if he is going to lose his job and I don't know what we will do then. We are getting married in less than three weeks and we had been hoping to buy a house. We've paid a deposit and everything, but if he loses his job, well, we couldn't get the mortgage.'

'I understand, Miss Golden, but I do not think you appreciate what I have been put through. This has gone on since November, getting worse every day. All that time I have had to endure a stream of people coming in here, prying into my private life, examining my books, thumbing through them, ostensibly attempting to assess their value. It is really only in the last couple of weeks that, at last, they are beginning to put it right. As for it being partly Mr Palmer's fault, I am afraid that I cannot agree with you there. I consider it to have been entirely his fault. I also believe that the company's senior management is of a similar view.'

'Oh, yes, I know, yes, they do, and I know you have been very badly inconvenienced, but if David gets the sack now, it won't undo what has gone wrong before, will it? It will just make him suffer as well. And me, too. It just seems that the result is out of all proportion. I am sure you would not want to cause all that if it could be avoided.'

'Miss Golden, your fiancé has made a succession of serious mistakes which he has neither attempted to rectify nor even taken seriously. He needs to learn from that.'

'But he has, Mr Mortensen, he has! I'm sure you're not a vindictive man, and I just feel that if only you knew how important all this is to us, what it all means to us, you would give David another chance.'

Her words still gushed out in a naive torrent that believed everything could be put right if she just said 'sorry'.

'How important is it, then?'

'Well, very important. You know, it means everything.'

'Everything?'

'Yes! If he loses his job, I don't know how he'd get another one, and we would lose the house and lose all our

3

savings that we paid as a deposit and then I don't know where we could live or what would happen. It really is our whole lives.' Her voice trembled away into silence.

'I see.' I considered this for a moment. Although I was not convinced the consequences would be anything like as severe as she presented them, she clearly believed that they were. However, although she was right in saying that I am not a vindictive man, I had been put to a great deal of trouble, prolonged over several months, and she did not seem to have any idea of the full consequences of her fiancé's failings.

So I considered the little figure huddled in front of me while she hoped and waited for me to relent. She tried to keep her eyes down but glanced up as often as she dared with such contrition, such pleading, that any heart would have broken. Her huge round eyes were almost bursting into flood; her fingers were wringing at the strap of her bag and a devil settled on my shoulder.

'All right,' I said, 'let's try this. Take off your blouse.'

'What?' For almost the first time, she stopped staring at her twisting, twining fingers and her great bright eyes were directed at me.

'Take off your blouse,' I repeated, keeping my voice soft and calm.

Her fingers were finally still and the expression of strangled incredulity intensified. 'I'm not going to do that!'

'Fine.' I stood up, disappointed, to tell the truth, and a little hurt at the rejection but still managing to keep an even tone. 'Fine, then kindly leave my house straight away and don't waste any more of my time with exaggerated stories of how desperately important all this is to you when in fact it clearly means less than a flash of your precious little tits. Goodbye.'

'But Mr Mortensen –'

'Goodbye, Miss Golden.' I held open the study door for her.

She picked up her bag, pushed past me and, head down, scuttled down the dim hallway towards the front door. There she reached up to the shining brass latch and paused. A second passed. Two seconds. She hadn't moved, and the devil rubbed his hands in anticipation.

'Do you really mean that?'

'Mean what?'

'Just what you said, you know, "a flash of my . . . of my breasts".'

'I didn't say breasts.'

'No.'

'What did I say?'

She hesitated. 'Tits.'

'What? Speak up, girl, don't mumble.'

'Tits,' she repeated louder.

'That's better. Now what is your question, exactly?'

She swallowed. 'If I let you see my breasts, would you agree not to go any further with your complaint? You'd have to promise just to look and not touch me or anything.'

I considered the little figure standing in front of me. 'Tell me, Lucy, how much do you think it would cost me to go down to the beach?'

She was puzzled. 'I don't know. It would depend how you went there.'

'Let's say I was lavish and took a taxi.'

'Well, I don't know. About ten pounds or something.'

'Right. And if I went to the beach, would I see many girls without their tops on?'

'Yes, I suppose so. Some.'

'So are you suggesting that the equivalent of ten pounds would be a fair compensation to me? Because if that is what you mean, why not just offer me ten pounds?'

She suddenly realised where this conversation had been leading her. 'No.'

'When this claim all started to go wrong, caused by the utter incompetence of your fiancé, I had no idea how long it would all take or how much worse it would get before I was able to continue as things had been beforehand. Every day, the business seemed to be getting more involved and I was paying a greater and greater price for a fault which was entirely caused by someone else. If you were willing to undergo a similar experience, then, yes, I would consider withdrawing my complaint. But, just as I did not know at the start how it would end, no more can you.'

She looked up at me, weighing up all the options. 'But I don't know what you will do,' she wailed.

'No. Just as I didn't. The only difference, Miss Golden, was that you had a choice. I did not. Goodbye.'

She hesitated again, then her hand dropped down from the latch and slowly she crept back into the study and placed her shoulder bag down on the chair where she had been sitting. The devil smirked and flew; his work here was done.

For a moment she was entirely stationary but then she glanced over and finally turned away to present her back to me and face the wall. I watched the movements of her arms as she unbuttoned the pale blue blouse and dropped it neatly on the settee. Across her narrow back stretched a thin white bra strap and after another fractional hesitation, her hands reached round, fumbled, and unhooked it. She slipped the bra off and dropped it down on top of the blouse. Then slowly turned to face me, her hands clasped together under her chin and her slender arms pulled up in front of her. Her lips were moving as if she wanted to speak, but then she suddenly committed herself and thrust her hands straight down by her sides. She continued staring down at the floor, not moving, and I walked round to sit back in the chair behind my desk.

'Come over here, Lucy. Stand in front of me.'

She walked across, little nervous steps, but resolutely kept her arms by her sides.

Her breasts were small, finely rounded swellings perched proudly on her slim chest and topped by pert little nipples that reacted to their sudden exposure by erecting delightfully as I watched. Most attractive of all was that although she was pale-skinned, a light golden tan showed where she had evidently been enjoying the weekend sun, and yet her breasts were as white as pure silk. This sign of her pure modesty demonstrated clearly that she was not in the habit of letting others see her. I made no secret of studying her, but smiled, enjoying the embarrassment in her eyes as she weakly smiled back and then quickly looked down.

'You have very beautiful breasts, Lucy. Very beautiful indeed.'

'Thank you, Mr Mortensen.' Her voice was little more than a whisper.

'Does your fiancé appreciate them?'

Her blush deepened even further. 'Yes, Mr Mortensen, I think so.'

'What does he do with them? Does he stroke them? Kiss them?'

'Yes, sometimes, Mr Mortensen. Both.'

'He kisses both of them?'

'Oh, no,' she corrected hurriedly, most embarrassed at her mistake. 'I mean he strokes as well as kisses . . .' Her embarrassment devoured her vocabulary.

'But not both of them? Only one breast? Why is that?' I pretended to misunderstand.

'No, I mean he does that to both of them.' Her voice was again trailing away in its confusion and increasing embarrassment.

'I see. Well, yes, in that case clearly he does appreciate them. And do you enjoy that?'

'Yes.'

'Good. That is nice to hear. Would you like him to be doing that to you now?'

'Well, no. I mean. Not here, not now.'

'Why not?'

'Well, I would be embarrassed with you here watching me.'

'Yes. I imagine you would. But if I weren't here, would you like him to do that?'

'Yes, I suppose so.'

'Because your nipples are very erect, aren't they?'

She said nothing, but bit her lip and continued to stare at the floor in front of her feet.

'Are they often like that? I mean, some girls,' I continued quickly, offering this up as a point of interest, although the topic was causing Lucy something closer to anguish. 'Some girls have nipples which erect very easily, in fact are erect

7

almost all the time, and others have nipples which hardly erect at all. Which sort are yours, Lucy?'

'I think – I mean, I suppose they are the sort that erect quite easily.' She whispered again, still not daring to look up at me.

'They certainly seem to. Yes indeed.'

Her arms were beginning to snake forward as she willed herself to keep her hands down by her sides when every instinct screamed at her to cover herself up.

'Keep your arms still, please, Lucy. In fact, it would probably be better if you put your hands behind your back.'

She obeyed, meekly, and glanced up at me again as I continued to study her breasts openly.

'Do you find this embarrassing, Lucy?'

'Yes, Mr Mortensen.'

'Why?'

'Well, I don't know you at all, and it just seems quite wrong to be standing here like this.'

'Are you quite shy normally, then?'

'Yes, I suppose I am.'

'But do you go topless on the beach?'

'Only once or twice. I don't normally.'

'Why not?'

'I don't know, I just don't like it. People stare at me.'

'They are probably admiring you.' She made no response. 'So you find it embarrassing that I am admiring you now.'

She said nothing, but nodded slightly.

'Hmm, I can imagine you do.' I paused a moment and looked at my watch. 'Yet, it is less than five minutes since you took your blouse off, during which time I have not touched you. I have merely looked at you and we have talked about your breasts. And this is just one day. Can you imagine how I felt when it was the other way around? When your fiancé, and several of his colleagues, came here and studied my private things? And I should tell you that their examination was not merely visual.' I paused, so that she could draw her own inference. 'No, they also fingered them.' She blushed. 'Handled them.' She flinched. 'Spent several minutes poking, prodding and poring over each one.' She hunched her shoulders together in defence. 'And not just on one occasion, oh, no. Let me see now.' I turned to check my desk diary while I considered an appropriate number: ten seemed too round, twelve perhaps too many. 'On eleven separate times that they came here. Do you begin to understand what I have been put through as a result of your fiancé's incompetence? The embarrassment I have felt at this intrusion?'

'Yes, Mr Mortensen. I'm sorry. I really am very sorry.'

'Well, I am glad to hear it, because I really think you should be.'

'Yes.'

'So how old are you, Lucy?'

'Nineteen.'

'Isn't that a bit young to be getting married? How long have you been engaged?'

She hesitated a moment. 'Eight months, but we've known each other since we were at school.'

'I see, and it's in three weeks, this wedding?'

'Yes. That's why it's so dreadful all this problem happening now.'

'Do you plan to have children? After you're married, of course?'

She blushed. 'Oh yes, I mean, not at first, because we can't afford to, but we would like to have some later.'

I nodded. The girl had obviously thought everything out. 'You mentioned that you and David are planning to buy a house. Do you not live together now?'

'Oh no! I live with my mother.'

'I see. And are you working, Lucy?'

'Yes, I work at the tea shop, along by the castle.'

'What do you do there?'

'Everything, I suppose. I mean, I'm a waitress, really, but I wash up and clean as well if they need me.'

'Why are you not there now?'

'I have just finished for today. I do mornings and lunchtimes in the week from ten o'clock until three o'clock and Saturday and Sunday afternoons until six.'

9

'I see.' I knew the Castlegate Tearooms only vaguely, because although I visited the castle itself quite frequently, having a friend and co-historian in the curator, Duncan McQuillan, I had not been inside the tearooms more than once or twice at most. I remembered it as a small place directly opposite the gatehouse with no more than a dozen tables and only a couple of staff on duty at any time. I certainly did not recollect ever seeing Lucy there, although I did recall that the waitresses wore the traditional black skirts with embroidered white blouses, lace-trimmed at the collar and cuffs. In all, very attractive to the more traditional taste. I tried to picture her in the uniform and decided I would have to go there more often in future. I would enjoy having her serving me and being able to recall, and doubtless find a way to remind her of, this pleasant afternoon when she had permitted me to study her breasts.

'Will that be all, Mr Mortensen? Please may I go now?' I realised I had been sitting staring at her, daydreaming for some time, and stumbled back to the present.

'No, not really, Lucy. I think I would like some tea. Kindly make some and bring it out into the garden; I will be working out there. Make a nice pot. You'll find everything in the kitchen. Bring a cup for yourself as well. No,' I added, as she moved to put back on her clothes. 'You can stay like that.'

'But somebody might see me!' she protested.

'Oh, yes,' I agreed. 'Quite possibly.' I picked up my book and headed out into the garden.

In fact she was in little danger of being seen because although my house is in the centre of the old part of town and fronts directly on to the street, as was common in the eighteenth century, the back garden is extensive and is entirely surrounded by a substantial brick wall over nine feet high. However, I saw no need for her to know that at this stage.

Once in the sun, I pulled a chair out to the centre of the lawn. Although the garden is almost half an acre, several mature trees, including the seven limes after which it is named, line the edges of the lawn, and consequently it

10

often receives full sun only in the centre. Here it was quite open and would certainly do little to reassure Lucy that she was unobserved.

Some ten minutes later I pretended not to watch as she appeared at the French windows, a full tray gripped in her hands and her breasts plainly visible behind the innocent arrangement of teapot, jug and cups. She hesitated before stepping out but, finally satisfied, put her head up and strode out across the terrace, down the steps and over the lawn to me.

'Ah, lovely,' I said. 'Bring up one of those chairs for yourself.'

Lucy carefully placed the tray on the low table and fetched a chair from under the cedar tree at the side of the lawn.

'Thank you, Lucy, that is very kind of you. Now, will you be mother?'

I watched as she carefully picked up the saucers, placed a cup in each, which rattled slightly in her grasp, and started to pour the tea, still ensuring that she did not spill a drop. It was as she handed a cup to me that I noticed something.

'Thank you. That is a very elaborate engagement ring.'

'Thank you. David doesn't like it much. He thinks it is a Victorian habit, as if he was my master and owned me. He thinks it isn't really suitable nowadays.'

'But you disagree?'

'Well, I understand what he means, but a ring is nice; it shows somebody is proud of you, I suppose, and maybe having a man to look after you is not so bad.'

In retrospect, I should have paid more attention to that comment, but at the time I was thinking of something else as I watched her pouring her tea and refilling the pot from the hot-water jug. 'I see you are concentrating hard.'

She frowned. 'Yes, Mr Mortensen.'

'Do you know how I can tell that?'

'No.'

'Because your nipples are no longer erect. They have at last relaxed.'

11

Of course this reference had the immediate, and intended, effect of so increasing her embarrassment that not only did the sweet nipples stand up again immediately, but she shook the saucer so hard that she slopped tea on to the tray and I had to send her inside again for a cloth. It was a real treat to watch her skirt flying as she scampered across the lawn on the way in, and her bare breasts shake and bounce as she scuttled back.

When we were settled again, and I had asked her to move her chair round to a position from which I could best view her nakedness, I returned to our earlier conversation – her breasts. 'Do you have very sensitive breasts, Lucy?'

She put her cup down and the familiar scarlet blush returned to her face. She looked down, still unable to meet my eyes when on this subject. 'I don't know, Mr Mortensen. I mean, they are, but I don't know if they are more sensitive than other girls' would be.'

'You said you enjoy having them caressed.'

'Yes.'

'And kissed?'

'Well, yes.'

'And suckled?'

'Yes.'

'And all of that is quite arousing for you?'

'Yes, Mr Mortensen.'

'Sexually arousing?'

'Yes.'

'It makes your vulva moisten, does it?'

'Yes, Mr Mortensen.' Her voice had not risen above a whisper since we resumed our conversation, but as my questions became steadily more specific and more personal, it all but faded away entirely.

'Tell me, then, what about exposing your breasts like this, and talking in this way. Is that arousing? Does that also make you damp?'

'It makes me nervous, Mr Mortensen.'

'So you think it is mostly the nervousness causing the dampness?'

'Yes,' she agreed hastily.

'But you are damp, are you, Lucy?'

'Just a little bit, just from the nervousness.'

'How can you be certain it is not at least partly from arousal?'

'I suppose it could be a bit, Mr Mortensen.'

'Yes, I would have thought so. I mean, even though we have never met before today, it cannot be wholly unpleasant having a man admire your breasts, can it? That must be a fairly pleasant experience?'

'Yes, I suppose so.'

'So that could well be why you are damp, couldn't it?'

'Yes, I suppose it could, Mr Mortensen.'

'How wet are you? Do you think you need to go and wipe yourself?'

'Oh no.'

'It's at quite a manageable level at the moment, is it? Nothing that your knickers cannot absorb?'

'Yes,' she mumbled.

'Good. Well, do tell me if you think you ought to wipe yourself. I won't mind.'

'Yes, all right. Thank you, Mr Mortensen.'

'Right. Now, getting back to the subject of your breasts, you said that your nipples are sensitive to your young man's loving caresses. Are they also sensitive to pain?'

At this she did look up at me with horror. 'Yes, Mr Mortensen. Yes, certainly!'

'More than average, would you say?'

'Well, I don't know, but I am certainly very sensitive.'

'Have you in fact ever experienced any pain on your breasts, Lucy?'

'Yes,' she muttered. 'Not often, but I have done.'

'In what way? What happened?'

'Well, nothing particular, you know. Just general things.'

'I'm afraid that I shall need you to be specific, Lucy.'

She paused, thinking. 'When I was younger, I had an older cousin who was horrible to me and once she pinched me very hard.'

'Where did she pinch you?'

13

'On my breast.'

'On the nipple?'

'Yes.'

'Which one?'

'Both of them, both together.'

'And this hurt a great deal?'

'Oh yes.'

'Was it not also arousing?'

'No!'

'Are you sure? I would have thought it should be, just a little bit. And I do notice, Lucy, that your nipples have become even more erect while you have been telling me this, haven't they?'

She sat in silence, considering how she was caught out by the evidence of her own body.

'Was it? Just a little, Lucy?'

'Maybe just a tiny bit.'

'Right. I want you to pinch yourself now. Do it as hard as you can stand.'

'But Mr Mortensen . . .'

'Yes, please, Lucy. On both breasts, and hold it.'

She hesitated again then looked at me and, hesitantly, reluctantly, her hands rose, fell a little, then rose again and finally closed carefully over her little nipples. She glanced over at me once then I watched as she pinched her fingertips together and held them, the soft flesh turning white in her grip as she struggled not to release herself. Her bottom lip was tucked into her teeth, but she held her head high, proud of her obedience and her endurance. I let her stay there for a few seconds, until a trace of moisture appeared in the corner of her eye.

'Well done, Lucy, very good. You may release them now.'

She did so immediately, and we both looked down as the colour quickly returned to her skin.

'It is half-past four now, Lucy, and I have thoroughly enjoyed our afternoon together. I must say you have behaved yourself very well and I am pleased. I know that this problem was not of your making and yet you have struggled very hard to make up for your fiancé's wrong-doing. You may get dressed and go home now. As you will remember, I asked no more of you than that you let me see your breasts and you have kept your side of the bargain; I will keep mine and withdraw my complaint to your fiancé's employer. You may rest assured that the matter will quickly be forgotten.'

'Thank you, Mr Mortensen. Thank you very much.' I could swear she almost curtsied as she scuttled away across the lawn. I followed slowly and found her struggling hastily back into her bra and blouse in my study. The moment she was dressed, she gathered up her shoulder bag and almost ran down the hall, where I caught up with her as she struggled with the big brass lock. I let her out as she muttered a hasty goodbye and stumbled down the steps on to Bridge Street, where I watched the top of her head bobbing down the pavement until she was lost in a cluster of people at the crossroads.

I gently closed the door behind her. I was extremely sorry to see her go, because it had been a very pleasant diversion, and I cannot see how any man could fail to find his afternoon enriched by having it decorated with a pair of beautiful nineteen-year-old breasts.

2

Tuesday

I was busy the following morning and had no chance to call at the Castlegate Tearooms, although I did make a phone call immediately at nine o'clock to Graham Worthing, the managing director of the insurance company, to say I felt on reflection that I had been too hard on a well-meaning boy and I would not wish him to suffer any penalty on my account. In fact, Graham is a man I have come to know well through our shared interests and when he expressed some disbelief at my sudden change of heart, I admitted that, following a discussion about the matter with the boy's fiancée, I had come to an arrangement which I felt would be adequate compensation. He was discreet enough not to enquire although I am sure he had some idea of the nature of the arrangement I had made. I was assured that no further action would be taken.

It was another glorious May day. Summer had clearly arrived and I spent much of the morning in the cool shade of the summerhouse verandah where I could work undisturbed by telephones or street noises and enjoy the view of my garden in front of me. In fact, the garden was starting to get rather out of hand. I do have a boy who comes to do odd jobs around the garden – wash the car and so on – and I would clearly have to put him on to the summer timetable of coming twice a week instead of only once as he did during the winter. I would tell him so when he came that afternoon. I take great pride in my garden, for I grow a number of rare species of roses and have an extensive

Victorian conservatory in which I grow melons, grapes and chillies as well as the more usual fruits and salad vegetables. I had eaten late and was enjoying this view at around three o'clock when my thoughts were interrupted by the jingling of the doorbell, and was most surprised to find Lucy Golden was again standing on the step.

'I'm sorry to trouble you, Mr Mortensen, but I have just heard from David that he has been told your complaint has been withdrawn.'

'Yes,' I replied, although I admit I was a little mystified as to the reason for her arrival. 'I told you I would do that.'

'Yes, I know you did, and I wanted to thank you.'

'That is quite all right, Lucy.' She was still hesitating, glancing nervously up and down the street, something else clearly troubling her. 'Do you have something more to say, Lucy?'

'Well, yes, Mr Mortensen. You see, I wasn't completely truthful when I was answering your questions yesterday, and I wanted to apologise. If you are not busy, of course.'

'There is nothing that cannot wait. You had better come in.'

As soon as the heavy door closed behind her, she appeared to relax a little, as if she found more safety within my house than standing conspicuously on its doorstep. Still she found no words.

'Would you like to come out to the garden again? I was enjoying the sun out there.'

'Yes, Mr Mortensen. Shall I make some tea again, or coffee?'

'Yes, coffee would certainly be very pleasant. You will find everything in the kitchen.'

I returned to my chair in the garden and waited curiously to see what she wanted to confess. I could not remember there being anything of any particular significance in our conversation.

Within a few minutes, I heard the rattling of the cups again and glanced up to see Lucy picking her way across the lawn towards me with the same tray held precariously

17

in front of her, laden this time with the cafetière and cream jug. However, the scene otherwise was just as it had been yesterday, for her breasts were again bare. Without my having asked her to do so, she had again removed her blouse and brassière.

'This is a very pleasant treat, Lucy,' I said ambiguously.

'Thank you, Mr Mortensen. Shall I pour?'

'Please do.' I watched her concentrating, although again I have to say that my gaze was mostly fixed on her nakedness, the gentle sway of her small round breasts as she moved, the soft delicate peaks of her nipples not quite so hard this time. When she had finished pouring, she sat down again in the same chair as yesterday, and glanced over nervously.

I made no comment about her state of undress. If she believed that this was required of her in my house, I was not going to suggest anything different.

'So, Lucy, in what way were you less than truthful yesterday?'

She put down her cup and saucer carefully and clasped her hands between her knees, still nervous and with just a very slight blush around her face.

'When I said about my cousin, who hurt me.'

'Oh, yes, what was it you said she did?'

'She pinched my breast . . . My nipples.'

'Oh, yes, that's right. Now, what about that?'

'Well, it wasn't just once. She did it several times. She said that if I didn't lend her a magazine I had, she would pinch me and so I deliberately said I hadn't got it even though I had. Then she gave me another chance and I said again that I hadn't so she did it again.'

'I see. Yes, you were really quite untruthful.'

'I felt that after you had been so fair, it was not right that I had been untruthful and took advantage of you. Because even though you were quite strict with me yesterday, you were fair, and you said how David or someone from the company came here eleven different times and you had to put up with all that, so it didn't really seem fair if I just came once, and then didn't tell you the full truth.'

Her words poured out in a flood, badly composed but spoken from the heart and deliberately rushed to avoid the head interfering with their course. Her face was flushed as she stared again at her twisting fingers, for she knew exactly what she had said, what it all meant.

'Well, my dear Lucy, although I am extremely annoyed to learn that you have lied to me, you have at least shown a little repentance. In the circumstances, I will not revoke my statement to the company, but I shall require some further sacrifice from you to make amends.'

'Yes, I understand.'

I considered the possibilities. A full afternoon stretched ahead which no-one but a fool would have wasted. 'As a first step, Lucy, I consider that as a consequence of your deceit, you have forfeited the right to retain the remainder of your clothing. Kindly stand up and remove the rest.'

She gasped, almost dropped her cup and stared at me in utter horror. 'No, Mr Mortensen, I just thought it would be all right if I stayed like this and you continued to ask me questions if you wanted to. I wouldn't mind and I would answer truthfully, really I would.'

I considered her carefully. She clearly meant it and had really not expected that she would be required to reveal herself any further. 'You say you would not mind?'

'No, Mr Mortensen, honestly, I wouldn't!'

'Do you think I minded when I was put to considerable trouble, embarrassment and expense over this business, not just once but, as you well know, eleven times?'

'Yes, I suppose so.' She was sounding a little less confident.

'Then would it be fair dealing if you were to do something that you "honestly don't mind" in restitution for what I most earnestly did mind? Does that seem just to you?'

'Well, no, I suppose not.'

'No, indeed. Kindly remove the rest of your clothing.'

I thought for a moment that she was going to continue to resist, but she finally blinked her little eyelashes, meekly stood up and reached for the zip at the side of her thin skirt. She fumbled over unfastening it, but then slipped it down her slender legs before hanging it neatly over the back of her chair. Her shoes were canvas slip-ons and these she kicked off and arranged under the chair. The tights she slowly peeled away, being careful not to tug at her knickers as she did so, and laid these out over the skirt. Then she turned to face me again, her hands clasped in front of her knickers, white and lace trimmed, but revealing a faintly darker triangle of her pubic tuft at the centre. She gripped her hands and shifted her weight from one leg to the other.

I cleared my throat. 'And your knickers, please, Lucy.'

'But Mr Mortensen, I –'

'Now, please, Lucy,' I interrupted, and raised my voice just enough to let her know she had no choice.

She hesitated another second, then hooked her fingers into the waistband and slipped them down her thighs. She stepped out of them and turned quickly, bundling them into a ball in her hand. She was about to stuff them in under her skirt when I stopped her.

'Give those to me, please.'

She stopped and looked over at me. 'They're my knickers, Mr Mortensen.'

'Yes, I know that. Hand them to me, please.'

'But Mr Mortensen, they –'

'Lucy, please do as you are told. Hand them to me.' I held out my hand to her but she was so slow, so reluctant, that I was in no doubt the prize would be worth the winning. Eventually she handed them across.

'Thank you,' I said. 'Now please turn and face me. Let me have a look at you.'

I continued to hold her knickers in my hand as she turned to me, and although she was trying to stand up straight, the urge to shield herself from my undisguised scrutiny clearly tormented her. I had no pressing appointments.

My initial focus was, naturally enough, on that part of her that I had not seen yesterday, and I was delighted in the innocent wildness of her pale golden bush. Even though she stood demurely with her legs tightly together,

her fair curls did not hide the little cleft at the top, nor that further down a small sliver of her inner lips was peeking out into the light.

Her hair was again held back behind her delicate ears in a little ponytail and she was managing to keep her shoulders back, though her skinny little arms were quivering and making the soft golden down shimmer in the light as she wavered in front of me. Her tender breasts rose and fell with each breath and her stomach curved down to a sweetly indented navel, crossed the line between tanned exposure and pale innocence and continued on down to that gorgeous little bush that I was already impatient to ruffle with my fingers. Her legs were long and slender, the feet turned inwards where the toes of one foot crossed over the toes of the other and wriggled as she waited. Beautiful, beautiful, beautiful.

She kept glancing over to me, waiting for my reaction or my next request, and sometimes her eyes darted down nervously to the incriminating little bundle she had dropped into my hand. While she watched, I carefully unfolded it and her face turned steadily a deeper and deeper scarlet. As I opened it out, the cause of her embarrassment became clear. The knickers were not just damp but positively wet, and so I opened them fully out and displayed the clear stain which so embarrassed her. I raised them to my nostrils to inhale her sweet scent while she stared at the ground, her cheeks a blazing bright crimson that spilled down her neck to her breasts.

'Please keep your head up and your hands at your sides, Lucy,' I instructed her, and she obeyed, appalled to see that I was still holding up her fragrant knickers. 'You should not be ashamed, you know. No sweeter scent exists in all the world than the natural intimate perfume of a young woman.'

She shuffled her feet but did not look up.

'Turn around, please, Lucy.'

'Why?'

I smiled at her terror. 'Don't be frightened, my dear. I want to look at your bottom, that's all.'

21

Slowly she turned and presented me with a bottom so pure and pale and unblemished I could have wept. The cheeks were round and firm, divided by a cleft that begged to be traced by a finger or a tongue. Her thighs met the cheeks in a neat horizontal fold that emphasised how slender were the thighs, how fulsome were the cheeks. The white mark from her swimming costume was as visible round her hips as it was around her breasts. Clearly she did not favour the high cut and alluring shape worn by many girls of her age, but its modest shadow was imprinted across the whole of her gorgeous bottom. I stared, bewitched. By what perverted standards does our society permit the display of a man's gross and flabby stomach and yet demand the concealment of something so exquisite and innocent?

I must have been staring for some minutes because the girl peered round over her shoulder anxiously. 'Is it all right, Mr Mortensen?'

'It is perfect, Lucy. It is quite perfect. Please turn round again. You know you really have no need to be shy; you are a very beautiful girl. I am sure that David is very pleased with you, isn't he? He is a very lucky man.'

'Yes, he's very good to me. Very kind.'

'I'm glad to hear that. Now, as I said, I have incurred a considerable amount of expense as a result of this fiasco and I think it only right that you go some way to working some of that off. For a start there is a good deal of work to be done in the garden. You can embark on the conservatory. It should be nice and warm in there but it all needs sweeping out and the shelves need wiping down.'

In fact I had been into the conservatory earlier in the day when it had indeed been pleasantly warm; from long experience I knew that it would now be extremely hot. The melons and chillies both required a high temperature and she would soon have the sweat running down her. I took her over to the conservatory, let her in and carefully shut the door behind us. The heat was incredible, like a sauna, while the humidity from the plants and water tanks all around us made the pressure even harder to bear.

22

'Good. Now I think you'll find a brush under the shelving there.' I pointed up into the corner, where an old and threadbare broom stood propped into the cobwebs. 'Could you sweep the floor out and then scrub down the shelves? You'll find some water in the tank at the end.'

I stayed to watch her get started and then left her to her work and returned to the cool of the lawn, deciding to give her ten minutes before going back to see how she was getting on. When I returned, I pushed open the door.

'How are you doing, Lucy?'

She turned and her natural good humour drew her face into a smile before she remembered. In her exertion, I think she had almost forgotten that she was entirely naked, but as I had expected, she was sweating profusely, her hair starting to fall out of its neat ponytail into rat tails around her pink-flushed face. Her body was already smeared with dirty streaks, leaving her hands unnaturally pink where they had been in the water. She had finished the sweeping and was starting to wipe down the shelves, but could barely reach the back. This would not do.

'I think it would be best if you get up and kneel on the shelves, then you can get right into the back.'

I did not help her. After all I did not want to get my slacks or shirt dirty. I watched carefully as she clambered up on to the shelves, an exercise which resulted in her having to part her thighs delightfully, giving me a first fleeting glimpse of her vulva.

Lucy obviously realised, once she was up kneeling on the waist-high shelving, that as soon as she leant forward, she would expose herself to my eyes even more. For a moment she waited, but then she twisted her hips away from me, dipped the brush into the bucket, and leant down to start scrubbing.

Of course, by turning her bottom away, she presented a profile which was no less alluring than the sight she had tried to conceal. Kneeling down with one hand on the shelf in front of her, the vigorous scrubbing caused her hanging breasts to swing from side to side until it was all I could do to keep from reaching out to cradle them in my hands, to feel the dampness of her smooth skin, the gentle weight

23

and the tender points of her soft nipples in my palms. Tearing my eyes away from that, I took a step behind her, where I was presented, only just below eye level, with her rounded bottom, equally glistening from her exertions. Her knees were spaced a short distance apart which had the effect of parting her buttocks slightly and displaying her neat pinkly puckered anus and below that the fat ripe lips of her vulva, a sparse scattering of pale down doing nothing to hide where the smaller lips were pushing through.

The temptation was so great that I was in serious danger of succumbing, and I did not want that, not yet, so I tore myself away and returned to my chair in the sun. If I had stayed there a minute longer I would not have been able to keep myself from reaching out for her, from taking her there and then among the pots and the boxes. It would have been heaven to have her sprawled on her back, her arms thrown out and her legs spread so wide that I could burrow my face between her thighs and drink from her swollen lips. Or positioned just as she was, kneeling on all fours with her small breasts hanging down into my hands and entry offered through either of her moist openings; it would have been paradise. But I knew that the moment I did either, although she would most probably permit me without complaint, she would regard her debts as settled and would disappear from my life, never again to grace my garden with her innocent nakedness.

If I was careful, and set a pace that she could handle, fast enough that she was always kept just off balance, slow enough that she did not stumble, if I led her step by step up the flight of pleasure, if I was cautious and wary and painstaking, she would follow me to the summit. If she was challenged but never overstretched, I would eventually win the opportunity to indulge myself completely, but I would also win prizes along the way. New experiences and delights were yet to be unveiled; familiar treats waited to be explored in ways that she had never imagined.

Yet that pleasure had a price, which was that today I must deny myself the joy of touching her. I must persuade her to invite me to that, and even then, I might refuse.

I returned to my books and was making good progress when I was distracted by a shaft of sunlight reflected off the conservatory door as it was opened. Without raising my head, I squinted up and saw Lucy emerging and turning to close the door carefully behind her. She glanced over towards me and when I did not move, assumed that she was unnoticed and turned to brush the dirt from her long pale legs, her arms and then, after another quick check to ensure she really was unobserved, her breasts. There was such magic in the contrast between the natural purity of her pale unblemished skin and the dirt and smuts streaked across it that I knew I would have to find other opportunities for her to work in this way.

She stayed there a moment and gazed round the garden, I believe admiring the array of colours from the last of the spring bulbs and the first of the summer blooms. The birds were fluttering through the bushes finding mates, building nests and calling out their achievements. All around us the trees soared tall and brilliant in their bright new foliage and in the midst of this, the small pale figure of the girl stood like a vision from an ancient myth.

She started fiddling with her hair, whose neat ponytail was now a straggling mess. Reaching up behind her head, she pulled off the band and shook the golden waves free in the sunshine for a few moments before she drew them back neatly and fastened the little black band again.

Then she turned her face up to the sky and spread out her arms to soak up all she could, and stayed there breathing deeply the scents, the cool breeze and the sunshine. I longed to find some way to keep her there always.

Finally she dropped her arms to her sides and turned in my direction. She was about to move when she remembered my being there and furtively glanced round. I quickly turned away and waited while she slowly made her way back to where I worked. I sat up with a start as she approached.

'All done?' I asked cheerfully.

'Yes. I've done that.'

'Good. Well done. Now, I need to get the wood shed cleared out and restacked. I don't think we will be having any more fires for many months.'

I led her over to the small shed under the oak tree and showed her how I wanted the logs pulled out and restacked, with the newest at the back where they would have another year to season, and the oldest and driest at the front and ready to hand. It meant taking most of the logs out before they could be rearranged and I allowed myself a few minutes watching her firm young muscles glistening from the sweat as she worked. The continual bending and lifting showed off her figure almost as well as in the conservatory, but the action kept giving enticing glimpses of her little dark cleft, glimpses that were lost the instant she stood up again. And as she turned and bent and straightened and twisted, her breasts shimmered in the sunlight, changing shape as she moved and begging to be held and kissed and worshipped.

Again, I forced myself away, but this time I stayed and watched at a distance from my chair and this time I did not even try to concentrate on my book. I don't believe I would ever have tired of watching her.

When that was done, I set her to weeding the end flower bed. It was in no particular need of attention, but I wanted to keep her within my sight, and the image she presented, again kneeling with her back turned towards me, and her round bottom pushed out as she worked, was too alluring to forego.

It was well after half-past four, and Lucy had just started on this task when I heard the side gate being unlatched. I keep this locked for security, but Alan, the gardener, has a key. This gives him access to the back of the house and he is therefore able to work in the garden whether or not I am at home. Alan is a convicted thief whom I met when he was trying to break into my house. However, we had a long discussion that evening about the problems he was facing and I was quickly convinced that he is not at heart a bad lad. I was able to help him out of the particular difficulty he was in then, and he repaid me by working. That debt

26

was long since paid off but I have kept him on and I now trust him entirely not to steal anything of mine, or steal from any of my guests. However, as soon as they step out of my door on to the pavement, he would consider them fair game again. I had presented that thought to him one day and he admitted quite cheerfully that it was the case, but he stressed that his sense of loyalty would forbid him causing, or allowing, any harm to come to me.

As soon as I heard the gate open and saw his head appear, I waved to attract his attention and signalled to him to keep quiet. He was puzzled but quietly latched the gate behind him and tiptoed over to where I was sitting on the terrace. I pointed down the garden and his eyes widened as he saw nothing but Lucy's broad, round, naked buttocks pointing straight towards us down the garden as she knelt over the flower bed. As the full realisation dawned, his cheerful face broke into a wide grin.

'Well, Alan, what do you think? We have been saying that maybe you need an assistant,' I said quietly.

'I'd have asked for one long ago if I'd known that was what you had in mind, Mr Mortensen. Who is she?'

'Her name is Lucy and she will be here for a few days.'

'Making up for past sins?' Alan asked, obviously thinking back to his introduction to my household.

I smiled. 'Well, yes, in a way, exactly that.'

We watched her in silence for a moment before I called, 'Lucy, could you come here a moment?'

Even from that distance we saw the sudden blush as she turned to look over her shoulder and discovered that someone else was with me. She must have realised also that her posture had given us both a perfect view of her bottom and even, where her cheeks had been parted by her kneeling down, right into her cleft, to the tiny brown puckered rosebud and the nest of smooth round lips. She turned a little and slowly rose to her feet, then walked nervously up the lawn towards us. Her breasts shook delightfully as she walked. The round muddy patches on her little pink knees and the smears of dirt over her arms and legs, across her belly and even on her breasts

27

themselves all emphasised her nakedness and vulnerability. She stopped in front of us, her hands demurely in front of her, trying to shield herself from our gaze.

'Ah, Lucy, this is Alan, my gardener. I think I mentioned to you he comes occasionally to work here.'

Alan greeted her cheerfully, still grinning broadly. 'Hello, Lucy. Lovely day to be out tending the garden, isn't it?'

Lucy did not glance up as she mumbled a 'hello' in reply.

'Alan will soon be planting out the summer bedding plants where you have been weeding,' I went on, 'and I think it would be a good idea if we get some of the leaf compost ready to dig into the beds before planting out. You will find a heap under the chestnut tree in the corner and perhaps you could bring a few barrowloads over to the main bed. You know where to find the wheelbarrow and fork, don't you?'

'Yes, Mr Mortensen. Please, couldn't I put on an overall or something? I am getting ever so dirty.'

'Don't worry, Lucy, you can have a good wash before you leave.'

She seemed about to say something more, but then just pushed her hair back off her face, in the process spreading yet another streak of dirt from the back of her hand. I watched as she turned and walked back to the shed and appeared a moment later, pushing the wheelbarrow. She paused by the end of the lawn and pulled on the big black wellingtons that I had given her to wear in the woodshed, before disappearing down into the trees.

Alan chuckled. 'Well, there's not much for me to do here, then, Mr Mortensen. I'd better leave you to it.'

'Oh, no,' I replied, 'it's not quite like that. I have just had her doing a little tidying up and weeding. If you could show her where to dig in the leaf mould, perhaps you could wash the car. I am going out to dinner this evening.'

Alan ambled down the lawn – he was never one to hurry – and waited for Lucy to reappear. I heard the low rumble of the barrow before she came in sight, her forehead creased where she was concentrating on her task and ensuring that the barrow, which she had hopelessly over-loaded, did not tip up. She glanced up and her expression changed to concern when she realised that Alan was waiting for her by the flower bed. She glanced from him to me then stopped, lowered the barrow and made her way gingerly up the lawn to where I sat.

'Please, Mr Mortensen, I don't mind working with you here, but I don't want him to see me. Could I do something inside, please?'

'Lucy, didn't I have to suffer the embarrassment of my personal life being revealed not just to your fiancé but also to his assistant?'

She paused a second and then, without a word, turned back, lifted up the barrow and finished her journey to where Alan stood waiting; her protest was too mild to be sincere, done for appearance more than anything else. I watched as she was sent to fetch two more loads and shown how to fork it well into the topsoil, an action which required Alan to put his arms right round her to show how the fork should be held, and I noticed that his hands accidentally brushed her breasts and bottom on every occasion.

Once this job was completed and Lucy had replaced the barrow, it was time for her to go. She came up to where I was waiting.

'Very good, Lucy. You have done very well.'

'Thank you, Mr Mortensen. Could I go and have a bath now? I am filthy.'

She had taken off the wellingtons and was now entirely naked again, so we both looked down at her body and could see she was quite right. Small bits of leaf were stuck to her damp skin while mud and dirt was streaked all over her arms, her legs and her body, her breasts and even her face. There were twigs and leaves in her hair, both that on her head and on her belly, and when she turned round, her back, legs and bottom were just as bad.

'Well, I'm sorry, Lucy, but I really don't think I can let you go through the house like that. You will spread dirt everywhere.'

'But Mr Mortensen, you said I could!'

'Well, I said you could have a wash. I certainly did not say you could trail dirt all through my house. Several of those rugs are very old and extremely rare and valuable. It would be best if you rinse off out here first, then go in for a proper bath. I'll fetch some water.'

I found Alan just finishing washing the car.

'Alan, could you refill the bucket – cold water will do – and bring the sponge? Lucy needs to wash off some of the dirt.'

He grinned again; this was proving to be the best working day he had ever known. I left him squeezing out the big yellow sponge under the stand-pipe at the corner of the garage block and returned to where Lucy was waiting outside the garden door. She shuffled impatiently, standing with her hands clenched together in front of herself, but when Alan, still grinning from ear to ear, strolled up with the bucket in his hand, she looked horrified.

'Here you go, miss. This will clean you up and cool you off.'

I had intended to leave Lucy to wash on her own, but Alan obviously had other ideas. He dropped down the bucket and dunked the sponge well into the water. He then raised it over her shoulder and squeezed a torrent of cold water down her breasts. She squealed in shock and turned away from him, clasping her hands up to cover and protect herself, but Alan ignored this. Recharging the sponge, he squeezed some more down her back and then rubbed the sponge down her, sweeping off the leaves and rubbing energetically at the smears of dirt across her shoulders, down her back and over her bottom. He rinsed the sponge again before tackling her legs and having finished each of them, left her standing in a growing puddle of water on the stone terrace.

'Bend over now, miss, and let's make sure all the little creases are clean.'

I really wondered whether Lucy would obey this, but she did, meekly moving her legs apart and bending down, her hands resting on the stone wall. Alan dunked the big yellow sponge again and lifted it up to squeeze out the water over her bottom before working the end of the sponge well into the crease between her cheeks and rubbing it liberally up and down.

At last he let her up. 'Right, turn round so as I can do the front and then we're finished.'

Meekly she did as she was told, turning round with her hands still clutched together under her chin. Her skin was covered in little goose bumps, her nipples were puckered into tiny knots against the cold breeze, and her fair pubic hair was matted flat against her skin, revealing even more of the fine plump lips from which water was still dripping.

Again Alan squeezed a full charge of water over her breasts and then, starting at the top, he sponged her down, working vigorously at the worst patches. He caught hold of each wrist in turn and pulled it up above her head to wipe down her arms and armpits. Then he moved on to her breasts, and did nothing to spare her feelings in slopping water over her and then brushing furiously at her nipples with the coarse sponge. He left them clean and glowing pink, but if they were also rubbed sore, Lucy made no complaint. She probably had no complaint left in her.

Moving down, he washed off her rib cage, across her stomach and belly button, then straight on down her legs and to her feet. Finishing that, he stood up and looked at her huddled and shivering in the shade.

'One more bit to go!' he remarked cheerily. 'You'd better bend your legs a bit, miss. Squat down so I can finish you off.'

She glanced over at me, but, when I did not contradict, she obeyed him, again shuffling her legs apart and turning out her thighs before she half squatted down. She flinched and practically leapt up as he slapped another cold sponge over her matted pubic triangle, but then, when he worked the sponge between her legs and ran it slowly but with a steadily increasing pressure, forward and back across her lips, her expression changed and she rested her hand on his shoulder to steady herself. Her eyes closed and lips parted as his attentions continued, and both Alan and I retreated

31

into as inconspicuous a silence as we could manage. For a few seconds her hips started to weave back and forth as if enchanted before she seemed suddenly to collect herself and pushed him away. She stood up straight and squeezed her legs together again, genuinely shocked, I think, at the strength of her own feelings and the ease with which she had allowed herself to be manipulated and abused in front of us both.

For a moment I was afraid that she might have been pushed too far and so I quickly sent Alan off to work down at the bottom end of the garden while I showed Lucy where she could take a warm bath. She kept her face turned away from me as I showed her the way upstairs to the bathroom and gave her towels. I left her alone.

By the time she reappeared, more than half an hour later, she was calmer and more relaxed, but as she came creeping down the stairs to fetch her clothes, still naked but almost hidden inside a huge bath towel, she shone with a warm glow. Watching as she dabbed one or two last damp spots, set aside the towel and climbed back into her clothes before disappearing out into the crowded street, I wondered how on earth she could have induced such a feeling of relaxed well-being all on her own. There was only one way I could think of.

3

Wednesday

Although the implication had been that Lucy would return
for eleven days, she had not specifically said so. After the
previous day's events, I was seriously worried that I had let
Alan push too far and too fast with someone so young, so
inexperienced and so unsure of herself. I decided to keep
his involvement in check, at least for a while. The previous
afternoon, once Lucy was dressed and had disappeared out
into the crowded streets beyond my wall, Alan asked more
about her. I told him little, but I did say that I expected his
discretion over what had happened and I certainly did not
want it being known around the town that she was there.
He was perfectly understanding about this; after all, in his
line of work, secrecy was the usual requirement.

I was most ill at ease that morning. The weather had
turned cooler after the glorious sunshine in the previous
four or five days and although I welcomed a little gentle
rain at last, I was still dismayed. After a succession of days
outside, I could not settle in my study to my translation
and I was feeling cooped up as well as nervous about Lucy.
If she did come, we would have to stay indoors for our
entertainment.

In the end, of course, I should not have worried. A little
after three o'clock, the doorbell, a sound I had once
detested for the interruptions it brought but which I was
now beginning to greet as one of the most wonderful in the
world, announced her arrival. I took her into the study
again, where she selected the same chair in which she had

33

sat on the first day. She started with a subject that was evidently close to her heart.

'Is Alan here?'

'No, Alan only comes a couple of times a week. He will not be here again until tomorrow. We are quite alone.'

'Will there be anybody else coming?'

'I'm not expecting anyone.'

She hesitated a moment, and then spoke so softly. 'Will you want me to undress again?'

'Oh definitely, Lucy. Unless I tell you otherwise, you must always undress immediately you arrive here, whether or not other people are here.'

I suppose that eventually, had I witnessed it day after day, month after month and year after year, it is possible that I would finally have grown tired of watching her undress. But I knew only too well that I would never get the chance to become so blasé, that every occasion was rare and precious and the luxury of indifference was beyond my reach. Her fiancé, the wretched and undeserving David Palmer, would enjoy that gift and I confess an intense bitterness at the thought that he would receive and disregard something I would have treasured so highly. He could watch her every day, every morning and every night, and yet he would not appreciate or even understand the riches he was given. He would watch that exquisite form flourish, ripen and mature and it would be as singing an opera to a deaf man.

I pushed these thoughts away and turned to savour what I had. On this day, only the third time I had seen her, it was as magical as ever.

She was still shy and still turned herself away as she pulled her sweater over her head. Then a T-shirt came away to uncover the thin pale back, the seductive groove that ran the length of her sweet spine, a groove that I yearned to trace with my tongue. Even the shoulder blades; what appeal can there be in them? On most people? None. On Lucy? Magic. They slithered like sensuous dancers beneath her velvet skin as her arms stretched round to unzip the skirt. When this too was arranged neatly on the chair, she still hesitated, glancing at me as if hoping I would tell her it was enough. But it was not enough, would never be enough, not nearly.

Today's underclothes were in a pale green, attractively trimmed in a colourful floral lace pattern. She slipped the bra straps off her shoulders and then peeled the cups over her breasts and twisted the bra round before unhooking the front. The knickers she quickly pushed down and stepped out of, before she padded over to me and offered them out. I had not intended to request them today, but I could not be so ill mannered as to refuse such a gracious offer, so I thanked her, opened them out and inhaled the sweet scent again as she quickly sat down.

'Now, then, how are you, Lucy? Not too worn out from yesterday's work?'

'No, thank you, Mr Mortensen, I'm fine.'

'And what did you make of Alan?'

'He's er . . . well, he's . . . he's quite determined.'

'Yes, I suppose he is. He works very well, and I should say that he is very loyal to me and will also be very discreet.'

'Thank you.'

'Tell me, Lucy, did you tell your fiancé you were coming to see me two days ago?'

'Oh, no, Mr Mortensen, I don't think he would have approved of that.'

'So he does not know you are here now?'

'No.'

'You do remember, don't you, Lucy, that you are going to be entirely honest in your answers?'

'Oh, yes. Yes, I am being honest.'

'Good. Now, I would just like to clarify something. Yesterday, when Alan was rinsing you off, that was not altogether unpleasant, was it?'

'It was very embarrassing.'

'Yes, but quite stimulating for all that?'

'Yes, a bit.'

'Just a bit?'

'Yes.'

35

'So when you went up for your bath, what did you do?'
She blushed. 'I had a bath, Mr Mortensen.'
'Nothing else?'
'I don't know what you mean.'
'Lucy, I think we both know that while you were up there, all on your own, you took the opportunity to masturbate, didn't you?'

Her head hung down, her hair, loose today, obscuring her face, and she was silent for so long, I began to wonder if she would ever speak again. Finally she mumbled an acknowledgement so softly I could hardly make out what she said.

'Please speak up, Lucy. I can't hear you.'

She threw her head up, her face as bright a scarlet as I had ever seen it, and looked straight into my eyes. 'Yes, I did.'

'But I hadn't given you permission, had I?'
'No, but ... Well ...'
'Did you ask for permission?'
'No. You didn't say I should.'
'I would have thought that was obvious.'
'Yes. I'm sorry.'
'Do you masturbate at home often?'
'No!'
'Why not?'
'Well, I mean, you shouldn't. It's wrong, and besides, I have David so I ... I don't.'

'Do you mean you don't get the chance, because he's there, or you have so much sex with him that you cannot face sex on your own?'

'Well, both. I mean neither. I mean I don't. You shouldn't. It's wrong. I don't do that.'

'But you do, Lucy. Yesterday, at the first chance you got, despite knowing that I was sitting down here waiting for you, you did it.'

'That was different.'

'Why?'

'Well, it's different here, isn't it? I mean everything's different.' Unable to find the words, she gestured round at

36

the walls and books and the whole universe that comprised my house. She was right, of course, and yet the difference was too intangible to be explored, in case exploration revealed there to be no real difference at all.

'I see. Well, I will want you to do it again today for me.'

She did not move, but her eyes widened. 'Oh, I couldn't do that, Mr Mortensen. I couldn't possibly go up and do that, knowing you were sitting here knowing what I was doing.'

I smiled. 'It won't be quite like that, Lucy. Besides, you have no need to be shy. I would be willing to bet you that when Alan went home last night, he did exactly the same.'

'Do you think so?' Her eyes were wide.

'Certainly. And I would bet that he was thinking of you while he did it.'

'Oh my goodness.' She clapped her hand over her mouth, in a classic but entirely unconscious gesture in which the shock and the shame and the pride glowed across her face.

'I'll tell you what. When he comes tomorrow, we'll ask him, shall we?'

'Oh, no! Please don't do that. It would be very embarrassing.'

'Nonsense. Alan wouldn't be embarrassed at all. In any case, I am perfectly certain it is something that most young people do, and since you managed yesterday, I think you could do it again today. Not yet, perhaps, but in a minute we will see if you don't feel more in the mood. For now, though, I think we need to consider something else. You were saying on Wednesday that you get wet quite quickly, weren't you?'

'Well, I don't know that I was saying that exactly. Just that I get, you know, wet sometimes.'

'But it seemed you were getting wet then.'

'Yes, but I was nervous then.'

'In any case, I think it would be best if you had a towel to sit on. I don't want my chair to be stained. In the corner cupboard in the bathroom where you were yesterday, you will find some small white handtowels. Fetch one of those, please.'

When she returned, she carefully arranged it meticulously on the wing chair opposite my desk in the study, and again sat down very quickly.

'Now then, Lucy ... No, don't cross your legs. Keep them both down on the floor and keep your feet apart. Good. Now, it seems to me that you are most anxious to remain sitting down. Why is that?'

'I don't know, Mr Mortensen.'

'Are you sure you don't?'

She looked down but said nothing.

'Please bring that little stool over here by me and stand up on it.'

She cautiously carried it over to where I sat, stepped up and balanced. It was low, no more than nine inches high with a neatly embroidered top, but it was enough to raise her to a height where my eyes were almost on a level with her sweet blonde triangle and her lips, already looking a little puffed up, were opening out to display the tips of her smaller lips within.

'Now, then, put your hands behind your back and tell me why you are so shy of my seeing between your legs. You must realise that I saw your charms quite fully yesterday.'

Her face was again flushed and her mouth worked up and down for a few seconds before any sound came.

'I don't know what you saw. I didn't want you to see. I mean, I hoped ...' And then she said no more, but broke down in tears completely, one hand in front of her face. The other had crept back to hide her little triangle.

'Lucy! Lucy! What is this?'

Her words came out between the sobs. 'I don't want you to see me. I know I'm wrong.'

'Wrong? What on earth do you mean, wrong?' The poor girl was clearly distressed. 'Come and sit down again.'

She returned slowly to her seat, but her tears were still flowing.

'Tell me, Lucy. Tell me what you mean.'

'You have seen me. You said you saw me yesterday, and Alan did, and you have seen me again today.'

I thought I was beginning to understand. 'What do you say is wrong?'

'I have bits, sticking out.' She finally blurted the words out.

'Your inner lips?'

She nodded, her mouth clamped tight shut.

'Lucy, how many other girls have you seen naked?'

'None! What do you mean?'

'Have you never seen any of your friends changing? Never seen other girls in the showers? At school? At the beach?'

'Well, yes, at school, and I know they were different, not like me. I mean I didn't look, but I'd have noticed if they had been like that.'

She was obviously most worried about this perceived defect. 'What about David, your fiancé? Has he said anything?'

She sniffed. 'I haven't told him.'

'But surely he must have noticed?'

'No!'

Her outrage filled in a few more pieces of the picture. 'Have you never slept with David?'

'No, of course not!' As far as Lucy was concerned, the answer was so obvious that she seemed to be looking for something more devious in the question.

'What about any previous boyfriends? You must have had many admirers.'

'Well, yes, I had a couple of boyfriends, but not, you know . . .' Her voice trailed away before she took a breath and found the words which were so terrifying her. 'I mean, we didn't make love.'

'So are you in fact a virgin, Lucy?'

'Yes, of course.'

'Has David not pressed you to sleep with him?'

'No! Certainly not.'

'I find that very surprising, Lucy. Are you certain?'

'Yes. The Scriptures state clearly that would be a sin.'

'Ah.' I now understood. 'I am pleased to hear you say so, but it is quite an unusual attitude for most young women these days.'

'I don't know. Yes, I suppose so.'

'Do you not wonder what you are missing?'

'No.' She considered a little more. 'Not really.'

'Are you not curious?'

'Well, yes. I mean Sam says . . .' But she trailed away. Whatever it was that Sam said was too scandalous to be repeated.

'Sam says?' I prompted.

Lucy swallowed and looked away, clasping her hands in her lap. 'Sam has a boyfriend and I know that they make love; sometimes she tells me things.'

'Things?'

'Things they've done.'

'And don't you feel left out?'

'Sometimes, but I promised my mother that I would remain a virgin until I was married. I could not go back on that.' She looked up at me pleadingly. 'Whatever happens, Mr Mortensen, I can't go back on that.'

I nodded. 'I understand.' I did. Her moist eyes pleaded like a spaniel's. 'I promise, Lucy, I won't ask you to break that promise.' She was trustingly relieved and although I would keep my word, I had no intention of making this the deliverance she believed. She had told me where the fence stood, the mark beyond which I could not go, and I had acknowledged the boundary. So anywhere on this side of the fence was permitted. A huge world of wickedness may be encompassed within the words 'whatever happens'.

She wiped her eyes as I sat and considered the little form huddled in front of me. Her thighs had crept back together, her hands had slipped down into her lap; she was hiding herself as much as she could. Sometimes you have to be cruel to be kind.

'Lucy, I want you to get dressed again and then go out and buy me something.'

She quickly stood up and dressed. I gave her a few pounds and sent her down the road to buy a magazine from the newsagent a few doors down.

'Which magazine?' She was obviously bemused by this.

'Well, any of them. I mean, any from the top shelf. "Men's magazines" they are generally called.' She flinched visibly as I expanded my request.

40

'Mr Mortensen, I can't go into a shop and buy one of those! Please don't ask me to do that.'

'I have asked you.'

'Please . . .'

'Lucy, you will please do as you are told, and don't take ages about it. It should take you less than two minutes to get there, one minute in the shop and two minutes to get back. I don't want you hanging about for ages hoping I'll change my mind, or waiting until there is nobody in the shop. So, don't dawdle, because if you're not back within five minutes, I'll make you go and buy another one.'

She shuffled out, and I watched the blonde head bob down through the crowds until it was lost to my sight. Well, within the time I had allowed her, she was back. I had her undress again immediately, but stopped her when she had only her knickers left.

'Come here by me,' I instructed her. When she came up close to where I was sitting, I reached up and took hold of the thin elastic waistband of her knickers and eased them off. My fingertips scraped down her skin, and although I did not attempt to go any further than was required to finish undressing her, it was the first occasion on which I had actually touched her skin. I think we both acknowledged the significance of the step. It meant that more intimate contact was inevitable, purely a matter of time, but time was plentiful, and I was enjoying too much savouring each step to want to rush her now. She rested her hand on my shoulder to keep her balance as she lifted each foot in turn and let me slip her knickers right off.

I had her take her towel and arrange it on the sofa and again I asked her to sit with her legs apart and the magazine opened up next to her.

'Now then, Lucy, the reason I asked you to get this magazine was so that you could look through it and see for yourself how many girls there are who also have full inner lips which extend beyond the outer lips. Point them out to me as you come to them.'

So she started to flip through the pages and of course several girls were shown with lips much larger than hers and several with lips much smaller. We looked at the photographs together, and I had her fetch my shaving mirror from the bathroom and sit with it held between her thighs so that she could examine her vulva as easily as I could. And we worked through the magazine, comparing each of the models with Lucy so that by the time we had reached the end, it had been necessary several times for Lucy to push her legs wide open and pull out her lips to see if they were as long or as wide or as dark or as pale as the girls photographed. We had seen the different shapes of the lips – those which offered full wrinkled rolls like tender leaves and those which were thin and smooth as velvet – and we had found those which hid away like a closed shell and those which offered an abundance of shamelessness, far too long and proud to be retained within any modest covering. We had seen the difference in the clitoris, where in one or two cases the pink round tip was just visible while on others, just like on Lucy, it was totally concealed under the thin hood. One of the girls was entirely shaved, and this intrigued Lucy, who had clearly never thought of doing such a thing, and we paused long at those few pages, working through them and then turning back to the start to consider them all again. A good number of the models trimmed their pubic hair, particularly along the lips, which made the vulva appear all the more prominently in these photographs. Again, Lucy was most interested and we compared the growth of hair between her legs and along her lips with that shown in the photographs. Although Lucy's hair was quite sparse, I got the impression she was beginning to like the entirely clean and uncluttered look of the models spread out in front of her. Towards the back was one collection of photos featuring two girls together in a pathetic parody of lesbian passion; nevertheless, Lucy studied this in silence and although she made no comment on the activities depicted, I kept quiet and noted her close attention.

By the end she seemed much less inhibited about touching herself and was quite free in exploring this previously unfamiliar area. I had looked and watched and searched and examined with her, but never once had I touched her: that was another day's delight. Yet I had noticed, although I had made no comment, the pink flush that had gradually spread over her lips as our investigation had continued, and the light sheen that now coated them. Finally Lucy moved away the mirror, closed the magazine carefully and thoughtfully and clasped her hands together over it.

'Good. Now are you happier about yourself? You are not deformed or ugly or weird; you are less richly endowed than some girls and more richly endowed than others. In fact, you have a very beautiful little pussy – sweet, tidy and compact.'

She moved the magazine away and looked down into her lap at the little tuft of pale hair covering the cleft we had just been so carefully considering, but said nothing.

'So, what I want you to do now is to stroke that pretty little pussy for me to see. You have already told me that you did that yesterday, so now do it again.'

'You mean here?' Her eyes were moist, wide and absorbing, but this time I am sure that excitement shone as brightly as dread. In the long ascent that I had set her on, she was beginning to take her own weight, but still doubted her own talent. 'I don't know if I can.'

'The first day you didn't know if you could show me your breasts, but you did. The second day you didn't know if you could show me your whole body, but you did. I believe you can do this too.'

Her face was still turned down and her shoulders shook but I could not see whether it was excitement or distress. I waited patiently, and slowly her hand inched across to her lap and ran down through the little curls to part her lips below. The tip of her forefinger eased in so slightly, as if the sin of the act would be reduced if the degree of penetration was only negligible, and her thighs slipped a little further open, ever so slowly, so that I am sure it was no conscious action on her part. Her delicate fingertip played daintily across the groove of her plump outer lips and then, inevitably and unstoppably, as her thighs continued to draw back, her knuckle hooked over as she circled beneath the little hood. For a moment, I let her carry on as she liked, as she relaxed into the comfort of her own creation, because already her face was a brilliant scarlet of embarrassment and too much attention to her actions might have prevented her inducing any pleasure at all.

'Lucy.' The instant I spoke, her movements stopped and her thighs clamped shut, pinning her hand in its sinful place.

'Lucy, look at me.'

She did, reluctantly, raise her head, and her eyes briefly flickered up to me and then down again. Her cheeks were still a brilliant red, and I think a little moistness lurked in the corners of her eyes, but her lips had been parted, her tongue flickering out and back with an impatience and a longing that her conscience could no longer defeat. Her teeth rasped across her lip in an agony of shame and impatience.

'Continue.'

Without opening her thighs at all, her finger resumed its slow movement up and down, a rhythmic flexing of just that one joint, so tiny a movement, and yet in less than a minute, a little sigh escaped from her lips and it was clear she was lost again. Once more the slender thighs opened like curtains to reveal the swollen glistening lips within. The tip of her finger was now catching more directly on her clitoris with every movement, and was pressing much harder each time it passed. Her inner lips too had swollen and parted, readying themselves for any attention she would give them, and so now her finger ran the entire length down to their join and back to the hooded pearl at the top. As I watched, the movements settled into a steady rhythm and her head dropped down to the side. All the muscles of her face relaxed, her eyes drifted out of focus and then fell shut, her mouth opened a fraction with another tiny but deeper sigh.

Her other hand still lay idle across the arm of the chair, but the fingers twitched impatiently and finally started to creep towards her breast. The first feather-light touch of her fingertips barely brushed over the surface, but the second pressed a fraction harder into the soft curve. Then the fingers closed gently round the nipple, and one single tiny fingertip took up a slow circling caress, little more than a light scratch of the fingernail around the rich darkness of the very tip of the swollen cone.

She pushed her bottom further forward on the seat towards me and another sigh escaped as her hips lifted up and flopped back again, her legs splayed wide open in complete abandonment to the irresistible demands building within her. Briefly her palm reached down along the expanse of smooth pale thigh, leaving her vulva open and unprotected. Between the eager chubby lips, the velvety wrinkled folds of her inner labia pushed out, so divinely pink and puckered. At the little triangular tips they curled over on themselves as if in modesty and then trailed away down either side of the demurely closed vagina. My fingers itched, quivered, to caress such pure and undisguised sensuality. I knew exactly how she would feel if I were to reach out my own coarse fingers and touch that most feminine of places: how warm, how sweetly soft and delicate. Like duck down. Like soft meringue. Like an angel's wings. Like innocence.

Her head was still turned away, lost somewhere in a dream, but her hand slid back up her thigh to the downy centre. The finger slipped down between her lips again, slid up and back, pressed so lightly at first on the soft ridges that they barely moved under her caress. Yet slowly, almost imperceptibly, the pressure of that single fingertip was becoming firmer, the lips were being pressed down and the movement was becoming more determined. No longer a delicate brush as light as silk across the surface, the touch was becoming resolute and purposeful. Still little response showed on her face bar the occasional flutter of her eyelids, but the growing purpose in the steady movement of her finger was clear indication of its effectiveness. It was faster now, focused and concentrated, little frantic circles around the bud concealed beneath those closed wings, and then

45

with her eyes tight shut and just that one small finger running in frenzied agitation at the top of her fold, her lips peeled open like a flower, glistening as they swelled and curled. Suddenly her hips twitched again and her fingertip's circles spiralled inward, more concentrated and more furious and then she stopped. It was all over in almost complete silence. Not a great event, not earth shattering, but it was one small mountain she had conquered all on her own. From now on, every new challenge would be easier as we moved up towards more demanding heights; it would be more rewarding for me and more satisfying for her.

Her eyes finally lifted up to me and a proud smile flickered through her mortified guilt. I smiled at her. 'Very good, Lucy. Well done. Now you can go home.'

She began picking up her clothes and I could barely bring myself to look. The steady concealment of such rare and innocent beauty seemed such a tragedy, such a waste, and it moved me as powerfully in its own way as had the unveiling those few short hours ago. I searched for an excuse to detain her a little longer, although in truth I knew that none was needed. An excuse would only be to ease my conscience; a simple command would be enough for her. I had only to say the word and she would stop; I could ask her to reverse it and show me everything again. She would do so immediately. But no. She had placed her faith in me entirely and I must not abuse that. I was as bound by our timetable as was she. She scurried off to her other life with scarcely a glance back, while I went to retrieve the warm, fragrant and very moist towel that still lay on her chair.

4

Thursday

The morning promised to develop into another bright sunny day, so I decided to stroll through the town and take the opportunity to call at the tea shop and watch Lucy at work. Partly I was attracted by the thought of her vulnerable innocence wrapped up in the severe uniform; partly I wanted to see the blush that would flare across her face when I reminded her that I knew exactly what she looked like beneath it. Those were the two reasons I gave to myself then, but I now recognise that in truth there was another. Already she had wormed her way into my life and dug beneath the tranquillity that the years had wrapped round me, a tranquillity that had been so easy, so unchallenging and so comfortable yet now seemed so shallow. Already I was building my days around the hours we would spend together. A bright day needs a bright companion and there was no-one brighter.

Accordingly, at eleven o'clock, as the last of the morning cloud was being burnt away by the new sun, I left the house and walked down Bridge Street, past the church and into Castle Street. Almost half a mile down, after the shops have given out and become houses, after the houses have given out and become spaces, the buildings all start again, cowering together as close as they can to the castle gate which gives the area its name. Right at the end of that huddle and immediately next to the gate crouches a gloriously ramshackle half-timbered building that jetties out over the pavement. It is a building which adorns many of the postcards, brochures and boxes of fudge that are sent out from this little town, and proudly proclaims itself to be the Castlegate Tearooms. I pushed open the door and walked in.

The low-ceilinged dining room was already quite full with a mixture of early tourists and locals meeting their friends, but a couple of empty tables still stood empty and I selected one in the front window corner where I could see the whole room and watch the comings and goings of the customers as well as the staff.

A woman of about 40, displaying all the arrogant dominance that showed her to be the owner, stood behind the counter, positioned centrally at the till, where she could maintain control over all that passed. She was a tall and well-built woman, whose severe style of dress and make-up warned that she accepted no nonsense from anyone. She was of the breed that had built an empire, and she ruled this domain with the stern rigidity that she would have applied to any minor colony.

She smiled at me coldly and turned to call back towards the kitchen behind her in a tone that expected immediate obedience. At once Lucy hurried out and stopped dead in her tracks the instant she looked across the room and saw me. She blushed deeply and the manageress looked up at her in some surprise, glancing from her face to mine to determine the cause. I just smiled in a friendly and welcoming way, so that the manageress brusquely instructed Lucy to get a move on. Lucy crept over to my table.

'Good morning, Mr Mortensen. What would you like me to get you?' She made no allusion to our other meetings and so I made no direct reference either.

'Well,' I said ambiguously, pretending to study the faded little menu card on my table, 'what do you do exactly?'

I looked up at her face in time to catch her eyes widening as she glanced back towards the counter. She didn't answer me, but we both knew what it was that she did, and I expect that she was picturing, as I was, her slim pale figure scampering about my house naked, or writhing in my chair as she fiddled and prevaricated and delayed but finally succumbed and brought herself to orgasm.

'We have tea-cakes or scones and a selection of different types of tea or coffee. We also offer various gateaux.'

'I think I will have a filter coffee and a tea-cake, please.'

'Yes, sir.' She hurried away again, glancing apprehensively at the manageress as she passed her on her way back to the kitchen. A little frown crossed the woman's face and I turned away before she could catch my eye.

Lucy emerged again quickly, bringing a prettily decorated plate bearing a tea-cake and a foil-wrapped square of butter. She also laid down a knife and a neatly folded paper napkin, but hurried away to another table before I could speak to her.

It seemed that Lucy was the only waitress on duty at that time, and she was kept busy flitting around the room under the gaze of the lifeless manageress. It was a pleasure to watch her work and every now and then to catch her eye as she emerged from the kitchen and could not control the nervous glance to check that I was still there. Like a butterfly she darted from table to table, back to her kitchen and out again, and I knew that in time she would come back to me. Yet I had seen her nipping about my garden quite naked, and flattering though this uniform was, sweet though she looked all brushed and neatly arranged, it could not compare with the sight to which I was growing accustomed. The manageress was busy attending to another customer's bill when Lucy brought over my filter coffee, and I picked up the napkin that she had laid out for me earlier.

'Excuse me, do you have any other napkins? I do not really like paper ones.'

'I'm sorry, Mr Mortensen, we don't have cloth napkins. Paper is all we do.'

'Is there nothing else? I was hoping for something rather less impersonal. Do you have anything of that sort? Perhaps a little scented and hopefully slightly moist?'

She shook her head. 'I'm sorry. We don't have any . . . Oh!' She almost squealed as she suddenly understood and hastily looked round to see if she had been noticed. She had. The manageress was staring across, clearly convinced now that something was going on in her tea shop, but quite unable to see or imagine what that might be.

Lucy quickly turned back to me. 'Yes, sir. I will bring them to you,' and she flitted away, squeezing past the manageress with her head down.

As soon as she was gone, the woman turned her puzzled expression back to me, and after a short consideration, marched across to my table. 'Good morning, sir, I am Celia Ackworth, the owner. I noticed you asking the waitress about something just now. Is there anything you need?'

'No, thank you very much. The waitress is looking after me most adequately,' I answered cheerfully, giving her no consolation and no clues at all.

'Oh, good,' she said, with little conviction. 'So everything is all right, then?'

'Oh, yes,' I replied. 'Absolutely fine, Miss Ackworth. You have excellent staff here. I imagine you are extremely pleased.'

'Mrs Ackworth, actually. Well, yes, I am pleased with the staff, but of course what matters –' She simpered ingratiatingly '– is that the customers are pleased.'

'If all your staff are as efficient, charming and helpful as this waitress, then I have no doubt they will be.' I smiled my most obsequious smile to show clearly that the conversation was now closed and I had nothing further to add. She snorted in frustration as if she would produce fire from her nostrils and stalked back to her lair beside the till.

A few moments later, Lucy appeared at the kitchen door again and waited while Mrs Ackworth stood watching closely, but as soon as she was distracted, Lucy scuttled over to my table, her hand stuffed down in the pocket of her apron. As she passed, she lifted her bundled white knickers out of her pocket and dropped them into my lap. I closed my hand over them as she slipped away to lay another table before returning to her post at the counter. From there, she looked over to me, a proud little smile on her face as I nodded my head in acknowledgement of her obedience and, as she continued to watch, raised the fragrant parcel to my lips to inhale her scent. She immediately turned and escaped into the kitchen.

I dawdled over my tea-cake, ordered a second coffee and read my newspaper, all the time keeping an eye on Lucy's comings and goings as she attended to the orders of other customers. When finally a suitably quiet moment arrived, I asked her for my bill and, as she stood beside me waiting for payment, rested my hand on her stockinged leg and slid it up her thigh on to the bare skin and then higher up to her smooth round bottom. I did not reach out between her legs, but I think that as she stood there by me, she was waiting for me to do so; she might even have been disappointed as she scuttled away the minute I removed my hand. It would have been natural, perhaps, and yet this was our first overtly sexual contact, and enough for the time being. We were both being tantalised by the slow progress and although we made progress every time, Lucy could never guess what form it would take.

I paid Mrs Ackworth, ignoring her suspicious frown, thanked her again for her kind hospitality and stepped out into the sunshine. The shop bell tinkled gaily behind me, the sun shone down from a huge clear sky and I felt so invigorated that I strolled right round beneath the castle's perimeter walls just for the joy of the day.

As soon as Lucy appeared at my house that afternoon, I led her through to the study and she began immediately to undress. However, she was curiously reluctant to remove her skirt and when she finally did so, instead of the glory of her naked femininity, I was disgusted to find she was wearing knickers again: huge, horrible, drab, baggy things. Lucy hung her head, immediately aware of my disapproval.

'Where on earth did those come from?' I demanded.

'Mrs Ackworth made me put them on. She said I couldn't go home without any.'

'Mrs Ackworth? How did she know what you were wearing?'

'I think she may have seen me give them to you. I know she has a little spyhole from her office where she can watch

51

the tables. As soon as you left, she told me to see her in her office and asked me what was going on.'

'So you told her?'

'No, Mr Mortensen, I didn't want to say anything, but she asked if you were my father and of course I said you weren't. Well, I lied a bit, really, because I said that you were someone that my fiancé knew from work. I think she realised that I knew you more than that, because she, well, she made me lift up my hem.'

'Why did she ask you to do that?'

'She said she needed to check that I was properly dressed.'

'And what did she do when she found that you weren't?'

'It was very embarrassing, because she made me hold up my skirt while she lectured me, and she kept looking at me, you know, down there. Then she said I was to come and see her again after I ended my shift.'

'What happened then?'

'She made me lift up my skirt again, and saw that I still had nothing on underneath and then she said I would have to put some other underwear on and that I couldn't go home through the streets without anything.'

'I see.' I was quite bemused. 'So where did these come from?'

'They are hers. She said she had a spare pair, except . . .' She tailed off.

'Except what?'

'Well, I'm not sure they were exactly a spare pair. They did not seem to be completely clean and I think they may be the ones she had been wearing herself.'

'I see.' Mrs Ackworth was starting to sound like a most intriguing woman whom I should perhaps get to know better. 'Well, take them off at once. They are quite horrible, but you had better leave them here. I will return them to her.'

'Oh, no, Mr Mortensen.' Lucy was hobbling on one leg as she removed the things. 'Mrs Ackworth said I must be sure to bring them back tomorrow. She said they are very expensive and delicate and I should not try to wash them or anything.'

'Did she indeed? How curious.' I took them from her and examined them. 'They look perfectly ordinary to me. Cotton, and not a particularly fine or unusual quality at that.'

I was musing mostly to myself and realised that I was staring, almost unseeing, as Lucy, entirely naked, stood shifting her weight nervously from one foot to the other. I waved her into her usual chair.

'So, tell me more about this, Lucy. Mrs Ackworth said she needed to check that you were dressed properly; is this something she does often?'

'Oh, no, not often, but she does do spot-checks occasionally. We have the proper uniform, you see, which she provides for us, and that includes the stockings, so she does check occasionally that none of the girls are wearing tights instead. Sometimes some of the girls do that – mostly the new ones try it – but she always seems to know, and she checks them and then she can get quite cross.'

'What does she do when she's cross?'

'I don't know, not always, but I know that when she found Amanda wearing tights once, she spanked her, like a little girl. Amanda was crying.'

'Has she ever spanked you?'

'Oh, no! But then I have always been careful to wear the proper uniform.'

A suspicion occurred to me. 'Do you have a changing room there, Lucy, or do you get changed in Mrs Ackworth's office?'

'Oh, no, we change in our little restroom, right next to her office.'

'I see.' Mrs Ackworth would certainly be worth speaking to. 'Now, if you have finished your tea, I think we should get to work. The fish pond really needs clearing out before the summer. It has collected a huge amount of leaves and mud over the winter. Let's have a go at that, shall we?'

Lucy followed me down to the great round pond as I explained what I wanted her to do and she complained bitterly and squealed delightfully as I made her climb down into the cold slimy mud at the bottom of the pond. The

53

water barely came up to her knees, but it was impenetrably murky and in no time her thighs and stomach were splashed with grubby smuts. The pond held the usual crop of tadpoles and I was confident she would soon find the newts, frogs and water-snails which also live in the muddy depths. I gave her a scoop and asked her to start to remove some of the muck from the bottom. In spite of the warm summer sun, the water was still extremely cold and she stood for several minutes shivering at the edge of the pond, her nipples pushed out tightly erect and goose pimples all over her body. Finally she edged further in, but I realised that I had omitted to warn her that a shallow shelf runs round the edge, and the pond then steps down another eighteen inches to the bottom. With a scream and a splash, she slipped down, almost lost her footing and suddenly found the water lapping not just round her legs, but right up to the tops of her thighs, and, as she slid a little further down into the pond, round her vulva. She stood forlornly holding the plastic scoop and pushing her long blonde hair away with the back of one grubby hand, the tip of that seductive little triangle of blonde wool just disappearing beneath the surface of the water. I could not remember ever seeing so divine a picture of sullied purity.

I left her to it and returned to the summer house, from where I could watch and hear her cries and protests as her bare feet encountered yet another slimy unidentifiable reptile lurking in the mud.

She drew out two bucketfuls and then clambered out. Long tendrils of green weed and slime slithered down her legs and she tried to wipe them away, leaving streaks where her pale skin shone through the black mud. Her hands and forearms were similarly smeared with mud and splashes even spattered her stomach, breasts and face. She abandoned trying to wipe it away and turned to cart the first load of slime down to the end of the garden. When she reappeared, she stared up at me accusingly before turning back to the pond, climbing gingerly back in and scooping up more of the dead leaves from the bottom. A scream a few seconds later caused me to turn back to see her scrambling out on to the stone surround and then squatting down to peer suspiciously into the black mire. When she saw that I was not going to investigate her distress, she delicately stretched out a foot into the water again and was soon back refilling her buckets. I watched her with amusement until she had repeated her trip six times and then had regretfully to tell her to stop. It was tempting to leave her working there all day, just for the joy of watching her clambering in and out and then staggering down the garden with a bucketful of mud in each hand and a clear black tidemark across the middle of her creamy bottom. However, the pond would never recover if she removed all the rich nutrients.

Finally I told her to stop and then, warning her that Alan would be back later, I invited her to wash herself off quickly before he came to help. She was just rinsing herself under the hose when he pushed his way in through the side gate. He grinned widely at seeing her there again, and nodded down to where she stood in a growing puddle on the flagstones.

'Will she want a hand, Mr Mortensen?'

Lucy started at the voice, blushed and turned away again. I let Alan continue watching her for a few moments before broaching the subject I had been pondering, keeping my voice too low for her to hear.

'I think I should explain, Alan, that I am training her.'

'Training her.' The mockery implicit in his flat repetition of my phrase showed his scepticism.

'Not as a gardener. I am training her in something rather more intimate than that. She is quite remarkably naive, and I am attempting to introduce her to a wider range of erotic pleasures.'

He smirked again. 'Well, you're the man to do that.'

'Thank you, Alan. I think you intend that as a compliment. However, the question I have to ask you is whether you would be willing to assist me in this. I have to say that you would find it, shall we say, pleasurable and satisfying, if perhaps unusual in the setting and less private than you are used to.'

He sniffed. 'In other words, you'd be there watching.'

It was my turn to smile. 'I don't mean I want you to throw her down on the grass and fuck her for my amusement.' I deliberately adopted a tone and vocabulary as blunt as his own. 'I may be there; I may not. Others may be present or may not. More than that, I am quite fond of the girl and would like to do right by her. So I'm not intending to abuse the trust she has placed in me and I would like to teach her properly the things she ought to know. That may come from description, or it may come from practical demonstration. As an example, for today I would like to ask her to examine your genitals. I do not think she really has much idea about male anatomy.'

We continued for a few minutes in silence as Lucy turned off the tap, recoiled the hose and then used her hands to sweep the surplus water off her body. Already she displayed a glorious confidence in the way she worked and moved as if she were clothed, and yet she must have known that every movement of her exquisite naked body was being watched closely by both of us.

'Well?' I asked Alan as the girl finally finished and turned to face us, her limbs wet and glistening in the sun, her nipples erect, her pubic bush moist and matted.

'Fine by me,' answered Alan. I had hardly imagined he would refuse.

Lucy was hesitantly making her way back towards us and she glanced nervously from one to the other of us as she approached. She had seen us talking and presumably assumed that she had been the subject of our conversation.

'All done?' I adopted an unquestionably cheerful tone.

'Yes, thank you.'

'Good. Now I believe there was something you wanted to ask Alan, wasn't there?'

'No!' she answered hurriedly. 'No, it doesn't matter.'

'Oh, I think it does. Shall I ask him?'

Alan was listening to the exchange with amused curiosity. 'Well, I certainly hope somebody asks me, because I'm dead curious now.'

'Well, Alan, it seems that young Lucy is rather shy. However, the question is quite simple. Do you remember last time you were here, you sponged Lucy down out here?'

56

'I certainly do. I won't forget that in a hurry.'

'Well, quite. The thing is, Lucy found that extremely exciting. Not just exciting, but arousing. So much so that when she went upstairs afterwards – you may remember she went up to have a bath – she could not resist the temptation to masturbate. I told her that she should not be ashamed, that such a reaction was perfectly normal and that in all probability you had felt quite aroused yourself by the experience.'

'I can't deny that, Mr Mortensen. If she'd like to repeat it any time, I'm more than willing.'

'Continuing on a step further,' I ignored Alan's generous offer, 'would I be right in thinking that you also masturbated when you later reflected on the events?'

Alan didn't even blush. 'Certainly I did. More than once.'

His openness encouraged me to press ahead. 'And might do again in the future?'

'Quite likely.'

'Because the event continues to excite you?' I looked from one face to the other – Lucy blushing already and trying to avoid his eye, Alan amused and perfectly composed.

'Bloody right.' His enthusiasm was undoubted, a response which came to him as readily and naturally as embarrassment came to Lucy when I raised the subject.

'Then would you mind if I asked Lucy to perform that service for you? Here? Now?'

He did falter a fraction at that. Like most young men of his age, he had not the experience on which total confidence is built and in spite of our friendship and trust, he hesitated to indulge so openly in my presence. He glanced not only at me, but also at Lucy, who still waited beside us, glistening wet and goose-pimpled, with her hands clasped together under her chin and her forearms pressed against her fine round breasts, concealing her nipples but revealing so much. Could any man refuse? Seeing those pale slender fingers wrapped loosely round each other and being asked if he would like them to be wrapped round his penis – could any man refuse?

'I'd be delighted.'

I caught her fleeting glance, a glorious mixture of terror, shame and relief all so tangled she could not have understood it herself.

'Good! So, why don't you settle into this deckchair here. Lucy, you come and kneel down in front of him. Now, then, unfasten Alan's jeans and see what you can find inside.'

Taking up the positions was easy enough; Alan settled back with a light, if rather nervous, smile on his face as Lucy knelt where I had indicated, but then she stopped. She sat there for some moments, frozen and unmoving as she stared directly at the bulge which waited in front of her. Alan slumped back further into the chair and swung his legs wide open, an expansive invitation which offered Lucy irrefutably the package in the front of his jeans, a package which she was being asked to unwrap.

She reached out towards him, one single delicate hand that hesitated as it hovered nervously over his stomach until, finally finding courage, it landed on his belt. She leant forward and unfastened the buckle, pulling the heavy leather through its loops with an assurance as if she had been doing it all her life. Then the stud on his waistband was free and, working steadily now, the tab of the zip drawn firmly down. She clutched the faded denim on both sides, pulled the jeans down and away and then, without even acknowledging what she was doing or what her actions were revealing, reached up to the waistband of his underpants and pulled these down too. She squashed the whole lot down into a bundle round his ankles and only then did she sit back to see what she had revealed.

Alan lounged back with a satisfied smirk on his face, swinging his leg idly to and fro just in front of her. The long tail of his thick shirt covered most of his tangle of pubic hair, and his penis stretched, semi-erect, across his stomach, the head also burrowed beneath the shirt. Nobody spoke and finally Lucy picked carefully at the heavy cotton shirt and lifted it away to uncover him entirely. His penis twitched and straightened a little further in response to the nearness of her fingers and the promise implicit in the completeness of its revelation.

She was staring fixedly and with concerned curiosity but when she glanced up, nervously willing someone to tell her what she should do next about this unfamiliar presentation, I caught her eye and smiled. 'Have you seen one of these before, Lucy?'

'No.'

'Touch it.'

She glanced up at me, at Alan, at me again, at the exposed pink penis waiting for her hand, and still she couldn't move. Once her hand twitched, almost managed, but she could not quite bring herself to reach out to it, to something so alien to her sheltered and naive upbringing.

Alan was becoming embarrassed too. He was a cheerful and appealing young man who I did not imagine ever wanted for female company and he had confided in me from time to time about some of his many conquests. Despite that wealth of experience, I am certain that he had never encountered this reaction from any partner he had ever lured to his lair. Faced with such inexperience and reluctance, and in the knowledge of my being there to witness it, his confidence was crumbling at the delay. He too looked anxiously at Lucy (who didn't move), at me, back at Lucy again (who still wouldn't move), and then finally he acted himself. He reached down, took hold of her wrist and placed her hand on his penis.

Once in place, and relieved of the shame of having herself brought the action about, she allowed her delicate fingers to wrap round him. Inevitably he began to swell at her touch, and as he did so, she slowly started working her hand up and back the steadily increasing length. The head was now fully exposed from the foreskin, and the whole organ started to erect properly, soon standing proud and primed while Lucy, with frequent glances up at Alan to gauge the reaction to her experiments, tried different speeds and pressures. After a few moments she brought her other hand to join in so that he was entirely encased within her little fists and settled to a steady rhythm that was clearly relentlessly effective. Alan gazed down at the girl, his hands toying with her hair as she knelt before him, with such admiration and devotion on his face that I admit I was jealous. Stupidly, of course, because it could have been me that I had commanded her to serve in this way, and it had been entirely my decision to use Alan instead.

I pushed the thoughts away; Lucy had more ground to cover. 'Stop a moment, Lucy.'

Her reluctance at releasing him was almost the equal of the reluctance she had first shown to start. 'Now, I want you to kiss him.'

She recoiled as if burnt, scrambled to her feet and stepped away, her hands defensively across her breasts. 'What? You don't mean kiss him there?'

'Of course I do, Lucy. I want you first to kiss Alan's penis on the tip and then take it right into your mouth.'

'But . . .' Her words failed. What could she say? All the grounds for objection were perfectly obvious and she knew that they would all be perfectly inadequate.

'I can't do that, Mr Mortensen. I just can't.'

'Yes, you can, Lucy. It is perfectly straightforward. Something almost any girl would willingly do for her partner. Or,' I added a little sweetener which was less an offer of a treat to come than it was an indication of the path down which disobedience might lead, 'or of course he might do the equivalent for her.'

At this appalling prospect, her hands flew down to protect herself there. I could see the battle being fought in her mind. Which was worse? To do something so disgusting to Alan, or be so shamed by having him in such close and intimate contact with a part of her body that she was only beginning to acknowledge existed?

She edged closer and knelt back where she had been, reaching out to catch the terrifying object which was weaving drunkenly in front of her before moving her head down. At first she paused, but then resolved to complete the task she had been set, and like a sparrow at a bird-table nodded down to drop the lightest possible kiss on the tip of the organ and whipped back again, already wiping the back of her hand across her lips. It was barely sufficient to discharge her instruction, but I had to let that pass; I had not specified a type of kiss.

Her other hand was still wrapped round Alan's erection, totally motionless as she continued wiping her mouth and staring at the thing. Finally she took a breath and, holding it now with both hands, leant down slowly until she was almost there – a couple of inches, an inch, half an inch. Her tongue appeared, lightly flicked out and back with the speed of a snake, but it had touched. She recoiled at once, but she was not struck down by a thunderbolt and was not consumed by fire, so she leant forward again. This time the lick was longer. It touched and stayed and rested and even lapped ever so lightly at the smooth head until eventually, because she was given no other choice, she opened her mouth and bobbed down the last little distance so that the whole head disappeared between her lips.

Her eyes swivelled up at Alan and round to me for approval at her achievement. Her cheeks were still flushed with embarrassment, but also distended by the huge and unfamiliar object inside them and some of the flushed look may have been pride at another milestone passed.

Her mission completed, she sat up again, pulling away to reveal the shining wet head of his erection which stayed joined to her for a moment by a glistening thread of saliva. The wetness extended down the shaft where her hands had resumed their slow caress, hypnotically rising and falling up and down the length of the shaft which she held, warily, at a safe distance.

I turned to Alan. 'How is that?'

He grinned, an ear-to-ear, what-a-stupid-question, sort of grin. 'Pretty good, actually, Mr Mortensen.'

'Would you prefer it different? Harder, faster or slower?'

'Well,' he considered. Since he was being offered à la carte, he had no need to settle for the choice of the day. 'She could squeeze a bit tighter.' He tousled her hair again. 'It won't break, love.'

She squeezed obediently, shuffled forward on her knees and settled into her task. A few seconds later Alan leant down and moved her thumbs round so that they pointed straight up the shaft and Lucy immediately absorbed her new lesson, shuffled another few inches closer and a warm smile of contentment spread across her face as she turned to me briefly for my blessing.

Alan was clearly having difficulty staying still. His thighs swung from side to side and he pushed himself further down into the chair, sliding his groin closer to Lucy, presenting his genitals unequivocally to her face, her mouth, her lips. She was watching in rapt attention and as his movements became increasingly agitated she glanced up at him.

'Will I have to put it in my mouth again?'

'Yes. Definitely.'

She looked at it anxiously. 'But will all the stuff come out into my mouth?'

'Oh, no. Trust me.' Alan grinned across at me and his eyebrows flicked up and down. I decided to let him have his way.

Reassured on this, Lucy was less hesitant this time. She simply leant down and when Alan pushed forward again, the round head knocked on her chin, on her lips, and she meekly opened up and let it slide inside. Her palms continued slowly masturbating the long shaft and Alan, taking a handful of her hair, indicated how she should also move her lips up and down the head.

'That's very good, love. But use your tongue as well. That's right.'

His grip on her hair was getting stronger and his thighs had now scissored wide open to expose as much of himself as he could to the caresses she was offering. His breathing, in spite of his attempts to give no warning, was also laboured, and then suddenly it was all too much. Both his hands grabbed her hair as Lucy squealed and pulled free, hauling his penis out of her mouth, dribbling and spitting as the jets spattered across her face, her cheeks and into her hair.

When Alan finally released her, managing to look a little sheepish, she quickly sat back, glaring at the hateful object which had done this to her and from which the last drops were still oozing and running down its length. She dabbed cautiously at her face with her fingertips and turned accusingly to me, her mouth still held open as she refused to swallow the residue of the first stream, but her face glistened, her eyes burned and she was a mess.

'I'm sorry about that, Lucy. Alan appears to have lost control.'

'Can I go and wash, please?' She was still trying to keep her mouth open.

'Well, not quite yet. I think you ought to clean him up first.'

She looked forlornly round her. 'What with?'

'Your tongue, of course.'

She stared at me in horror and then across at Alan, where he lounged unashamedly. His penis, glistening with her saliva and his own semen, was wilting but still blatantly displayed.

'You don't mean lick it now?'

'Yes, I mean exactly that.'

'But it's all mucky.'

'Yes, and I want you to lick that off.'

She turned to stare at the thing for a moment. 'And swallow it?'

'Of course.'

'Sam told me once she'd done that.' She seemed to be musing to herself more than to us. 'You know, let her boyfriend do it all in her mouth and then swallow it. I said I never would.' But she leant forward, carefully picked up the soft object with her finger and thumb and examined it for a moment. Finally she ducked down, started to lick and, after a few tentative laps, gave in and took it all into her mouth. I watched the movement of her bloated cheeks, for a moment later she released it again, shining but now clean.

She turned to face me, made sure I was paying due attention and then swallowed. She licked her lips. 'I suppose it's not so bad.'

5

Friday

Everything I had learnt about Mrs Ackworth intrigued me; I was impatient to meet her again, to beard her in her den, return the dreadful knickers and probe deeper below the conservative veneer of the bizarre establishment that she had set up in so unlikely a place. The woman clearly took an unjustifiably close and tyrannical interest in the girls in her charge, and I was anxious to discover just how far she had gone. My inclination was to assume a great distance, but then we always judge others by our own standards. Moreover, it would be entertaining to take a leisurely cup of coffee while both Lucy and Mrs Ackworth hovered about me. Each, for her own reason, would be horribly uncomfortable in my presence while neither could have any confidence as to my intentions.

Eventually my impatience overboiled and after lunch I decided to go up to the tea shop before Lucy finished work for the day when I could take the chance for a chat with Mrs Ackworth and have the pleasure of Lucy's company for the return journey. I made my way out there, picked through a tangle of bicycles that littered the street outside and pushed open the door into bedlam: the place was awash with lycra-covered bodies. The colours were bad enough – black, fluorescent greens, yellows and pinks – but the shapes were even worse – a range of bony knees and elbows, sweaty torsos and scrawny buttocks that could have modelled for Hieronymus Bosch. Not one with any justification to be so blatantly displayed. They had overrun the place with alien garishness as if they owned it and, worst of all, like tourists in a sanctuary, had defiled it and driven away its proper inhabitants: there was not a sign of either Lucy or The Dragon. However, another girl, equally young, not quite as pretty but charmingly chubby, was smiling fixedly from over the top of the counter. As I reluctantly pushed through to the only remaining table, she came hurrying over.

'Good afternoon, sir. What can I get you?'

She scurried off with my order and I watched the gaggle of cyclists sorting out who had drunk what, who had eaten which of the biscuits and who should settle each of the dozen or so individual bills before they eventually all swarmed off and the tea shop returned to something closer to its normal tranquillity. As yesterday, I had ordered coffee and a tea-cake which, as yesterday, arrived accompanied by a neatly folded napkin: a paper napkin that lay on the dull little side plate. It mocked me.

When the waitress returned with the coffee, I opened a conversation, discovered she was indeed the Sam that I had heard so much about, explained to her that I was a friend of Lucy's and asked whether she was available.

'No, she had to run down to the shop to get some more milk. With the sudden rush –' She waved towards the tables still littered with the leavings of the cycling party '– we almost ran out. She'll be back in a moment.'

'I see. And Mrs Ackworth?'

'No, she isn't here at all, I'm afraid. She's had to go to collect her sister this afternoon. Can I give her any message?'

'Her sister?'

'Yes, her sister, Mrs Kewell. She comes to stay for a few days sometimes.'

One harridan was interesting; a pair was intriguing. I was about to see what else I could glean when Lucy pushed through the door clutching two bottles of milk, panting and flustered and doubly so on finding me there.

I dawdled over my coffee until Lucy had finished, changed out of her uniform and was ready to join me for a sunny stroll back to my house. Before we had travelled more than a few yards, I was stopped by my name being bellowed from a passing car: Duncan McQuillan was waving at me excitedly.

'Alex! Stop right there! I have made a discovery that will bring music to your life.'

I was accustomed to Duncan's excess of enthusiasm for his subject, but a day which shone so bright could not be dulled even by his insufferable jollity. Lucy and I waited dutifully and within a moment he had parked his car and come galloping down to us with a sheaf of papers flapping insecurely in his hand.

'Alex! How splendid! I have just come from your house!' He grasped my hand and shook it enthusiastically, as if I were a long-lost friend he had not seen in years. 'This really is magnificent. You will never guess what I have found! Come up to my office at once!'

To Lucy's great amusement, I allowed myself to be hustled towards the castle as I made the introductions. 'Duncan, I should explain, is a fellow historian and the castle curator, nationally recognised as an expert on the early seventeenth century.'

He paused briefly and beamed at her, grabbed her hand too and squeezed it eagerly, then bustled us into the gate-house, past the stands of gifts, fudge and postcards towards some stairs at the back and up to his office on the upper floor. His discoveries, he explained with a mischievous grin, were not for public ears. At the top of the winding staircase, he ushered us into his tiny office, closed the door and scrambled about clearing a couple of chairs of the mess of books and posters and lumps of stone that littered every available flat surface. Lucy and I waited at the little row of small leaded windows looking out over an expanse of neat grass within the castle's outer walls until Duncan called proudly to indicate that he had managed to make room for us to sit down. He returned behind his own little desk and pulled a notebook from the bottom of a heap of other books which he placed, neatly closed, in the tiny clearing directly in front of him.

The man's eyes were burning with a childish delight, but I had to pause. 'Before we start, Duncan, I take it none of the staff normally comes up here, do they?'

'Very seldom, almost never unless I ask them. Why?' Although I knew Duncan to be reasonably broad-minded – indeed, we had collaborated on a few ventures in the past when the historical content was sufficiently high to justify what, to him, was the intrusion of an erotic dimension – he was primarily a historian whose interest tended to the theoretical rather than the practical. He was therefore puzzled at my enquiry and agitated at the delay.

'Usually, you see, when Lucy comes to visit me at home, I have found it pleasant to have her naked during our afternoons together. I thought, if you don't mind, I would continue that way.'

She looked round at me with a start and wrapped her arms round herself defensively. I had never before asked her to undress anywhere but in my own house and, Alan excepted, never with anyone else there. 'Please, Mr Mortensen, I don't want him to see me.'

'Nonsense, Lucy. You know you have nothing to be ashamed of and I am certain that Duncan would not object.'

'Well, no. I have no objection. That is, I'd be delighted. Please! Go ahead!' He clasped his hands together in front of him but the agitated way his fingers twirled around each other suggested the delay was tolerable but not desirable.

The stillness stretched out as Lucy gazed down at the floor. Below us we could hear a few tourists making their way through the shop and ticket office into the castle grounds. Voices and sounds drifted up through the sunny afternoon: children being reprimanded and quietened down; crockery clattering in the tea shop: a grinding cement mixer where some workmen were repairing a section of wall. Still Lucy didn't move. It was such an ordinary vanilla life down there, of families behaving as families do, while up above we sat and watched and waited while Lucy digested my instruction and decided whether she would take off her clothes for us.

It was slow and reluctant, her final surrender. She crossed her arms in front of her and pulled the sweater up over her head, draped it neatly over the back of her chair and then stooped to untie her trainers and pull off the little white socks. Next came the jeans. First the stud unpopped and then the zip was undone before the thick denim was pushed down her long legs. This caused her knickers to be tugged askew, and even though she would soon be removing those as well, she immediately stopped to readjust them. The jeans were draped over her sweater and she glanced over at me. She tossed her head back, swinging her blonde ponytail clear before sliding down the shoulder straps of her bra and peeling the cups away from her breasts. The little nipples appeared so pink, so clean and scrubbed, and yet I was beginning to know them better, to recognise their different stages. They were not completely soft, but appeared just slightly erect, promising a tender firmness to the touch, a delicious resistance to any fingers that stretched out to sample them. I resisted.

She twisted the bra strap round to unhook it, her hands nudging gently, but perhaps unnecessarily at the soft undersides of her breasts as she did so. The bra was laid neatly on top of her jeans and as she reached up to take off the last item, I stopped her.

'Lucy? Go over to Mr McQuillan. I'm sure he would like to help you with those.'

She shuffled across to his chair and stood meekly in place as he picked carefully at the thin elastic waistband and drew the knickers down and off. He immediately handed them to her and turned back to me to resume the saga of his discovery. Lucy seemed disappointed at his offhand treatment, so I had her bring the knickers over to me so that I could sample their sweet scent. The end of a long hot day, culminating in a dash to town and back to fetch milk, produced a perfect reward: aromatic and incomparable.

'How wonderful, Lucy, dear. Please sit down.' The girl scuttled back to her coarse over-stuffed chair – which clearly prickled her delicate skin as she settled into it – and tried to make herself comfortable. 'Now then, Duncan, what did you have to tell me?'

He was watching us with a look of bemused curiosity, like a proud schoolboy who finds his confidence challenged; who wonders, secretly and unexpectedly, whether another boy's toy really is better than his own. Finally he pulled himself together, and as his tale gathered pace, it cleared his mind of everything else.

'Ah, yes! Well, I have been working on Cecily Markham's diaries and have started to transcribe them. They really should be published, you know, because they paint a most illuminating picture of life at that time. Perhaps some of the later volumes concerning her time at the priory and the events leading up to her expulsion may be a little strong for public consumption, but I'm certain they would appeal to the more refined palette and would be specially entertaining to someone of your tastes.' He smiled to show his comment was good humoured, but we had never agreed about his wretched priory. Despite the local council's vain attempts to promote it as a tourist attraction, it was now just a heap of blackened stones up on the headland, which Duncan incessantly argued needed a proper study and excavation.

'However, the particular item I wanted to tell you about is much earlier when she was, as we suspected, living in your house, it being at that time the rectory. And that bizarre tangle of straps that I found? The ones I told you about? Well, it seems you were perfectly correct; that was indeed a harness made for a young woman, but it is a much older object than we thought.'

He pushed forward on his chair, glancing uncertainly at Lucy, seeming startled to be reminded that she was naked, but his enthusiasm overcame his discretion and he eagerly hurried on with his tale. 'The first volume of the diaries, as you know, is missing but the second volume starts just after the girls, Cecily and her unfortunate sister, Anne, became Sir Charles Cobden's wards, although perhaps ward is not entirely correct because there is a suggestion that they were in many respects little more than bonded slaves. It appears that Sir Charles may have acquired them from their father as security for a gambling debt which the poor man had been unable to pay before he died. In any event, Sir Charles seems to have treated them both very poorly, but Anne, who was evidently the prettier of the two, suffered the worse, mainly because she was thoroughly obstinate and refused to succumb to his desires. Finally, he issued an ultimatum, but still she refused and so he had her whipped and –' Here the man's eyes sparkled in delight '– strapped into that harness! Cecily describes the scene quite explicitly. Shall I, er . . .?' He looked to me for an answer, then Lucy and then me again. 'Shall I read it?'

Lucy beat me to the reply. 'Yes. Certainly.'

'Cecily describes . . . Where are we?' Duncan started rummaging through his notes and finally opened the notebook at a slip marker. 'Ah! Here it is!'

In the stillness of the afternoon, Lucy leant forward as he started to read.

' "Sir Charles had on this night called together some six or eight of his companions and when they were assembled did he have Martha bring us both down to him, where he yet sat at table with his friends as they had dined and were merry. So we both descended to him in some fear and I stood by the by, but dear Anne, being then but nineteen years of age, was brought out unto the midst of the company. There doth Sir Charles relate that she has often times disobeyed him and vexed him and must be punished for her sins and he asks her yet one final time whether she will now repent and oblige him with the completion of his desires. Still doth she refuse at which, against all my anticipations, he seemed not angered but mighty pleased at her reply. Forthwith doth he have her stripped quite naked of every cloth that she had ever had covering her body sparing her not the slightest scrap that might cover her person. Then he calls to four of his companions, who straightway lay their hands on her, stretching her out in that condition and holding her thus, with her face pressed down upon the great table that be in that room, and her body and her posterior lifted upward, and when she be arranged to his liking, Sir Charles doth himself make mockery again. At last, he doth take up his own riding whip and doth whip her hideously and in full measure the full length of her body even from her fair knees to her shoulders.

' "All the while doth Anne cry out most piteously at the torment, but he takes no note of it and continues in the same fashion until all her flesh be reddened and sore and all her skin be raised up in furrows such as no man could countenance upon the body of one so young and gentle. Then he doth rest and examine carefully both her back and also her buttocks which he doth peruse most privily, as do his companions, freely laying their hands upon her nakedness, and acting their wanton pranks with such unbounded licentiousness as if she were but a common harlot, often making careless and coarse mockery of her protestation at the pain that she doth suffer and the shame of her treatment.

' "Once that be done, he doth have those same men turn her upon her back, so that all her nether intimacies be laid open to their lustful eyes and then doth he whip her again across her body, from her neck down to her knees, till all her front be made a fine match for her back, being all over reddened and striped. Even so, be this not enough to quell his cruelty, for he spared neither her tender bosom nor yet her feminine parts, and indeed extracted most particularly upon those undeserving places the fullest force of his fury. And again doth he stop and examine carefully all the results of his work, both he and his company passing their hands often times across her body and insinuating their hands even between her privy parts which, two among them hauling hard upon her ankles, he doth cause to be freely exposed to all of those gathered in attendance.

' "In this part doth Sir Charles tarry long, remarking that she be so moist and do flow so plentifully as if she did spend of the exertion put upon her. At this, all his companions also gathered round and marked the place, discoursing loudly how plump and juicy, how succulent and ripe for plucking, be that part of her which by modesty they never should have known. And all the while, Anne doth turn her face away as tears flow from her, but I yet stood by and beheld it all, and (to my shame) felt in that part of me where the sense of feeling be so exquisitely critical, a strange tickling heat such as I had not till that evening known and which grew to a fire that did consume me till I felt quite faint and would have fallen had not I held fast to the mantle to save me. The others being entirely taken in their examination of Anne's body, I thank God that none observed it.

' "Presently one of them, turning from Anne and marking that I still be by, doth bid me come forward and questions Sir Charles why do not they compare whether indeed we be as like as sisters in those parts of my person which be not then visible to them. At this Sir Charles doth laugh merrily and agree that this should be fine sport. So they do pull me out also to that table the while that one of them doth tear at my silk kerchief until my bosom is laid quite bare and he doth make free of my bosom with his hands, pinching at my person and making with me as if I were but a she-goat to be milked upon that day. Then another of them doth pull at my skirts and they two together do lift me up upon that table beside dear Anne, mindless of my begging and my protestations until finally I do call that they may not do this for it be my woman's time and the flowers be upon me. On hearing this do they let me go. I am much ashamed at this, for my claims were not truth yet did I by a lie maintain my modesty.

' "Presently was Anne released from her holding but Sir Charles did bring forth a harness that he had ordered to be made and which were put upon her and this harness be of the lewdest type that were ever devised and that do but display her body most wantonly. For forty days hath she been kept in this way, without ever a single scrap of clothing, nor any covering at any time, but each day must she attend Sir Charles in the dining hall, no matter what servants or visitors be present, and there doth he examine the stripes upon her body. All the while that he doth examine her, laying his hands all upon her with no

72

modesty, he doth acquaint her that on the very day when the last mark can no longer be discerned, will he have her whipped again. Nor does he make any endeavour to guard her modesty, for her intimacies are so freely displayed by this foul harness that the matter is much spoken of in the village and many men of little quality and most disagreeable in their persons do find some pretence to be at our house each day to witness her shaming and to partake to what extent they may in the scrutinies that are inflicted upon her nakedness." '

Duncan paused while we digested this account and I looked across to gauge Lucy's reaction to so vivid and anguished a tale. She shivered, staring at the book that Duncan still held in his hand and yet gazing with an awe that was more than terror. There was something of empathy, if not of envy, as she digested the details of the event, blinking in embarrassment and turning away while Duncan carefully closed the notebook and severed the bond that for those few minutes had tied her so intimately to that other girl across a distance of almost 400 years.

'Eventually,' Duncan continued, 'it seems she was rescued by her lover and they eloped and were married, but Sir Charles, furious at this challenge to his authority, had a series of carvings made which he displayed over his mantelpiece and which show him with both the sisters and his own wife. According to the sketches, the two sisters both appear bare-breasted and Anne, the central figure, is depicted in the harness itself. The carving was in Sir Charles's dining room, that is to say, your dining room, and quite scandalised the local gentry in that rather prudish time. Eventually, on Sir Charles's death, his widow determined to be rid of the outrageous object and the panels were removed by a cousin by the name of Samuel Baldwyn, who may have been present on the night in question, and who apparently intended to take them back to his own house. Whether he did so or whether they were destroyed, of course we now have no idea. From the pictures, I can scarcely believe that putting them on public display would have been possible, but I suppose we can always hope they still exist somewhere. I have had the sketch photographed and enlarged.'

He passed across a large black and white reproduction of a pencil drawing. The stone fireplace I recognised immediately from my dining room, but above that, in an area which now has only the plainest of panels that is thoroughly out of keeping with the rest of the ornate room, there are shown four carved panels, the middle two being somewhat grotesque heads and the outer two possibly coats of arms. However, at either end of the panels, and in the three borders between them, are five carved figures, all well rounded but all stopping at hip height. On the extreme left is a woman, her arms neatly folded in front of her, then a stern-looking man, bearded. On the extreme right is another woman, her arms also neatly folded in front of her, and although she is clearly wearing a skirt below the waist, her breasts are bare. Next to her is another man, similar and quite possibly the same one, but he is shown in little detail.

However, it is the figure in the centre that immediately catches the eye and that the artist has depicted in the greatest detail, as well he might. This too is a woman, but she is not merely bare breasted, she is entirely naked, and whereas all the other four figures are shown with their arms tidily in front of them, forearms neatly parallel with the floor, the central figure has her arms behind her and she is wearing what can only be a leather harness. A collar encircles her neck from which a wide strap runs between her breasts and joins another encircling her waist. A further strap extends below that, where it would doubtless have passed between her legs and joined again at the waist behind her. Her arms disappear behind her in a pose which is totally unnatural and would not be adopted by anyone unless their wrists were held in that position. In my life I have seen many such harnesses, and many girls wearing them, and this was identical to several modern designs I have encountered and even used; I never thought the pattern to be so old.

I was amazed to see this depiction of the young woman, grim but unbowed, as she was displayed next to her tormentor, and even more so to think that she had been strapped in that way, harnessed, exposed and doubtless humiliated and whipped, in that same room, in front of that same fireplace where I had myself indulged in remarkably similar pleasures.

I passed the shiny photograph across to Lucy, seeing her shiver as her head bent over the image, before turning back to Duncan. 'And the harness? You think that is the same one? It scarcely seems possible.'

'Why not? Why else would it have been so carefully hidden away? I am sure of it. I have been soaking it in oil for the last four days so it really should be ready by now. I shall fetch it.'

When he returned with the bowl, the leather was dripping with oil, but it was at least sufficiently supple that we could at last straighten it out and unfasten the buckles, one on the collar, one on the waist, one on the crotch strap and one on the wrist strap. Unquestionably this was the same harness that was shown in the sketches. The embossed fastenings on the front of the collar and front of the waistband were quite unmistakable.

'Her rescue was interesting,' Duncan continued as he carefully wiped the ancient leather with a cloth, 'because it seems that each night he had the harness attached to a thick ring in the wall of her bedroom but, one night, her lover crept into the house and covered her entirely with goose grease so that she was able to slip out of the harness.'

'That hardly seems possible,' I argued. 'The leather seems far too tough.'

'Very hard to say,' he answered, but even as he was speaking, my mind was filling with an idea.

'We must try it! There is no reason why we should not. We will put Lucy in the harness and try it out.'

They both objected to this immediately. Lucy's grounds were more heartfelt but less well founded than Duncan's, who was concerned at possible damage to the harness, but he was clearly enthusiastic once persuaded that this was a valid historical reconstruction. I sent Lucy down to the tea shop to see what we could use instead of goose fat, while Duncan and I finished wiping clean the rest of the harness. By the time she returned with a vast tub of butter, our job was done. I decided it would be good for her to experience being handled by another person, so as Lucy stood forlornly in the centre of the room, undressed again, I left to Duncan the task of carefully wrapping the straps around her.

The first went round her neck, the second round her waist, and then he fumbled the long tail through between her legs. This started as a single broad strap but, just about level with the top of her pubic triangle, the strap split into two narrow belts, which both passed between her legs and were then fastened to separate buckles spaced several inches apart at the back. The result was that these thinner belts each nestled snugly against the inside of her thigh alongside the outer lips of her sex and thus the harness could be worn for extended periods without having to be removed to allow the wearer to go to the toilet. Equally, of course, access to her vagina was also possible. These belts were pulled up firmly between her legs and buckled securely behind her. Her arms were drawn back and fastened in the figure-of-eight strap attached to the back of the harness.

Within moments it was on, and buckled up tight. As Duncan and I stood back to assess the picture presented, Lucy was as vulnerable and defenceless as poor Anne Markham herself. She was held entirely helpless, her breasts completely exposed and accessible and her belly and pubis openly visible. Duncan was utterly entranced and I even permitted him to photograph her from all angles so that he could compare this with the sketches.

He returned from replacing the camera. 'Now the grease?' he asked.

'Please continue.'

'The buckles, you see, would have been easy: anyone could have unfastened them. It is only the waist strap, secured by a lock through the two large rings at the back, which, in the absence of the key, would have required the

76

application of grease.' He spoke as he spread layers of newspaper on the floor, arranged Lucy in the middle and opened the plastic tub.

She eyed him warily as he pulled up his sleeves and scooped out a good handful of pale yellow slime. Once started, he did not hesitate but simply slapped the whole mess on to her stomach and started to work it liberally over, round, and (in particular) under the leather harness. In spite of his comments that the top part could be easily unbuckled, he still slapped several generous handfuls on to her breasts, working it over the skin and sliding his fingers through the gooey mess and under the straps, across and round her nipples until the insistent attention caused them to project eagerly from their revolting coating. Moving down, he applied more around her waist, in front and behind, frequently slipping his fingers beneath the strap to work it all round her waist. The reason became clear when he moved down still further. Having set the fashion, she could hardly complain when he had her spread her legs and another good handful of butter was slapped between her thighs and then liberally worked into all her most intimate folds beneath the straps, slipped across her bottom and pushed even into the crease between her buttocks.

By the time Duncan was done, Lucy looked the most repulsive offering imaginable. Her face and hair were still relatively clean, but below the neck she was entirely covered in a thick grease, which completely obscured her breasts (although the tips of her eager pink nipples poked through the layers), matted her pubic hair and hid her crease totally.

'There! What do you think?'

Who could doubt what Lucy thought as she waited miserably in the middle of the room for our verdict? For any young woman, raised from childhood in cleanliness and elegance, taught to present herself at her best at all times, the necessity of standing so hideously besmirched and fouled was humiliating. To be naked was worse. To be the only one naked, and not merely naked but trussed in such a way that she had no means of attempting to hide herself, to be the only one so soiled, and on top of that to be standing awaiting our scrutiny was heaping insult on to her shame. Yet that was what made the vision so compelling. She was caused no pain, yet her misery at the loathsome treatment, the indignity as Duncan so freely rubbed the grease all over her, as if he were unaware of her sensitivity or modesty, and the contrast between her usual standard of care and this utter mess, all combined to make an image so haunting, so captivating, so entrancing that I wanted to keep her like that always.

Yet Duncan, ever the scholar, demanded to complete the experiment. I had no choice but to let him so he set to, unfastening every available buckle until Lucy stood with the greasy harness hanging down all round her like seaweed from a mooring buoy, and he began to wrestle with the thick waist strap. However, I could soon see that his experiment was going to fail since he could not slide it either down over Lucy's hips or up over her breasts without its being unfastened. Whether this was because she was a different size, whether the leather had shrunk over the years or, as Duncan suggested, the original victim had become so emaciated over the period of her detention in the harness that it would slip off her without problem, nobody could tell. In any case, I eventually persuaded him to give up the struggle and, since the castle had now closed and was empty, we unfastened the belt and took Lucy out to the castle courtyard where a pump above the old well still brought up crystal-clear water from 150 feet down in the chalk. There she stood, shivering naked on the cobbles in the fading evening, as Duncan gleefully washed off the grease, ensuring that none was left in any of the awkward places that a man with more decency might have left unexplored. Eventually, he finished rinsing her off and left her standing dripping while, unseen by either of them, the three stonemasons whose work I had heard earlier, watched silently from the top of the north tower. Once done we returned to the gate-house, and I waved cheerily to the men above us as we left them, yet I wondered as I did so whether similar workers in similar circumstances

400 years before had paused in their work to watch a young girl brought out naked to the well to be cleaned of that day's trial and prepared for the next. In any case, they did not return the acknowledgement.

Lucy was quiet as we made our way back up Castle Street to the town. At the cross, she stopped.

'I turn off here.' A hint of uncertainty quivered in her voice, as if she were unsure whether today's lesson was over or whether she would be required to accompany me all the way back to my house.

'I see. Right. I'll see you next time then.'

Still she hesitated, drawing uneasy lines in the dust with the side of her shoe. 'Is that possible, Mr Mortensen? That someone would allow themselves to be treated like that, almost as if, well, they enjoyed it?'

'I'm sure it is.'

'And what Anne's sister wrote in her diary? Becoming so excited at watching someone else suffering so much, specially someone so close to you?'

'Yes, indeed, specially someone so close, someone you love. These are early days, Lucy, but a whole world waits for you on that subject.'

She grinned at me, no misgivings at the prospect of what I promised, and I watched her turn and scamper away towards, presumably, her own home, tempted for a few moments to follow and see where she lived, but I thought better of it and checked myself. I should not allow a whim to become an addiction.

6

Saturday

I arrived up at the Castlegate Tearooms soon after they opened at ten o'clock. I was the first customer through the door and settled in the bay, at the same one I had taken yesterday. Lucy was not there, of course – she had told me that on Saturdays she only worked in the afternoons – but nor was Sam. Today's waitress was again different. Perhaps not quite as appealing as the two I had previously encountered there, but young and almost as pretty; I was beginning to recognise Mrs Ackworth's pattern. The girl quickly came to take my order and soon after she had bustled away, Mrs Ackworth herself appeared at her vantage point behind the counter. She glowered round her domain and stopped dead when she saw me; her response to my cheerful smile was strained.

Business was evidently pretty slow, the schools having recently gone back for the summer term and the tourist season not really started, cycling parties excepted, but I didn't dawdle and on finishing my coffee, walked up to Mrs Ackworth at her till.

'Good morning, Mrs Ackworth. Another lovely day.'

'Yes.' Thursday's appetite for conversation seemed to have departed her.

I settled my bill and dropped a coin in the tips bowl. 'I wonder if I might have a word with you, Mrs Ackworth, if you are not too busy.'

She looked round, guilt painted across her face, and tried to assume a doubt that such an imposition could be accommodated. However, she was looking at an almost empty room; her single waitress was more than enough to deal with present demands. There was no reason, no possible excuse, to refuse, but as she turned back to me, I could see her mind hunting for an escape. I pressed on.

'In your office, perhaps? I have something of yours that I should like to return to you.'

She glanced sharply round, guilt beginning to turn to unease, muttered agreement and led the way through, taking her place safely behind a large desk. I closed the door behind me and then handed the bag over. She glanced inside and blushed. Her eyes flicked up to me for an instant and then she hastily bundled the bag and its contents away into a drawer.

'I can, of course, explain. You see, it is entirely innocent, Mr . . . I'm sorry, I don't know your name.'

'Mortensen. Alex Mortensen. Please, Mrs Ackworth, do not be alarmed. It appears, from what Lucy has told me of the way things are run here, that we are of similar tastes, you and I.' She relaxed a little, although not entirely. We were both in a delicate situation.

'Let me be blunt,' I continued. 'Lucy has told me a little of what has been going on here and although, in her innocence she has not understood, I think I have. Putting two and two together, I believe you have been spying on the girls changing. You have demanded that they display their underwear to you. You have even on one or two occasions abused your position to discipline the girls in your employment.' Her face was colouring brightly as she waited for me to finish.

'Had I been in your position, I would have done just the same. As you now know, I asked Lucy to remove her knickers when I was in here on Thursday. You gave her those in replacement, a fact which I discovered because when she came to my house after work, I made her strip naked, as I always do. As I say, Mrs Ackworth, we have similar tastes. We have no need for pretence, either of us.'

She smiled at last. 'I'm very pleased to hear that, Mr Mortensen, and also pleased to meet a fellow connoisseur.'

After that the floodgates opened. She told me of watching the girls changing: how she had steadily introduced ever more detail to the uniform and how she had been desperately trying to find a style of top which would demand their removing their bras while they changed, and dreamed of finding a way to require them to change their knickers.

She showed me the deep cupboard in her office whose back was the two-way mirror through which she watched. She invited me to peer through into the (then empty) room. She showed me the video camera that she had used to film them; she showed me the tapes and offered to play one for me. Within a quarter of an hour, her whole enterprise had been opened up to me. She displayed the same enthusiasm as any collector of fine works and yet it seemed that hers had been a lonely pursuit and her delight at finding a companion on whom to pour her tale was uncontrollable. The years of caution and silence were swept away in a torrent of unrestrained revelation. I allowed her full rein until she had finally talked herself to a standstill and was reclining in her chair, her face bubbling with pride for her collection.

'But discipline, Mrs Ackworth?' I needed to delve to the bottom and adopted a tone of incredulous eagerness and stunned admiration. 'How have you managed that?'

'Not as difficult as you might imagine, Mr Mortensen,' she responded smugly. 'I mean, there are precious few job opportunities around here for unskilled girls, and almost all of those depend to some degree upon the tourist industry. If a girl gets no reference from me but is dismissed with the suggestion she has been stealing from the till, well! Frankly, Mr Mortensen, that is something no girl can afford. This is a small town where I know personally the owners of almost all the other establishments and a word from me carries some weight. A bad reputation will be remembered for a very long time. So, if they don't want the sack for whatever sin I may have discovered or –' She squirmed in a manner that was meant to be alluring '– let us say, devised, they generally agree.

Once they have accepted punishment once, I find they make much less fuss a second time.'

'But has none ever threatened to report you?'

'Oh, yes! Practically all of them do that. It is the automatic first reaction. However, they soon realise that it would be my word against theirs and that I have some standing in the town; after all, I am a member of the Parish Council. No-one would ever believe them. However, I would say that I am careful in assessing who might respond well and who might prove, what we might term, dangerous.'

'This does seem a little harsh, though, Mrs Ackworth. I mean, threatening to expose them and sack them unless they agree to be spanked by you.'

She laughed. 'No girl ever came to any great harm by having her bottom spanked, Mr Mortensen. Indeed, one might think that the female bottom was designed for the purpose. No, a good spanking takes them down a peg or two and teaches them a little respect. And, yes, it is mostly spanked, but if I find it necessary to repeat the punishment, I may use a slipper or sometimes a belt. I take care not to be too hard on them, you see, because very few girls these days have any experience of receiving proper corporal punishment, so I start quite mildly and those who come back for a third time are those who are not going to make a silly fuss about it. Of course, some will always continue in refusal, and they, well, they can always look for another career for themselves. It may not be easy, but they should consider that before they argue.'

'Well, you have my admiration. I have to say that if I hadn't heard it from your own mouth, I would not have believed it.'

She smirked, yet again. 'You are too kind, Mr Mortensen. However, you are also too modest. It seems you have made some progress with Lucy, who is a girl I had ruled out, with great regret, I may say, as completely unresponsive.'

'Oh, yes, I'm sure she is. I mean, she certainly wouldn't accept a spanking or anything of that nature.' I did not want the woman blundering on to my ground and frightening the quarry. I needed to keep her on her own terrain, perhaps by increasing her pride in that pathetic acre.

'But how do you start? How do you broach the subject?'

She smiled, smug superiority dribbling from her face. 'It's mostly a matter of establishing the correct atmosphere, getting the tone right. Once that is all prepared, they generally follow wherever you choose to lead, provided you don't rush them too fast. Taken at the correct pace, there is really no limit. Of course the skill lies in preparing the ground, and that, well . . .' She paused. 'Would you like a demonstration?'

'Yes, indeed.'

She stood up and made for the door. 'You understand that, given the time available, this can only be an illustration of what can be achieved. Young Sarah, the girl I have working here today, however, does seem most promising. She has been with me for a couple of weeks now and it is probably time to start laying down the ground rules. I had not intended to start for another week or so, but today could be as good as any.'

A few minutes later the girl had been summoned, the office door had been shut and Mrs Ackworth was back behind her desk. The girl, Sarah, stood terrified in the centre of the room, unsure whether the retribution which she was evidently convinced was about to fall on her would come from Mrs Ackworth in front of her or me behind.

'Sarah,' started Mrs Ackworth, 'Mr Mortensen is considering purchasing some of the same style of waitress uniforms that we use here and I suggested he might care to see how they look worn. You don't mind, do you?'

'No, Mrs Ackworth.'

'Excellent.' The spider smiled at the fly. 'Turn round so he can see from all sides. That's good.'

The little pirouette completed, the girl stood between us again. 'I always think the detail is important in these things; the stockings and underwear, for example, must be right if the uniform as a whole is to convey the proper

84

impression. Sarah, dear, lift up your skirt and let Mr Mortensen see the underwear.'

'Here?' The girl was appalled.

'Yes, come along. There is no need for any false modesty here, girl. Get on with it.' The tone was exactly that of a schoolmistress, and like a good schoolgirl, Sarah was entirely in her power. I have to confess, Mrs Ackworth's bearing was such that disobedience seemed quite unthinkable. For Sarah, it was clearly impossible. She shyly lifted her hem until her legs, her stocking tops, her thighs and finally her knickers were in full view.

'Higher than that, girl. Let him see the whole thing. In fact, it would be best if you take the skirt right off, just for a moment.'

Sarah glanced from one stern face to the other, looked to be on the point of protest but finally reached round, slid down the zip and stepped out of it. She stood with the skirt dangling forlornly from her hand. Her blouse only just reached her waist and below that was revealed a sweet pair of neat white cotton knickers, stretched tight across the smooth curves of her bottom.

'There, you see? What did I tell you?' Mrs Ackworth could have been referring to the underwear; the girl clearly believed she was.

Mrs Ackworth glanced at me, licking her lips, and I realised she was preparing to tighten another notch. 'Hand the knickers to Mr Mortensen as well, Sarah. Let him see them.'

'But Mrs Ackworth . . .'

But what reasonable objection could there be to so utterly unreasonable a demand? In the slow quiet stillness of that office, reason had gone, driven out by the seasoned certainty of the woman's tone. Eventually the girl simply reached up, hooked her thumbs in the elastic waistband and pushed them down her legs. She stepped out of them and handed them across, before scurrying back to cross her hands inadequately in front of the pale tawny bush that had so fleetingly been revealed to us. Mrs Ackworth immediately interceded.

'Hands behind the back, dear, and turn to face me.' I am sure her purpose in that was pure selfishness and nothing else. If a young girl were to be exposed half naked, then Mrs Ackworth would want to see it. She kept her there for only a couple of moments, turning her just once but even so, I was treated to a pretty sight, both front and back, of soft warm fluff, of little half-moon buttocks, of pure unblemished skin, the whole made all the more alluring by the evident reluctance of the display. She was quickly allowed to dress again and return to her duties and, once she had gone, we settled back in our respective chairs, Mrs Ackworth as complacent as anyone I have ever seen.

'There you are, you see. A girl of what? Eighteen? Nineteen? Admittedly the standard of modesty among these young trollops is very different from what was expected in our day, but even so, this is still entirely new to her. And yet! I bring her in here. I make her lift up her skirt. I make her remove her underwear. She did not want to, of course, but I have made her do it anyway. All in the power of the voice, Mr Mortensen. I confess she was more amenable than I had anticipated, so next week, I think I shall probably spank her.'

'Tell me, then, how long has this been going on?' A sweep of my arm took in the secret of the deep cupboard, the video tapes, the spot where the girl had been standing to undress.

'Well . . .' Mrs Ackworth smiled, folded her arms over her fine bosom and started on the tale.

That evening I phoned Alan. 'Alan, I have a particular favour to ask of you that requires the exercise of your other talents.'

'Other talents?'

'A little night work, Alan.'

'Mr Mortensen!' He feigned shock. 'Do you mean a touch of burglary?'

'Exactly.'

'Good! Tell me what I can do.'

7

Monday

The weekend dragged by without Lucy appearing once while I drifted aimlessly from room to room like a schoolboy in detention. Even the sky took away its favour and loured down at me, grey and unwelcoming, while the garden merely dripped, dank and misty, conscious of the sprite it was missing. We had made no specific arrangements about her visits and her absence unsettled me so that I swung between fears that she might never come again and self-induced reassurances that she simply could not get away so easily at weekends and by Monday everything would be back in order. I acknowledged that I was starting to look forward to her coming, to depend on her visits, and the house was already feeling empty without her. It was too big for me on my own, and needed the presence of a younger person to bring back life to its aged walls. I dreamt of having her with me always, of being able to look up at any time and see her sweet slim body, quite naked, of course, flitting through the rooms and down the garden. What more attractive an adornment could possibly be contrived?

So by Monday morning I was feeling almost lonely, something that I have not known for many years, and was sorely tempted to go the tearooms again to see her sooner. It was not the sort of lonely that comes from being without people in general. Although I live alone, that is something I choose for myself, assured that my work will always bring me into enough contact with others for me not to

87

miss other company. No, this was a quite specific feeling of missing one particular person and the joy which that one person would bring into my life.

When it came to two o'clock, I was pacing in the front sitting room, looking out for her. This room, intended as the drawing room, has a magnificent bay window with a full outlook on to Bridge Street, but as a result is unpleasantly noisy and so is not a room that I often use. Yet here I paced, searching anxiously up the street towards the town centre and down towards the river. I knew so little about her – how she got here, which way she came from, not even where she lived.

Then suddenly the familiar pale ponytail came bobbing into sight behind the cars parked down the far side of the road, and she emerged, glanced both ways and came skipping across the road towards the house, glancing up at the severe brick walls. The doorbell sounded almost immediately. I use a real bell, not a hideous electric intrusion, and I waited until it was almost still again before going down the hall and opening the heavy wooden door.

She smiled at me so sweetly, so joyously, that I wanted to wrap my arms round her and kiss her. For a moment I almost did, curious what her reaction would be to such a gesture, but no; that was not our relationship. I had to remain the strict master, in spite of the tenderness I was feeling. She had to remain the reluctant servant, in spite of the enthusiastic anticipation which had been evident in her tread as she arrived, and evident too in her repeated returns.

I tried to put some harshness into my voice. 'Good afternoon, Lucy. Please come through into the study; you can undress in there.'

I led her back down the dingy corridor. During the course of that long and bleak weekend I had considered instituting a regime in which she would undress immediately upon arrival, leaving her clothes on the coat-stand in the porch, but eventually I decided against it. Although I liked the idea of nakedness being the natural uniform for my house, a uniform that she would assume as a matter of course the instant she came in, I would have missed watching her undress in front of me. There might also, occasionally, be times when I had somebody there who I would not wish to know of this arrangement, or alternatively somebody who would enjoy watching her undress as much as I did myself.

After so long a denial, I was eagerly looking forward to the vision and so was particularly irritated when, just as we walked down the hall, the telephone rang. Mark Stenning, a literary colleague with whom I was planning a new venture, wanted to agree a timetable, but I had also wanted to invite him to dinner that week. While I was standing speaking to him, Lucy hovered in front of me. For a few seconds she mimed a question but eventually she simply dropped her shoulder bag casually on to the floor and started to undress. It was almost impossible for me to concentrate on my conversation because I was so enraptured at the easy way with which, completely unbidden, she shivered out of her clothes and laid them one by one over the back of a chair. There was a wonderful fluidity in her movements, a natural grace and agility as her slender young limbs turned and bent to their task. Although still deliciously modest, she was already less inhibited than on previous days, and barely hesitated before removing her blouse to reveal a thin cream-coloured lacy bra whose delicate embroidery so smoothly cradled her round breasts. This too was swiftly unclasped and removed and her skirt slid down her legs. Her short socks followed and then, standing in just the delicate cream matching knickers, she did just pause a moment, glancing across to me for some reassurance. I merely smiled and she slid the knickers down her pale thighs and folded them neatly on top of the pile of clothes.

Finally, after lightly riffling out her little pubic bush, she wandered idly over to examine my bookshelves. The afternoon sun was just working its way round to the study windows, but as she stood, half turned away from me, her pale figure was lit by a single square shaft of sunlight that pierced the narrow sash windows, illuminating her slender back, her smooth shoulder and one delicate nipple. The shadow of the central window bar fell directly across the middle of her bottom, emphasising the curves and suggesting other stripes that I could – and perhaps one day should – lay across her immaculate skin.

When I finished the call and settled back in my usual seat she returned from her examination of my books. 'Should I fetch a towel again, Mr Mortensen?'

'Do you think you are going to need one?'

'Well, I think I might, yes.'

'Yes, all right then, Lucy, I think that would be wise.' It was such a pleasure to see her turn and scamper out of the room and to hear her bare feet pattering across the solid oak floor, up the old staircase and across the landing above to the bathroom.

When she returned, she carefully arranged the towel before she sat down and then smiled up at me expectantly.

'This is a really lovely house, Mr Mortensen. Is it very old?'

'Yes, I think so. As you know from Friday, Duncan is researching the history because this seems to be one of the oldest houses in the town. The main part where we are sitting now was built in 1729, but that was tacked on to something much older. The rooms on the other side of the hall certainly existed during the civil war but there is a date on the fireplace of 1573 which seems to be authentic. The street frontage is of course much newer – 1835 or so.'

'It must be wonderful living here. Do you work here as well?'

'Yes.' I left it at that, knowing she would not be satisfied, knowing such inquisitiveness would not rest till it had pried further.

'My fiancé mentioned . . .' She stopped suddenly, probably wondering whether she should have mentioned him, given the background, but then carried on. 'My fiancé mentioned that you have some very old books. What exactly do you do?'

'I am in part a historian and in part a translator.'

'That must be interesting. What do you translate?' I assumed she would have a pretty good idea of my specialisation from her fiancé's reports, but she was obviously keen to explore the subject.

'Well, I translate a variety of things. Partly technical papers, engineering particularly, very dry stuff like agricultural machinery maintenance manuals, that sort of thing. I also translate fiction and I specialise in erotica, particularly late medieval texts.'

'Oh. I see.' Now that the devil was loose, she was unsure how to deal with him.

'I imagine David told you of some of my books, didn't he?'

'Well, yes, he did a little bit,' she admitted. 'He said some of them were quite rude.'

'Perhaps rather outside his experience?'

'Yes,' she agreed and quickly changed the subject. 'I really like old houses. Our house is quite old, Victorian, but nothing like this. Could you show me round your house sometime? I'd really like to see it.'

'You can go and explore now, if you like. I need to make another couple of phone calls since, as you will have realised from that call just now, I am planning a little dinner party this Friday and need to call some people. I would, incidentally, very much like you to come. Is that possible? In any case, please make yourself at home and feel free to wander wherever you like; you will find no dead bodies locked away. Just don't go into the attic, if you don't mind. I keep one or two of my more personal items in there. Other than that one room, please enjoy yourself.'

I had been watching her closely, and noticed her start, her eyes widening and narrowing again quickly as I mentioned the attic, so I added a little extra bait. 'I will only be twenty five minutes or so, half an hour at most.'

So she scampered off again and left me to the phone. I am not normally much of a one for entertaining, but with memories of the Markham sisters' diary fresh in my mind, and having Lucy's regular attendance at my house, this was too good an opportunity to miss. I knew of one or two among my circle of friends who would be intrigued to meet her, so a dinner party for a select group of friends would be most appropriate. More than that, we would gather round the same table across which poor Anne Markham had been stretched and beaten. One person had still to be contacted, Graham Worthing, a fellow collector, and one who already knew something of Lucy's history so would be especially interested to meet her.

So I made the necessary call, which I knew would take no longer than five or ten minutes at the outside, and I was perfectly certain from her reaction that Lucy intended to make straight for the attic, secure in the knowledge that she had a good fifteen minutes of safety to pry where she should not.

I heard her go up the main staircase, a wonderfully carved piece, whose every tread creaked as she climbed. I also heard it creak a little less as she continued up the second flight into the attic. Clearly, she was not used to staircases of this age, which almost invariably creak when the weight is applied to the well-worn centre of the tread, but barely give at all if you take the trouble to step on the very outside of the tread, where the joints are less worn and much stronger next to the wall.

I set off, quietly, in search of Lucy. Following up the stairs, I carefully climbed the outside of the staircase, and avoided entirely the three stairs which I knew from long familiarity creak wherever you stand on them.

I paused at the door of the attic. A sound of rustling came from inside and a little gasp, then the quiet scrape of a drawer being carefully pulled open. It was not immediately closed again, so I could guess which drawer this was. I waited for a count of ten and then pushed the attic door open and marched in.

Lucy was caught red-handed, and although she whipped round in guilt and horror the instant she heard me, it was too late. She was kneeling in front of the Dutch mahogany curio cabinet. The top display drawer was open and she was holding in her hand a pale carved ivory phallus. She was so shocked at being caught that she stayed motionless for several seconds before contritely turning and carefully replacing the object in its place on the thick velvet lining of the drawer.

92

'I'm sorry, Mr Mortensen. I just wanted . . .' Her words petered out. We both knew what it was she wanted and there was no point in her attempting any lies or explanations.

'Well, Lucy, all I can say is that I am thoroughly disappointed in you. I have allowed you the run of my home and asked that you respect one small area of my privacy. Your reaction to that is immediately to trespass in the one area that I have asked you not to.'

'I am very sorry, Mr Mortensen, truly I am.'

'Please close the drawer and come downstairs with me.'

I watched her carefully and then stood aside so that she could slip past me. I followed as she slowly made her way back to the study. I think I had known what I was going to do next even before I had set off up to the attic in search of her. Following her neatly rounded bottom down the stairs confirmed my ideas.

As soon as we were in the study, I sat on the chair at my desk and gazed at the slim, timid figure standing in front of me.

'Well. It seems that a refusal to observe proper decencies runs in your circle. First I have your fiancé, now you. Both of you unable to respect the privacy of others, both unable to obey simple instructions. It seems I have been too hasty in agreeing to your request that I withdraw my complaint. Rather than withdrawing it, in fact, I should better make another. Now, perhaps.'

'No, Mr Mortensen, please don't. I am very sorry. I was just looking.'

'No, you were not, young lady, you were also handling. Do you know what that was, that item you were so carelessly playing with?'

'Well, no, not exactly, but I think it is a sort of ornament.'

'No, Lucy, it is not an ornament. It is not for decoration at all. It is for practical use, use by refined ladies for purposes of masturbation. It is in fact Japanese, of the finest carved ivory and over a thousand years old. That item has been used in the beds of some of the richest families in Japan, quite possibly in the Imperial family itself. We cannot begin to imagine how many women have taken pleasure from that beautiful carving. Literally hundreds have brought themselves or each other to orgasm with that warmly held between their feminine lips. It is a rare antique of considerable value.'

She was still staring down at the floor, and whether her deepening colour was embarrassment at the details I was reciting or shame at her discovery, I could not tell.

'Yes. I'm sorry. I won't do it again.'

'That is quite inadequate, I'm afraid. You had said you would not go in the attic at all. You did. Having done so, rather than quickly rectifying your mistake by leaving, you stayed and pried about in my personal possessions. Now you say you will not repeat it, but given the history so far, how can I possibly believe you?'

'I won't. Honestly, Mr Mortensen.'

I paused and considered for a moment.

'I will teach you a lesson, Lucy, that you will not forget, and you may then go home. Whether you return tomorrow is of course your choice. I sincerely hope that you will, but if you do, it must be on the strict understanding that you obey my future instructions to the letter. Is that clear?'

'Yes, Mr Mortensen.'

'Right. Now come here, over my knee. I am going to spank you.'

Her eyes widened and she stared at me in absolute horror. For several long seconds not a sound came from her mouth. Finally she could manage only a single word. 'What?'

'You heard me, Lucy. I am going to spank you. Come and place yourself across my lap.'

'But, Mr Mortensen, you can't do that!'

'Indeed I can. You have behaved like a selfish, ill-mannered child. You will be punished as a selfish, ill-mannered child should be. Had your parents been more severe when you were a child, you might perhaps have learnt better before now. However, that is of no consequence. Come here.'

The girl shuffled forward until finally she was standing beside me. She waited for further direction, but when I made no move to help her, she had to take responsibility for her debasement on herself. She reached out, resting her little hands on my thigh, leant forward and finally lowered herself down across my knees.

At last she was there. Spread before me, stretched across my lap with her smooth pale bottom presented immediately in front of me. For a few seconds I simply gazed and then reached out, rested my left hand in the small of her back and my right across the round cheeks. She flinched immediately at the touch, not quite our first physical contact, but the first truly intimate touch, and then slowly she relaxed.

Her skin was delightfully cool, quite dry and silky as I gently ran my palm over the smooth curves in what, finally, was undeniably a caress. So much was offered here: the sweet cheeks themselves, the deep groove which separated them and hid – somewhere deep within – a tiny puckered brown rose that had been so beautifully, so innocently and so enticingly displayed to me last week. My palm continued circling, running down the long expanse of unblemished thigh and returning to the pink perfection of her bottom. I wanted to prolong the moment, to delay for as long as possible the moment when I would have to stop and release her, and so I also delayed the moment when I started. Besides, I had so much there to savour. This was no prosaic presentation of one part of a person's body: this was a total surrender of all rights. She had abandoned her dignity and allowed me access to everything. She was mine.

And as I sat there and contemplated the view that she now offered me, I considered what I may do. In one sense anything and everything; in another, by handing me the reins, she handed me also her trust and that limited my actions more than any other constraint ever could.

And yet . . .

And yet she had been delightfully embarrassed during our discussion of her breasts, exquisitely mortified at our discussion of her vagina. Why should we not discuss her bottom and see what reaction that could produce?

'You have a very beautiful bottom, Lucy. Quite flawless. When were you last spanked?'

Her reply was almost inaudible. 'Never.'

'Oh, come now! Never?'

'No.'

'I find that most surprising. Surely your parents must have had cause to spank you at some time?'

'My mother said she doesn't believe in it. She never spanked me.' Her words were being muttered down towards the carpet as my fingers continued trailing lightly across her skin.

'What about your father?'

'I never knew him. He left my mother soon after I was born.'

'I see.' I continued my slow gentle circles as I digested this latest revelation. So it seemed she was telling the truth: virginal not just in the strictly physiological sense, but also innocent, unsullied, untried. The delectable fragile body that she had undressed for me had been revealed to no-one else. Those sweet pink nipples which had erected so wilfully under my gaze had been examined by no-one else. This pale round bottom which now lay awaiting my hand had been punished by no-one else.

And I faltered; old enough and sentimental enough to be moved by the sacrifice she had made with so little dissent, I was shamed and I held back. I had so utterly failed to perceive the size of the gulf between us, and yet she had seen it, understood it and tried to accommodate my standards because she knew I would not accommodate hers. On that first day when she came to my house, I had glibly equated her exposing her breasts with any other girl doing the same on a public beach. Only now did I grasp how unfair had been the comparison, and how much greater had been the price she had paid. Knowing that, could I still take such advantage of one who had already offered so much?

Yet how could any man resist so complete a submission? Total surrender of her body to my will? With no more than the mildest protest she had turned her face away and spread herself naked across my thighs. She was allowing me, inviting me, to inflict whatever discipline I chose, whatever level of pain I determined, whatever humiliation I considered would be sufficient to erase the wrong she had done. The wrong that she had done me. What trust she had placed in me! What purity! What innocence!

I lifted my hand and brought it down again as hard as I could on the smooth white skin.

She yelped, kicked out, wriggled and tumbled off my lap on to the floor. She sat there, sniffling, staring accusingly up at me and rubbing her injured bottom.

'That hurts, Mr Mortensen.'

'Of course it hurts. What use would be a punishment that didn't hurt? Now, please return to your place.' I smoothed out the creases on my trousers as she slowly climbed to her feet then turned and draped herself back across my lap.

I resumed my slow caress of her bottom. A magnificently clear handprint gleamed across one cheek, every finger clear, outlined in a thin scarlet, and I traced the outline with my fingertips before running the backs of my fingers down the long central crease. The cheeks clenched up tight at this action and I stopped. It would have been so easy. All I needed to do was to rest one hand on the top of each swollen curve, press down a fraction and then ease the curves apart to reveal again the sweet multi-wrinkled star. Yet I had to resist that for now. One treat at a time for me. One agony at a time for her.

She was sniffling still, and the handprint was darkening as I watched. I lay my hand exactly within it, raised and smacked it back down again. She cried out again, such a plaintiff, mild little cry trying so bravely to be held back that it would have broken any heart. It almost broke mine and so I smacked her again. Three times now I had done it and the tangled line of fingerprints was dissolving into a red blotch that covered the whole of that single perfect cheek. Already it felt warm to the touch as I lay my hand over the surface and squeezed so gently at the softly resilient mound. A loud sniff sounded from beneath the tousled hair that was hanging down on the other side of my knees and she pulled one hand up to wipe her face. What would that sweet face look like, red-eyed, tear-stained and so sorrowful? I was resisting every temptation I could, but was under no constraints to deny myself every available pleasure and sat back.

'I have not finished, Lucy, but you may get up and fetch a tissue before we continue.'

The acknowledgement was barely audible as she slipped off my lap and without looking at me turned to trudge out of the room. As she walked away, the two sides of her bottom moved in perfect symmetry, one as pale as cool ivory, the other as pink as a ripe peach.

Lucy returned, still sniffing and wiping her eyes on the white scrap she clutched in one hand. The other arm had reached round behind her to soothe her injury, leaving her front entirely exposed to me. Her neat round breasts quivered with every sob, her slim chest and stomach heaved as she sniffed and the soft bush of down was openly displayed to me. Just once she glanced up at me from under her mop of hair before she stopped on the edge of the rug.

'I don't think this is fair, Mr Mortensen, really I don't. I've said I'm sorry. What else can I do?'

I considered her question. 'Frankly, Lucy, you can do nothing. Not now. Before you broke your promise, before you disobeyed my request, you could have asked yourself whether you were right to do so. Presumably you didn't stop to consider or, if you did, you decided to do it anyway. Now you must take the punishment.'

She was still for a moment, brushing the hair back out of her face and staring at me, defying me to justify my decision further, but I had nothing more to say, no more justification to give. I knew what I had done before allowing her the run of my house and sending her on her way. I could recall exactly the sequence of words that had passed between us before she went up those stairs to explore. I could remember exactly now: I had known exactly then. There is one room in which you may not go.

There is one tree whose fruit you may not eat. Name me one woman who has been able to resist disobeying such a command.

She dropped the tissue in my wastepaper basket, shuffled up to where I was waiting and lowered herself over my knees again. Her hands reached down to the floor on my left, her legs stretched out straight on my right. In the middle was her bottom, waiting for me to continue.

I caressed the smarting skin again, stroking lightly with the backs of my fingers across the vivid red ridges that those same fingers had made. Already the skin felt hot to the touch, radiating a precious glow that proved the effectiveness of my action. The cheek nearer to me was still entirely clear, and I ran my open hand across its cool surface and down the firm muscles of her thigh. As if I were merely pulling her more securely on to my lap, I curled my fingers round her leg and drew her nearer to me, but whether she realised this or not, the action only served to separate her legs and allowed a glimpse into the valley between her soft buttocks and beyond to the round plump lips of her vulva.

I turned my attention back to the unmarked cheek, running my hand up and down its smooth surface but allowing my fingertips to trail down into the warm crease just beyond. All the while my palm rested there, she was relaxed, but the moment I lifted it away, she clenched up again in anticipation until I returned to the caress.

I had not told her how severe the punishment should be, but I had decided in my own mind that she should receive six. It is a traditional number for these occasions and, when laid on firmly from the start with no gentle warm-up, is sufficient to show we are not just playing games while not so severe as to discourage her from disobeying me again. She had received three on one side. I no longer had any grounds for deferring the second set.

I laid them on in quick succession, one on top of the other on the unmarked cheek and she squealed at the first, howled at the second and was snivelling and sobbing by the third. Her contortions had opened up several fleeting glimpses between her thighs before they settled again, still trembling slightly and still just teasingly parted, just enough to show me the temptation within. Afterwards I kept her there, watching as the handprints swelled up out of the pale skin and the deep flush spread across the whole surface, admiring the gentle contours, the tender resilience, the array of colours. The conceited Mrs Ackworth had been perfectly right in her assessment: the female bottom might have been designed for spanking.

It would have been most gratifying to have delved further but I was determined not to push too far too fast. As a compromise, under the pretext of examining the marks, I eased the girl's buttocks upward and apart a fraction. In her naiveté she permitted the action, and so revealed the plump lips and between them the delicate slivers which had caused her so much embarrassment a few days ago and which were now undeniably fuller and darker than then. More than that, the sparse fluff scattered over the area was now matted and glistened ever so slightly in the light. My fingers itched to stretch down an inch, just one tiny inch and collect a touch of the moisture, but I held back. I must resist temptation, even if I was the only one who did.

I realised she had stopped sniffling and I let her climb off my lap and stand up again. She turned to face me, the wet trails running down her face while she rubbed sorrowfully at her bottom.

'There now,' I said, trying to put a more approachable jollity into my voice. 'That was not too bad, was it? A very light spanking indeed.'

'It hurts,' she grumbled, 'and I don't think I deserved it.'

She could barely bring herself to look at me, as if she were both ashamed of her sin and resentful of her punishment. Without prompting or permission from me, she went across to the pile of clothes on her chair and turned her back on me. I watched in silence as she picked up the white knickers from off her little heap and pulled them up over her long legs and with, I thought, a rather exaggerated awkwardness, over her glowing bottom. As she picked up the next item and the next and ever more of that divine figure disappeared beneath the layers of mundane and modest clothing, I was hit by the realisation that this could be the last time I would ever be permitted to see it. Away from this house, clear of the unique world that we had created, how might the day's events appear? I feared that her indignation might grow in the long hours that we would be apart until it generated a barrier that would seem too hard to cross. What then, when tomorrow came and she finished work? When she walked up from the little tea shop and reached The Cross, which road then would seem the more appealing? To me or to the comfort of her own home? After a night and a day to brood on her indignation, perhaps alone or perhaps shared with her friend Sam or some equally inexperienced confidant, which way would the inclination favour? How easy to decide, in a spirit of defiance, that she would not come to me that day. Yet if she failed once, if she missed one day, she would never return.

'There!' I said, still as if treating a child. 'Now the slate is wiped clean. Why don't I speak to Mrs Ackworth and see if you could have tomorrow off so we can have all day to ourselves, and have a treat to cheer us both up? What would you like? Shall we go to London? Perhaps we could go shopping, and maybe to the theatre?'

She looked round, sullen suspicion and resentment still painted across her face. 'What theatre?'

'Or anything else? What would you like?' She looked up at me, held my gaze for a second longer than usual and sniffed. For the first time, I really felt that she was sensing her power. The characters we played each day were not equals, but in the relationship behind those personae, the balance was much less tilted in my favour. In that, she could take some of the little decisions when she liked, and the biggest one was always ultimately hers: at any time she could decide never to return.

I watched the little fingers moving nimbly as she finished buttoning her blouse, considering silently.

'A ballet?'

'If you like. Yes, a ballet. I know just the one.'

8

Tuesday

'Are we going to have the pleasure of young Lucy again today, Mr Mortensen?'

This was Tuesday, one of Alan's usual days, but he turned up before lunch, long before his usual time, grinning from ear to ear and looking about hopefully. I immediately knew why and was surprised at how much it unsettled me so that I had to be careful that my response remained calm. He had a perfect right to be interested, even eager, given all that I had allowed last Thursday and virtually promised him that I intended to build upon. Yet I was disturbed and angry, and found myself inexplicably pleased to be able to tell him that although she would be coming, we would not be staying as I was taking her to London for the day. He pretended he was not concerned, but I found him hanging round close to the house tending beds which needed no attention at all so that I had to send him down to the vegetable garden where he could start to prepare the fruit cage and stay well out of harm's way. He stamped off like a petulant child.

Yet an hour or so later Lucy came sailing through my front door and the sun shone again. What a day! What a trip! She bubbled like a Lakeland brook that has only just discovered gravity, chirping and giggling and loving everything we saw and passed. She adored the car, the CD player, the air-conditioning, the upholstery. All those things that I take for granted were new and exciting to her, and she played with them endlessly, squirming against the leather seats and treasuring their feel, finding such joy that I was similarly swept up. As we drew nearer to the city and the traffic became steadily thicker, she explained why my suggestion of a ballet had been so appealing. As a child she had taken ballet lessons for a few years in a dismal church hall but had quickly grown frustrated by the teacher's refusal, borne no doubt of incompetence, to take the class beyond the most basic of movements, the most banal of settings. Lucy had felt something of the sensuous provocation of true ballet, had longed to go further than her teacher would permit, yearned to witness the real thing, and although she had watched them on television, she had never been able to see one live. It was the one thing she had always dreamt of and always been denied.

Not only that, she had been to London less than half a dozen times in her life. Her only experience of West End theatre had been a school trip to *The Winter's Tale* and so now she was ready to love London too. I drove her past Buckingham Palace and the Houses of Parliament, along Whitehall and round Trafalgar Square. We went through Hyde Park, saw the Tower of London and St Paul's Cathedral, the Bank of England and Old Bailey. I think she would have been happy just to have been driven round to see all the places she had only ever heard of but she did eventually allow me to stop and we made for an underground car-park not far from Covent Garden where I was able to leave the car safely directly under a security camera.

It lifted me to spend these hours with Lucy, although being out in public deprived me of the supreme pleasure of seeing her scampering naked around me. I had survived the weekend, two days of enforced famine, but yesterday had been curtailed and today I was denied again. The craving was unbearable and when she reminded me about my suggestion of shopping, I happily hailed a taxi to take us up to Oxford Street. There ought to be some opportunities there.

We bought jackets and dresses and skirts and blouses and sweaters and underclothes of every description. In the first changing room I made her strip completely and from then on I retained her underclothes so that even if I couldn't see her naked, I could know she was. I put her into a scandalously short skirt and watched her shuffling nervously through the crowds, terrified that any careless movement would shame her. Ultimately we found an evening dress suitable for Covent Garden, long and demure but superbly shaped so that her beauty was clear to everyone as she glided through the crowds. I let her have her knickers back, but kept the bra and tights, warm and snug in my pocket.

The dinner was good, a little place that I had never been to before, but I found it easily enough from the directions I had been given. As a consequence of its theatrical connections, it understands many of the requirements and happily serves the first two courses of a full dinner before a play or concert and allows diners to return for the desserts and coffee afterwards. The food was excellent and I ordered frogs' legs for Lucy because she had never eaten them before and so assumed they would be revolting; of course she liked them when they arrived and the sweet sensuality of watching her mouth and chin gleaming with butter as she licked each fingertip in turn is a memory that will stay with me forever.

She loved Covent Garden, loved the opulence of the auditorium, the glass and wrought iron of the atrium, the atmosphere of excitement and tradition and the sophistication of the rest of the audience. She could barely sit still as we waited for the show to start and when the lights finally went down and that magnificent curtain swept away, her gurgle of excitement drew smiles from several people around us. The show itself, an entirely new and – according to what I had been given to understand from the reviews – extremely liberal and daring interpretation of *Sleeping Beauty*, was danced by an Eastern European company, from somewhere in the former Soviet Union.

Lucy enjoyed it all and watched spellbound. When we reached the interval, she was impatient for the interruption to be over so that the performance could continue. Towards the end of Act II came the scene I had been waiting for her to see. For a hundred years, Princess Aurora had slept on her couch with a single fairy at her feet to attend her. Prince Florimund finally hacked his way through to the castle to waken her with a kiss and, before doing so, he pulled her up off the bed and danced with her round the stage. This pas de deux was quite magnificent because the princess, still supposedly in a deep sleep, was utterly relaxed and totally loose. The way she flowed into his arms was extremely clever and highly sensual. She slid like syrup through his grasp on to the floor and, when he gathered her up again, washed over his shoulders and back on to the bed. It was beautifully done, but it was something else that had caught Lucy's attention. From the moment that the princess was pulled up from her bed, she could be seen to be wearing a long flowing nightgown of the sheerest gauze and she could be seen to be wearing nothing else. She was visible to the entire audience and to us, only five rows back, she might just as well have been totally naked. As she was turned through the lights and swept across the stage, her tiny breasts were perfectly visible and her nipples unashamedly erect and firm. The girl sagged limp in the prince's arms, her eyes shut and her head lolling to one side, but the enervated glow was visible on her cheeks, and it brightened further when she was allowed to slide through his arms and his hands ran freely right up and over her breasts. When the prince held her against his chest, we could see quite clearly the curve of her bottom, and the narrow line of the valley between her delicate cheeks. When he turned her round to face us, we saw – through the thinnest veil imaginable – the dark narrow stripe where her pubic bush was neatly trimmed. Even that was not enough, for when he lifted her up on to his shoulders, the delectable peach of her vulva was revealed. After turning her gently so that, with her legs slightly parted, all had seen her entirely, he lowered her slowly to the stage while her skirt was caught on his fingers. As she slowly slid down him, the gown stayed up and her legs, her thighs and finally her bottom emerged, entirely naked from under the hem of her gown. The dance was unashamedly erotic, devised to display not just the girl's flexibility and fluid grace, but also to show her off physically, to reveal her body as near naked as could be allowed, and as near naked as made no difference. At the end, the princess was finally carried back to her couch, arranged on her back and with many caresses across her breasts, her legs and even down between her thighs, he finally leant down to bestow the kiss that would awaken her. It was stunning. The entire audience was motionless and hushed and the dancers received an outpouring of applause at the end such as I have never heard before. Still that was not the limit, for the ballet continued with the chorus of her attendants and bridesmaids preparing her for the wedding ceremony, dressing her in her magnificent wedding dress. Even this was done on stage, although she kept her back to the audience while two of them removed the gown up over her head and left her for too few seconds entirely naked on the stage before another two arrived with the flowing white wedding dress which poured languorously over her shoulders.

It was undoubtedly a beautiful dress and she danced in it most gracefully, but at the end, as the minor characters lined up for their applause, the princess silently slipped away to reappear a few seconds later for her own curtain call and for this, she had changed back into that same diaphanous veil and stood proudly centre stage to take her bows and receive armfuls of bouquets in the full harsh lighting of the entire auditorium.

Lucy was in raptures and over the second half of our dinner I realised that her excitement had now found a quite specific focus. 'But, Mr Mortensen, she was practically naked! I mean, you could see everything! How could she do that, in front of all those people? I would be so ashamed.'

'Would you?'

'Yes! Of course!' Her eyes and cheeks glowed at the vision. 'I could never do that!'

I smiled. 'I'm sure you could. You have done many things in the last few days that you thought you could never do, haven't you?' She considered this for a moment but something over her shoulder distracted me and I pressed on. 'What do you think that girl is doing now?'

'Now?' She considered briefly and then blushed brilliant crimson. 'No! You don't think she's . . .' The memory of what she had done herself suddenly flooded back and overwhelmed all conscious thought.

'No.' I laughed. 'No, I don't think she's sitting alone and masturbating. For one thing, unless I'm much mistaken, she has a good friend in her leading man who would be only too eager to provide any assistance that she might need in that direction. For another, she has just walked in and is standing right behind you.'

Lucy whipped round to see the dancer being bustled through the restaurant. She was now wrapped in a great black coat which almost entirely swamped her, while her escort, a ferocious-looking woman who might well have been the national shot-put champion, kept a protective and possessive arm wrapped tightly around her as she steered her charge between the tables. The change from her earlier costume was so complete that even if any other diners had seen the ballet, they would have been unlikely to make the connection. In any case, nobody recognised the girl, so when I stood up and addressed them, they could hardly ignore my presence.

'An excellent show, this evening, ladies. May I please congratulate you on a magnificent performance.' Laid on with a trowel: show me an actor, dancer or singer who will not respond to such an approach.

They thanked me, and then acknowledged Lucy's flattery, but Lucy had turned away from the minder and addressed herself directly to the dancer, a girl who we could now see was no older than Lucy herself, no taller and in every other respect very similar.

'You are so brave to dance like that. I would never have the courage, but it was magnificent.'

The girl smiled. 'It is not so brave. When first we danced this tour, I wear a body stocking beneath my dress. After a month, I leave the stocking behind. After some weeks, I leave away the brassière. Today, is the last night, so today

I leave the panties. If we had stayed longer?' She laughed again. 'Who knows?'

'But you could not go any further!' Lucy was outraged, but sidled up closer in anticipation of being let in on something more.

'Perhaps. I like to keep my audience guessing; that is why they come to see me at the theatre. That is why they come here tonight.'

Lucy responded to the lure, so that I did not need to direct. 'Tonight? What happens tonight?'

'I dance again! Here! Upstairs! You do not know? It is traditional in my country, one last dance for the company. You do not come for that? Pity! I would dance well for you.'

The girl trailed her fingers down the length of Lucy's arm and Lucy looked round at me, curious, intrigued, hooked. 'Can we go to see, Mr Mortensen? Please?'

I raised my eyebrows to the woman lurking behind her: minder, trainer or chaperone, I could not say for sure what was her role, but the decision was unquestionably hers. She shrugged and it was settled. The dancer took Lucy's hand as they weaved between the crowded tables and we trailed behind. A few eyes followed me, more followed the girls, but the curtain quickly fell back behind us and as we climbed a narrow flight of stairs, the sounds from the restaurant below were soon lost in the sounds from the celebration above.

Here we found most of the dancers already assembled and the rest drifted in, in twos and threes, together with another 40 or 50 people, men and women, patrons of the ballet, sponsors, directors and choreographers, until the room was completely full. Lucy had been swept on and away by the ballerina and although I caught occasional glimpses of the top of her head, the single blonde in a sea of black crowns among the dancers, she was utterly engrossed and never looked back once. I made my way to the buffet table, took a glass of champagne and settled to the side of the room. A couple of times I was approached by one of the corps, hoping no doubt that I was a producer of some influence who might assist them on their path. In the way of these things, I was left in no doubt that, whether male or female, their bodies were available if I so wished, but they quickly drifted away when I declined. Finally chairs were brought out and we all settled in neat circles as a stage was prepared in the middle of the room, a couch was arranged, sprinkled with flowers from all the bouquets collected earlier, the room darkened and the familiar music began again, albeit this time recorded.

When the low sweep of the cellos announced the dawn, the lights brightened enough to reveal the interior of the enchanted castle just as it had been on stage only an hour or two before. The princess reclined in that same gossamer dress, sleeping for a hundred years. At her feet, a fairy attendant lay curled in the shadows as the prince crept in through the gloom.

Yet as the light continued to brighten, following the prince's uncertain progress across the floor, he reached first the fairy and again he stopped there, but this time he stayed. He lifted her hand as she too slept; then the second arm was lifted, then her body and as she rose from the foot of the couch, I could see it was Lucy, dressed in a gown as thin and transparent as the princess's own. The prince lifted her up, held her for a moment and then let her slide back down while he held tight to the dress so that she slid out entirely naked. When he pulled her up again, the audience gasped as she came up out of the shadows into full light, and I saw Lucy blush. For a second her eyes flickered open and she could not hold back the little grin before she pretended to sleep again. The lights were full now, and the audience was treated to a totally unimpeded view as the prince lifted her in his arms, held her out, an offering of unblemished nakedness to us all, and slowly conducted her round the circle, less than an arm's length away from the front row of seated watchers. The progression was exquisitely slow, stopping frequently for her to be turned and pressed over backwards – the better to display her breasts – or forwards – the better to show off her bottom. Her legs were pulled up to reveal her sex to us all, and her escort ran long inquisitive fingers down the crease of her bottom and her delicate lips until she could not hold in the tremor that rippled across her. The gaze of all those sitting so close, both men and women, was fixed on her, silent and enraptured, hankering to reach out and touch, to caress and enjoy the pure pale skin, the ripe nipples, the soft cheeks and downy cleft, even the moist lips that sometimes peeked out and smiled at us all.

I could see that Lucy was in heaven. When her arms were lifted away from her chest, she pushed her little bosom out a little further. When she was bent over, she twisted her legs open a little wider. When she was pushed out practically into the lap of one of the rapt watchers, she edged in a little closer still. Eventually, at the end of the circle, the prince kissed her and she woke, then scampered back through the audience, weaving between the chairs and squeezing through the forest of earnest hands that reached out to touch and squeeze and stroke before she found her way back to the princess's couch. There she sat, her knees hugged up to her chest, watching as the prince approached his sleeping princess.

Their dance was similar to that which had been performed in the huge auditorium, except that before the first circle had been completed, the gossamer dress was stripped away to reveal the princess entirely naked. The dance continued, again displaying every private cranny to the silent audience, and although she was perhaps seeping a little more generously, I do not believe that she was any better displayed nor any more deserving of the attention than my own Lucy had been.

When eventually he returned her to the couch, briefly trailing his hands across Lucy's breasts as he passed her, he lay the princess down, spun away and in a single movement, stripped away his own clothes to stand naked before us all with a fine young penis proudly erect as he paced in martial splendour across the floor. When he passed Lucy again, he took her hands in his and made her caress him briefly and she clearly needed little urging to hold him between her palms and work her tiny fists up and down his eager horn. But then he turned to the princess again, laid her over on her back, splayed wide her legs and with little preparation entered her deeply. So close were we that we could miss not the slightest detail of the action. The prince picked up his love in his arms and held her, even brought her round in front of us all, his penis still unmistakably embedded deep within her, until he finally lay her down on the couch again, arranging her head in Lucy's lap so that she could stroke the girl's thick hair as they brought their lovemaking to its natural conclusion. The girl had entirely abandoned any pretence of sleep, but she reached out to entwine her fingers with Lucy's as every thrust of the young man's hips shook her little body. The mounds of her breasts quivered and the breath battered out of her in a gratified grunt at every crushing lunge. Her gentle sighs deepened into anguished gasps and his own rasps grew stronger and deeper and coarser. No longer unresponsive, she clawed at his back, wrapped her long legs round him and hooked her ankles together to clamp herself more firmly to him. Inevitably, this opened her even better to our view so that we could now see with perfect clarity the boy's penis, first deep inside the girl, then drawing out of her delicate lips as he pulled back, sleek and shining, before driving in again with a tantalisingly controlled patience that his partner was urging him to lose. With every thrust, his heavy scrotum bounced against her bottom, knocking at the taut wrinkles of her tightly closed little anus.

The young couple were captivating enough, but I was hypnotised by the look of ecstatic wonder on Lucy's face as she witnessed the intimacy of so private an action played out so publicly and so close in front of her. What finer sight could there be than two people in the throes of real love? So young, so fit and so beautiful, they complemented each other perfectly and when, with a roaring savage intensity that denied any suggestion of pretence, he finally filled her to the brim, the appreciation and admiration of all of us assembled round them was unstinting. Even so, he pulled away, opened her legs out wide again and then invited all of us to come near and see the clear proof of his climax in the wilting of his glistening penis and the trickles that were already beginning to run down his partner's thighs. So the audience converged on the couch where the two lovers still lay, a bizarre gathering of young dancers in casual sweaters and running pants mixed in with the more traditional Covent Garden audience, mostly much older but all in severe and formal starched suits and long dresses. Several among them, the women as much as the men, reached out to touch the girl, to feel the sticky wetness for themselves or probe the hot channel that still seeped its gift. Just as many, the men as much as the women, reached for the boy, to nurse the heavy testicles and touch and fondle the slippery softness of his fading erection. Several reached out to Lucy, to stroke her breasts, to fondle her round bottom or to slip their hands between her thighs where a fluff of warm gold covered her swollen lips.

Even after another champagne cork had been popped, glasses passed through and the three performers had been applauded and toasted, they made no move to cover themselves. Instead they reclined together naked on the huge bed in the centre of the room for the rest of the evening where they continued to receive the most generous of congratulations and the most intimate of caresses from a circle of bewitched admirers.

It was almost one o'clock by the time we said our goodbyes, Lucy having put on her dress and knickers. She was warmly hugged and kissed by practically everyone in the room, and we eventually made our way back down the narrow stairs. In the restaurant, one of the waiters interrupted his unenthusiastic mopping of the floor to let us out into the stuffy night and quickly locked the door behind us again. The streets were emptying at last so that we had the pavement to ourselves and a black taxi actually slowed as he passed us, offering business instead of hurrying away.

Lucy skipped down the street ahead of me and then turned to run backwards so that she could face me, could embrace me in her beaming smile, snatching my hands to pull me faster down the road to the next excitement.

'Wow!' Her eyes sparkled and she let go briefly to turn a graceful pirouette among the litter and the cars. 'I have never felt so naked, so exposed and so alive!'

The car-park was practically empty, and as we passed the attendant in his solitary booth, he barely glanced up in response to my greeting. On the third level, mine was almost the only car left and Lucy danced her way across the floor towards it, stopping to twirl beside it while she waited for me to catch up. Her face was still aglow.

'Can I undress again?' Her whisper echoed round the deserted concrete chamber.

'Of course, if you like, but come round to this side.' She was starting to unzip her dress even before she was round the car, and hauled it over her head before tossing it gaily on to the back seat. Her knickers followed (I still had her bra and tights in my pocket) and then she was naked, swooping, gliding and swirling across the filthy floor as if she were still on the most magnificent of stages. In front of me she stopped and threw her arms out wide as if to embrace the whole world and enfold it in her newly awakened sensuality. Then she turned away and bent and twisted, as celestial as the dying swan, and her hands kept running down to stroke across her breasts and dive between her thighs to rummage through the soft moist folds. She grinned at me, all shame and embarrassment evaporating as she watched me watching her.

'I feel as if I've been born all over again!'

I caught her again and turned her round so that her back was towards me and then pointed out the little red light slowly blinking on the security camera above her head. She didn't care.

'Do you think he's watching me?'

'I'm perfectly sure he is.'

She flicked her hair away and then ran her hand down her body. 'I wish there were more.'

But there were. Another car could be heard coming up from the level below, and after a second's hesitation, Lucy pulled away with a frightened but excited little squeal, hopped through the open back door into the car and climbed over the seat into the front. I fetched her a rug out of the boot before starting the car and heading slowly down the ramp.

At the dingy ticket booth, the attendant was now much more alert and stared past me to where Lucy was curled up on the front seat under her rug, her little fist clutching the edge and only her head poking out. The man's eyes never left her while he took the ticket and the money and handed back my change, and equally, although Lucy's face carried a crimson blush the entire time, she never once looked away. Finally, as I pocketed my change, I reached across to take hold of the edge of the blanket and as soon as her fingers had released it, I lifted it away and tossed it over into the back. Lucy didn't move, but just let the stranger stare while he marvelled at the unaffected honesty of her display and she lapped up his speechless admiration and awe.

After I had driven away, she climbed over the back of the seat to retrieve the blanket but didn't wrap it round her at first. Indeed, she took huge delight in clambering from the front to the back and vice versa as we passed through the crowded streets and several times paused halfway between the two so that though her head was hidden somewhere below the level of the car windows, either her breasts or her upturned bottom was fully visible to those caught up in the traffic queues behind and immediately alongside us. For the rest, she lay stretched across the back seat, her hands clasped behind her head and her legs wide apart so that in the frustratingly inadequate light, not only I, but any others who glanced in, could just make out her naked form spread proudly open and available.

Finally, safely outside the belt of the M25, as the street lights thinned out and then stopped altogether, she returned to curl up beside me beneath the rug and eventually the fidgeting stopped. After we had driven for several minutes in a still, warm silence, I glanced over to watch the little form covered by its woolly rug. One pale shoulder was visible poking out and her hair spread over the seat and spilled across her face. She caught me watching her.

114

'Mr Mortensen?'

'Yes?'

'I'm getting married at the end of next week, you know.'

I hadn't known it was then, but I had known that it was sometime, that it was soon and that it was hanging like a sentence of death over our newfound freedom and schooling. I had refused to consider the event or its implications and had been pushing the prospect into the back of my mind. It was a bitter morsel to have to swallow on this of all days.

Yet this was her life, her future, and the boy whom, presumably, she loved. She had every right to be looking forward to the event. I had no justification to be uncharitable. 'That's nice.'

'Yes.' It was so unenthusiastic a response that I glanced over again but as soon as I turned she twisted away from me, presenting her round back and, now, the other little shoulder.

'Can I ask you a favour? I mean, I know I have no right, but I would appreciate it.'

'Of course.'

'Well, you know my father left us, so I don't have anybody to give me away at the wedding.' She paused. 'Would you do it?'

I understood how great an honour this was, of course I did, yet what greater torment could there be than that? After so many days during which we had shared so much, to be asked to stand beside her and hand her over to that unimaginative, undeserving adolescent with whom she would go on to share the one rite that would always be denied me? How could I spend a day surrounded by such smug happiness on that boy's face as he anticipated the pleasure he had still to come when I had been so close myself? Yet she had made the limit clear when she first arrived; I had no ground to ask for so much and could not voice such disappointment. I first tried an evasion.

'Don't you think you should ask your father anyway? It could make a bridge.'

'I did invite him, all of them. Do you know, I have a half-sister called Helen who I've never even met? Anyway, they haven't bothered to reply.'

She was already putting a brave face on one hurtful rejection and I couldn't make a second. 'Well, if you're sure, of course I will.' I even managed to add some icing. 'I'd be honoured and delighted.'

'Thank you. You've done so much for me already.'

'Nonsense!'

'Oh, you have.' She paused and when she spoke again her voice was quieter than ever. 'You see, I had been so frightened. I knew so little about that side of being married – you know, physical things.' I smiled that we could share so much yet she could still be so shy. 'You've taught me so much.'

'You still have much to cover.'

'What?' She turned to stare at me. 'I've done practically everything! What more is there?'

'Lucy, we haven't even scratched the surface.'

She lapsed back into silence, huddled down in the blanket. Her breathing was slower now, so that for a moment I thought she had fallen asleep, except that I noticed a gentle rise and fall of the blanket where her wrist was lazily working between her thighs.

'Mr Mortensen?'

'Yes.'

'Are you watching me?'

'Yes.'

'Good.' In the long silence we both concentrated on the slow caresses until, with a deep sigh of total contentment, she turned over on to her back, the blanket slipped down and one breast appeared, the nipple peeking over the braided edge as if peeping out to witness the night. She opened her eyes for a moment and stared at me, but her hand did not stop.

'Did you know the dancers would all be there? In the restaurant?'

'Perhaps I did. Perhaps not. I shouldn't tell you every-thing.'

She laughed lightly, pulled the blanket up over her shoulder again and peered out at me through eyes that glistened and then glazed over as the movement of her arm accelerated and intensified while I transported her on through the night.

9

Wednesday

It was well after four o'clock before I heard the timid little ring on the doorbell which announced Lucy's arrival. She was clearly flustered and words were flowing almost before she was inside the front door.

'I'm sorry to be late, Mr Mortensen, but Mrs Ackworth had to go out unexpectedly this afternoon and so I had to stay and look after the shop until Maureen arrived and she does not get there until four o'clock.'

Her agitated apology was so appealing I had great difficulty assuming the stern reprimand that the circumstances required. 'I see. I have been kept waiting all this time. Please ensure you are not late in future. Now, take your clothes off, bring some tea through into the drawing room, and be quick about it.'

I waited in the hallway to watch as Lucy quickly scrambled out of her clothes, first pulling her sweater over her head and throwing it down on the hall chair, to be joined by her blouse and tiny, flimsy bra. Her shoes were kicked under the chair and then the skirt and tights were added to the top of the pile. She hesitated then, and looked up at me as she clutched the lacy white knickers, unsure whether I would want to take them down. I did.

'Yes, come here, please, Lucy.'

She meekly padded down the cold wooden floor in her bare feet and I squatted down in front of her. Her skin was so clear and smooth across her slim stomach, her belly button a little oval eye winking at me over the elastic waistband of the white knickers. I took hold of the edges of the elastic and pulled them slowly down her legs, revealing straight in front of my eyes the little mat of pale golden wool pressed flat against her mound. She lifted each foot in turn to let me pull the knickers off, but I didn't stand up immediately. Instead I again held them to my mouth and inhaled her sweet aroma. She was still unused to this, and blushed every time I did it, quickly looking away but then unable to resist looking back, just to check in case my expression showed disgust or nausea. It never did.

This seemed a good time for another small bridge to be crossed.

'Can you touch your toes, Lucy?' I continued to nurse the delicate cotton in my hand.

'Yes, Mr Mortensen.' Her reply was cautious.

Still squatting, so that my eyes were on a level with her hips, I asked her to turn around with her back to me and then to bend over.

'Keep your legs straight, my dear. Move them wide apart and reach right down to your toes.'

She was clearly very supple, as we all were at that age, and she easily leant forward to reach her toes. This stretched her firm round bottom tight and pushed out her plump little vulva between her thighs, its two inner petals also peeking out to me. Above that, her pale pinky brown rose was curled tight and closed and this was my object for today. I reached up and with one hand on each cheek of her bottom, gently peeled her buttocks further apart. Immediately she clamped up and started to stand up, but I ordered her firmly to stay still.

'Now just relax. I am not going to hurt you.'

She breathed out, a slow gentle sigh, and the round cheeks of her bottom softened gradually, until I was able to ease her bottom hole open just a little, just enough to show her that this too was available to me if ever, whenever, I wanted it. I pushed her down even further and gently trailed my fingertip down the central crease, pausing to press lightly on the small wrinkled star though it automatically clenched as tight as a clam in response to the touch. Then I let her up.

'Good. Well done, my dear. Now go and make the tea and bring it into the drawing room, will you?'

Without a glance back, she scampered down the hall to the kitchen, and I returned to my chair in the drawing room, placing my finger over my lips to ensure that my guest, of whose presence Lucy still had no idea, continued to keep silent.

We waited for no more than a few minutes, exchanging the occasional smile as we listened to the clatter of crockery in the kitchen, and, before long, the steady tread of Lucy's bare feet down the hallway. I quickly gestured my guest back into the wing chair behind the door as Lucy came in and carefully lowered the tray on to the Korean hibachi I keep in the centre of the room.

'Thank you, Lucy. Most delightful. Ah, we will need another cup, but you know Mrs Ackworth, of course.'

Lucy looked up at me in horror and spun round to see Mrs Ackworth smiling happily at her from her vantage point. Immediately she tried to cover her breasts and little fleece with her hands, but Mrs Ackworth only laughed.

'There is no need to be shy, Lucy. Mr Mortensen tells me that you are quite at home here, dressed like that.'

Lucy turned to me, her hands still clasped in front of her. 'Please, Mr Mortensen, could I just stay in the kitchen?'

'No, certainly not. There is no cause for that.'

'Precisely,' added Mrs Ackworth. 'I have never found any reason at all for young girls to display false modesty over these things. Now, run along and fetch another cup like a good girl.'

Lucy ran out, and eventually returned with the third cup. She started to pour the tea, her hands quivering as she realised how closely she was being examined. She tried to shuffle round to expose less of her breasts, and only realised that she was exposing more of her bottom, so she shuffled back.

Eventually she took up the cup and saucer and carried it carefully, but rattling at every step, over to Mrs Ackworth.

'What on earth is this, child?' The woman stared with indignation at the proffered cup. 'You've slopped half of it into the saucer.'

'Sorry, Mrs Ackworth. I'll get a cloth.'

She hurried out, and as soon as she was gone, the woman settled herself comfortably further into the chair and turned to me.

'You know I really think the girl deserves a spanking for a thing like that. It is sheer carelessness. Wouldn't you agree?'

For all her bravado, she needed my permission before she could spank Lucy. She would not take so much on herself, so I smiled at her: sometimes it is so easy to part a baby from its candy.

'I'm being guided by you on matters of discipline, Mrs Ackworth,' I answered. 'If you think a couple of spanks are appropriate, then who am I to disagree?'

She smiled and was still smugly victorious as Lucy returned with the cloth. She carefully wiped the saucer and the bottom of the cup and hurried out again. As she returned, the woman called to her.

'Lucy, come here.' The little naked figure scuttled over in front of her and waited. 'It simply isn't good enough that you slop the tea about in this haphazard way. I've noticed you doing the same thing in the shop. It looks so slovenly and I consider it should be dealt with. Mr Mortensen shares my view. You will please lay yourself down across my lap.'

Lucy looked to me for support, possibly even rescue, but I said nothing. She did not know and could not yet know that I was sending her into the cage not as quarry but as bait.

With the most mournful and accusing stare that any soul could stand, she turned away from me, shuffled round beside Mrs Ackworth's chair and then stretched herself out along the woman's lap. Mrs Ackworth drew her tighter in

121

and then rested one hand on the girl's shoulders and the other on her bottom. Her sigh was pure possession.

There is something so sacrificial about that posture. It is so unambiguous an arrangement, devised purely to present one particular part of one person's body to another. To offer up the smooth round curves of the victim's bottom to the hand or the strap or whatever else has been chosen to the other party. The bottom is there. Presented. All objections quelled, all rights surrendered. It is no longer the victim's property. She – it is almost always she – has relinquished all prerogatives and permitted full licence to the other. To hurt her. To beat her. To pry open the clenched cheeks and examine the anguished anus within. To slide an inquisitive hand down between the thighs and gauge the excited dampness seeping from the lips squeezed between her trembling thighs. Perhaps to press a long finger deep inside the narrow channel she tries to deny.

Or not. Perhaps simply to tickle the fingertips across the surface, to play round the curves, toying with the nerves and courage of the victim.

Or to strike out and turn the smooth pale skin to a vivid crimson of pain and fire.

Mrs Ackworth's hand rested on the surface, the finger-tips curving down timidly into the central crease but not daring to delve where they so clearly yearned to go. Lucy was stretched out, her long slender thighs on one side, her arms reaching down to the floor on the other. Her hair, loose today, tumbled round her face, but I thought I caught a slight sob from behind that perfect golden screen. Mrs Ackworth's left hand rested across Lucy's back, tucking her up on to her lap but at the same time seeking courage to inch its way further round where it could reach the little hanging breasts. Courage didn't come.

'What a very fine bottom she has, don't you agree? Quite beautifully clear and unmarked. I do enjoy having such a perfect specimen available to me and contemplating how thoroughly I will punish it in a very short time.'

The woman smirked at me again from the cosy comfort of her armchair, and I let her have back a shallow smile.

She patted her hand a couple of times on to Lucy's little round cheeks, reminding me so clearly of the sweet resistance they posed, a pressure I had felt just two days ago when she had been stretched that way for me. I could hardly bear to watch.

I turned back as the first smack, swiftly followed by the first squeal, echoed across the room. The clear print of Mrs Ackworth's fingers was painted across one cheek of the upturned bottom and the woman was tracing its outline with those same fingers. Two other slaps followed before Lucy first pleaded to be released. She was ignored and another dozen or so had landed before the first little plaintive cry.

'Oh, keep quiet, girl. I've barely begun.'

The blows continued raining down in a steady merciless torrent and Lucy's pretty bottom darkened slap by slap, second by second, until it was as red as I had made it myself. It was then I called a halt.

'I think that'll do for the moment, Mrs Ackworth.'

She jerked up as if she had completely forgotten my existence and stopped in mid stroke, her hand held up stupidly by her head.

I smiled at her. 'You don't want to wear yourself out and we have plenty of time yet.'

'Oh, yes. Yes, of course.'

Lucy struggled to her feet and one hand wiped away her tears while the other reached round to rub at her injured bottom. She glared accusingly at me for my failure to protect her as Mrs Ackworth straightened her skirt and picked up her tea cup. I noticed her massaging her palm when she thought I was not looking.

Lucy edged back to her seat and sat down gingerly, refusing to look at either of us, and for a few minutes I made small talk with my visitor. When I was finished, I addressed Lucy again. 'You remember that chest up in the attic, Lucy?'

She looked over at me, shame at being reminded of her disobedience on that occasion, the incident which had led to her first spanking, and distrust in equal measures wrinkling her face. 'Yes.'

'In the second drawer, which means the drawer immediately below the one in which you found that item which so interested you a few days ago . . .' The girl blushed and turned down her eyes but whispered 'yes' softly. 'You will find a selection of straps, canes and crops. On the right-hand side of the drawer is a narrow black wooden case which contains a reddish-brown three-fingered tawse. Could you please fetch that down for me?'

Her face went white as she listened to me. 'But, Mr Mortensen, I haven't really done anything. I just spilt the tea and that only went in the saucer and anyway I've already been punished for that.'

'Please don't argue, Lucy. The tawse.'

'But please, I'm so sore already.'

'Now, please, Lucy.'

She slowly got to her feet and walked to the door, but as she left she presented her neat round bottom to us, so red and glowing that I was deeply tempted to call her back and hug her. I listened to her slow steps dragging their way across the hall and up the stairs. Mrs Ackworth interrupted my reverie.

'You know, I have to say that I find something so much more satisfying about a punishment in which the recipient is entirely naked. It establishes the authority in a way that nothing else quite manages. I know some people like to see the knickers neatly arranged across the thighs, but personally I much prefer them off entirely. Don't you think?'

'Well, I suppose we all have our different fancies, but, yes, I do think I agree with you there.'

'Especially with girls who are argumentative, which is the case with so many of them these days, don't you find? In my day we would never have dreamt of arguing if we were given a clear instruction like that. We wouldn't have dared! Besides, as my nanny always used to say, the female bottom must have been designed for punishment and it certainly never comes to any harm from a thrashing. I received a few in my younger days and it never did me any harm.'

'I'm sure you're right, but I have to admit to retaining some misgivings about the propriety of threatening public exposure if the selected victim refuses a punishment. Are you sure that's all right?'

'Oh, Mr Mortensen, you're too soft! We must take what opportunities we can or we would get nowhere; no girl is likely to come up out of the blue and ask to be spanked, is she? No, it is up to people like us to raise the matter. As for the victim, as you call her, the tears last only a few minutes and the stripes no more than a day or two. A great deal of fuss is made about nothing, if you ask me.' She smirked at me over the rim of her tea cup.

When Lucy returned, she crept reluctantly through the door and offered me the thin black box. I didn't open it at once although, knowing her natural curiosity, I assumed that Lucy would already have examined its contents. I lay the box carefully on the small table beside my chair, conscious of Mrs Ackworth's covetous eyes following me.

'Are you ready, Mrs Ackworth?'

'Oh, yes. Yes, indeed.' She looked eagerly across at where Lucy stood with her head bowed, her face hidden beneath her hair but her fingers twined together and her shoulders lifting and falling with every sorrowful breath.

'Fine. Lucy, I think the footstool would be best. Please bring it out into the middle of the room.'

She hesitated a moment, but didn't look up and didn't speak. Then she shuffled away to collect the round leather footstool from its home in the bay window and dragged it forward to the position I indicated in front of the fireplace. She stepped back, staring down at it forlornly, and awaited the inevitable.

'Now, Mrs Ackworth. Your turn, I think.' Lucy looked round at me in hurt dismay and Mrs Ackworth beamed with surprise and delight: the ecstasy of anticipation. She stood up as I continued.

'You have explained your approval of physical discipline in appropriate cases. You stressed the importance you attached to punishing transgressors. You even confessed that as a girl you had yourself been a recipient and that it had never done you any harm and indeed is a great deal of fuss about nothing at all. You have used your position to chastise a number of girls in your charge and you told me clearly that you saw no harm in threatening the sack and public disclosure to any who attempted to challenge your rule. Am I right?'

She confirmed that I was but a shadow of puzzlement, an inkling of disquiet, was starting to tremble across her forehead.

'Then as I say, I think it is now your turn. Kindly remove your clothes and bend over the stool.'

She stared at me in motionless silence for several seconds. Could she have heard me correctly? Had I been making an extremely tasteless joke? Was even that conceivable or had she simply imagined the words? I watched the bewilderment spreading over her face and she even glanced across at Lucy, grasping for bearings in a predicament that had suddenly, inexplicably and unfathomably, twisted out of recognition. When she turned back to me, her words were calmly controlled, soft and measured, as if she were still unsure whether so ludicrous a suggestion even merited a response, but with just the slightest uncertainty that she had heard right. 'Mr Mortensen! I will do no such thing. How dare you?'

'How do I dare? I dare, Mrs Ackworth, because that pile of video tapes you may see on the table beside you comes from the cupboard in your office at the tearooms. They show the girls, including poor Lucy here, in various states of undress as they changed for work. In three instances they go further – they show girls being spanked. For which event I note that you required two of the girls to take down their knickers and the third one was made to strip entirely naked.'

Her mouth opened and shut like a goldfish, but Lucy had turned from outrage at the revelation of Mrs Ackworth spying on her to glee at the way the tables had been turned.

Mrs Ackworth's cheeks had turned a brilliant red as she turned to pick up her handbag before addressing me in as steely a tone as I have ever heard. 'I am sorry to disappoint you, Mr Mortensen, but I have absolutely no intention of complying with your insulting, not to say disgusting, proposal.'

I smiled at her with a superiority which must have been infuriating. 'I seem to recall your saying that the initial reaction of all your victims has been something similar. However, perhaps I could also remind you of one or two of your other comments when we first talked in your office? That the minimal discomfort of a spanking is nothing compared to the humiliation of public disclosure? That in a small town like this, a person's prospects can so easily be permanently ruined by such a scandal? That nobody would believe complaints from any of the girls because of your position on the Parish Council? And I see congratulations are in order – you have been elected Chairman of the Chamber of Commerce. However, Mrs Ackworth, I don't think you can be quite so confident that my evidence would be so readily dismissed. Certainly not with the disgraceful testimony of these tapes on my side.'

'How did you get them?' She hissed like a snake.

There seemed no harm in being entirely frank. 'I had your office broken into last night and had them removed.'

'Then you are a thief as well as a blackmailer!'

Again I smiled. Her outrage was richer than I could have hoped. 'A thief? No. I did not steal them. Someone else did that and I have no intention of keeping them. My intention is to hand them in to the police and explain that I found them. As for a blackmailer, well! If I am, then so are you since I am offering the same bargain as you have made yourself several times.'

She looked surprised, even shocked, at my candour, but as I stayed calmly waiting for her response, the woman seemed to start to realise that further blustering was not going to open up a way out. She glanced around, fixing her eyes on the cowering naked figure of Lucy for several long poisonous moments before turning her face to me but addressing her words to Lucy.

'Lucy, kindly leave the room. I need to discuss matters confidentially with Mr Mortensen.'

'Yes, Mrs Ackworth.' She was used to obeying, but her tone revealed her disappointment at missing the scene.

'Please stay where you are, Lucy. I'm sorry, Mrs Ackworth, but I do not wish Lucy to leave and besides, we have nothing to discuss or negotiate. You need to consider your position quite carefully and then you have a decision to make. You are entirely free to collect your things and leave the house right now. Alternatively, you can take off your clothes and bend over that footstool. You know perfectly what consequences will follow in each case so please don't waste time in trying to dream up other options; there are none. Now then. Which is it to be?'

She sat blinking at me in stunned silence as she examined the choices. Finally she put her handbag down on the floor again. I saw the flutter of joy ripple across Lucy's face. 'I will agree, Mr Mortensen, on the understanding that . . .'

'No, Mrs Ackworth. No understandings or provisos or bargains. You stay or you leave.'

She swallowed. 'I'll stay.'

It was all I could do to keep the smile off my face. 'Good. I'm sure that is the most sensible decision. Lucy?'

'Yes, Mr Mortensen?'

'Could I have some more tea, please, while we wait for Mrs Ackworth?'

The tea was much quicker arriving than any clear indications of Mrs Ackworth's willingness to obey. Eventually, after Lucy had long since returned to her seat, the woman finally leant down and pulled her shoes off, placing them neatly beside her chair. She looked over at me once, just momentarily, with a face of such thunderous loathing that I wondered whether she had been entirely truthful in saying she had herself been beaten in her youth.

Staying primly seated, she unbuttoned her jacket and blouse before she at last stood up. Moving quickly and efficiently, she slid off both of these, uncovering a plain white slip, and draped her clothes over the chair. The skirt was unzipped and allowed to drop away before she stepped out of that and, without a single glance round her, she pulled the slip up over her head. Her bra was also white, a substantial item, designed for work not show, and it supported a bosom which could now be seen to be larger than I had thought. Beneath that, the sensible white knickers, similar to those that Lucy had arrived home in last week, were visible through the thicker weave at the top of her tights.

She sighed and then reached round behind her, unhooked the tight wide strap of her bra and pulled this off over her breasts. I realised at last what she was trying to do. She was utterly humiliated at being made to strip in front of us: me a stranger, Lucy her employee and subordinate. The only way to counter that humiliation was to refuse to recognise it. She would behave as briskly and efficiently as if there were nothing unusual in her actions. If she had to undress, she would do it in just the same way that she would if she were in the privacy of her own bathroom. She would give us nothing. I only now understood this, so I interrupted.

'Just a moment, Mrs Ackworth.' She paused, warily, in the act of dropping her superb bra on to the pile of clothes. 'I think it might be better if you kept your knickers on. Just remove the tights, please.'

She glanced over to me bitterly, and then peeled away the thin elastic waistband of her tights and pulled them down her legs before adding these to the pile. She turned to face me, waiting for further instructions, and now that I had broken her rhythm and could re-emphasise the roles, I gave her instructions.

'On second thoughts, Mrs Ackworth, I realise I was wrong and you were right just now.' I paused and she glanced over, hardly daring to hope for reprieve, but anxious for any remission. 'There is something so much more satisfying about a punishment in which the recipient is entirely naked. Would you take your knickers off as well, please?'

She scowled as she peeled them down her legs. We understood each other. I sat back to consider her, and made no secret of doing so.

She was not, to be brutally honest, a particularly attractive woman, although I had grown somewhat spoiled and blasé by having become accustomed to the slim youthful perfection of Lucy. Mrs Ackworth was, after all, at least double the girl's age. In the circumstances, the distinct sag to her breasts, the thickening of her stomach and the beginnings of a crease through her belly button were perhaps understandable. Her pubic bush was thick and dark, as dark as the hair on her head, so that when she stood with her legs together, it entirely concealed her sex. I might have to do something about that, I thought. Her arms and her thighs could not be termed plump, but they were beginning to turn that way, and the little dimples in the skin revealed the softness developing beneath the surface.

However her nipples were dark and strong, standing out firm and proud from the smooth round curve of her ample breasts. She followed the direction of my eyes and perhaps saw my admiration for she pulled her shoulders back a little further. That wouldn't do; she was not entitled to any pride. I peered more closely.

'Do you have children, Mrs Ackworth?' The blackness that fell across her face could not have been darker if I had slapped her.

'Yes, Mr Mortensen. Two.'

'Ah. I thought you must have. One can always detect an added radiance in the nipples of a woman who has suckled.'

'The boy,' she continued with increasing bitterness, 'is seventeen and the girl is nineteen.' The coincidence was not lost, but she turned anyway to direct her bile at Lucy.

'Really?' I was not sure how well Lucy could take this level of fire and felt it better to restore the relative positions. 'How delightful. Now, would you please bend over as I requested.'

For a minute it looked as if she would argue again, but she changed her mind and made her way up to the waiting stool. At last she bent down and curved her full naked bottom out towards me.

I let her stay there for a moment while Lucy and I both admired the ample round shape that was offered. Finally I stood up.

'Now then, Lucy. Time to continue your education. You have been on the receiving end a couple of times; now you can experience the opposite. First, consider what we have presented here. Mrs Ackworth's bottom.' We would have time enough later to move to first names; for the moment the irony of so formal an address to one in so ignominious a position added a relish which I am sure was not lost on her. 'Mrs Ackworth has a very good round bottom, quite plump as one would expect of a woman of her age, but an excellent target for any implement that you may choose to use upon it. Today we will settle for the hand and the tawse, but on another occasion I should perhaps like to try her with the paddle and then the cane.' A muffled protest came from Mrs Ackworth, but I ignored this.

'When the miscreant is bent over as she is here, you have the whole surface of the bottom well presented and if she offers any resistance or misbehaviour during the course of the punishment, you can move the strokes down from the surface of the bottom here –' I gave each cheek a resounding slap with my open palm, which caused the whole target to quiver spectacularly '– to the backs of the thighs here.' A sharp slap on each thigh left proud red prints of my hand and produced a hissed complaint.

'However, benefits can also be drawn from requiring the miscreant to stand with her legs parted. Mrs Ackworth, would you oblige, please?' We had a long wait before there was any movement on her part. Finally she obeyed, but I had already decided that however wide she moved them, I would demand more. In the event, she made it easy for me so that I was able to drag two more concessions from her before I had to admit that I was satisfied.

'Good. Now, Lucy, if you move a little further round here, you will see the advantage of this position. Although the bottom is rendered a little flatter this way, you can see what is revealed to us. Not just the bottom, but now also the vulva. Here you can plainly see the plump outer lips, already parted, and emerging from within, the inner lips, which you will see are much looser and thicker than your

131

own; that is to be expected in a woman of this age, particularly after she has borne children.'

Mrs Ackworth was remaining commendably still in the face of this humiliatingly detailed description of her vulva. Time to tighten the rack another notch.

'However, we can also see not just the victim's buttocks, but even the anus itself. This is, as I am sure you will appreciate, an area which is extremely sensitive, and one would not normally apply punishment just there.' I took a good handful of the woman's bottom and squeezed it in a rolling grip that could have been massage as easily as it could have been punishment. 'Except in extreme cases.'

I released her and gave another full slap across the surface. 'It is also generally considered the most intimate area, which even a married woman such as Mrs Ackworth will probably have exhibited to few other people, if anyone at all. Quite possibly not even her own husband will have been privileged to have the view we now see so there is an extra piquancy in requiring the miscreant to exhibit it now.'

A weak strangled sob rose from the figure in front of us and I caught a quick grin flash across Lucy's face.

'If you look carefully, you will see that the anus is tightly closed. This is the normal condition, but it is exacerbated in this case by fear. She knows that it is quite within our power to insert any object we please into her and although the process will be painful, depending upon the size of object we choose, the pain and discomfort is nothing to the humiliation. So, while it is normally, as I say, closed, in some cases you may find that the anus opens a little, particularly if the woman indulges in anal intercourse. It seems that Mrs Ackworth probably does not.'

Another choke came from between us and Lucy could no longer contain her grin. When I caught her eye, I smiled too.

'However, it may be worth investigating this a little further. Lucy, place your hands on the cheeks of Mrs Ackworth's bottom and peel them apart a little, will you? Then we can see how easily the aperture opens.'

Lucy did not need a second invitation. She spread the waiting cheeks apart with such gusto that another protesting grunt was torn from Mrs Ackworth's lips.

'Well, now. In spite of that enthusiastic performance, no movement is visible from the anus at all. We may conclude then that Mrs Ackworth is either a virgin – anally, that is – or she is particularly nervous as to our intentions. I wonder which. You may release her bottom now, Lucy.'

She turned to me imploringly. 'Can I touch it? Her, you know, bottom?'

'Yes, of course, my dear. If you like. You can do anything you wish.'

I perched on the edge of my chair as I watched Lucy press an enquiring finger against the firmly closed and tightly puckered star, but she lacked the resolve to demand entry where her rival was determined she should get none, so although she pushed against the clustered wrinkles and circled round the target several times, she did not finally breach the entrance.

Lucy stepped back and I considered the next move. Mrs Ackworth knew she was to be spanked and probably assumed it would be done by me. She may have guessed she was also to be strapped, since Lucy had been asked to fetch a tawse, but we had time enough for that.

'You may get up now, if you wish, Mrs Ackworth. Turn round and sit on the stool.' Her cheeks flared red as she turned to face us, doubtless relieved to have reached the end of the ignominy she had been suffering but aware that although seated, her body was still exposed entirely naked to us. To be fair, so was Lucy's, and she was standing. I was the only one dressed, as I always would be, but found a delightful contrast in the two figures before me.

Mrs Ackworth sat down, her hands folded in front of her mature round stomach and resting coyly in her lap where they could, to some small extent, shield her pubis from our gaze. Her breasts swayed full and heavy, the proud dark nipples protruding conspicuously, and Lucy stared intently as if she had never before seen another woman naked. Her glances kept flitting from

Mrs Ackworth to me and back again before she finally summoned the courage to speak.

'Mr Mortensen, did you really mean that? Can I really do anything I want?'

'Yes, yes, of course. What had you in mind?'

'Well, I . . .' Her nerve failed her at first but then she leant across and whispered in my ear. 'Can I?'

'Yes. An excellent idea.' My pupil was galloping now. 'Go and fetch them.' Our victim glowered suspiciously from beneath sullen brows as Lucy dashed away out of the door again and rattled up the stairs, then turned her grim face back to me. I smiled sweetly at her.

'Please sit on your hands. I shall require you to stay still for the next few minutes; will you do that or shall I ask Lucy to fetch some handcuffs?'

She spat her words at me. 'I will stay still, damn you to hell.'

'Thank you. I understand that you feel a little aggrieved at the current course of events, but I would advise you not to antagonise me too much. Furthermore, this is just the first day of our friendship, Mrs Ackworth. You may feel that today Lucy is being allowed unpardonable liberties, but I assure you that I will give proper opportunity for revenge if you care to return on another day.'

Her eyes gleamed and she turned to contemplate Lucy as the girl returned. 'That might warrant my returning, I suppose. Certainly I can think of nothing else that would.'

'No, indeed,' I answered her gaily, untempted by her bait. 'Now, remain still. Lucy, please continue.'

The girl approached her, disentangling the chain as she came. Mrs Ackworth could not stay silent. 'What in hell is that?'

'They are nipple clamps. Have you never seen them before?'

Mrs Ackworth's eyes widened in horror as she heard the words and for a moment her hands started to slide out from under her bottom. She faltered and then stopped as she remembered my instruction and contemplated the humiliation of having her wrists cuffed if she failed to obey.

134

She tucked her hands back, took a deep breath and her lips tightened further as Lucy approached, eagerly opening and shutting the jaws of the little clips. For a moment their eyes met and Lucy blushed and looked away but the venom in the woman's eyes followed Lucy's every movement. The girl reached out her little fingertips to the woman's nipple and gently drew it forward, but I wanted more.

'They work best if the nipple is fully erect, Lucy, then the clamp can be fitted to the back of the nipple. I suggest you massage her breast a little longer. That's the way.'

I cannot say who was the more humiliated, Lucy at having to stroke the dark nipple or Mrs Ackworth at having to sit and suffer the attention while others witnessed the clear irresistible signs of her arousal. I cannot say who was the more aroused, Lucy at being able to toy with her boss's breasts in whatever way she wished or Mrs Ackworth at having this pretty young teenager caressing her so tenderly.

We all watched the nipple swell beneath the delicate stroking of Lucy's little fingertips until it was the size and colour of a ripe raspberry, as long as the last joint of Lucy's finger and certainly fatter. The unmistakable contrast with the girl's own small breasts and delicate nipples only made the process all the more appealing. When it seemed as plump and hard as it would ever become, Lucy squeezed open the jaws of the little clamp, fitted it carefully round the swollen nib and released the spring. Mrs Ackworth immediately twisted away, sucking in her breath in a sharp whistle and grunted out an agony of pain before she could straighten up again.

Lucy watched, utterly fascinated by the effect her actions had created, but with an entirely callous inquisitiveness like a small boy tearing the wings off a butterfly.

'Now the other one,' I said.

The action was repeated – the long, slow caress as both women stared down at the nipple and it erected between Lucy's slim fingers. Then the approach of the open jaws, the careful placement, the release and the immediate contorted grimace and yelp as the woman struggled to keep her hands in place.

135

It does not take long for that initial shock to pass and soon Mrs Ackworth was facing us again with only the slightest glistening in her eyes. Lucy reached out to the thin chain which connected the two clamps and shimmered with every breath, and she lifted it up and away. The clips, being of the tweezer type, dug fiercely into the soft peak of Mrs Ackworth's breasts and when Lucy pulled lightly on the chain, the jaws were pulled tighter even as they stretched the long nipples out into clearly agonising points. When she released the chain, they fell back into their pinched distorted shape. When she tugged again, they stretched out once more, crimped and twisted like an over-taxed spring.

'When you have quite finished, Lucy –' The girl started round at me in mischievous glee '– I think we should move on. Kindly stand up and turn round again, Mrs Ackworth. And Lucy? Perhaps you would pass me the tawse.'

10

Wednesday (continued)

It has to be said that in both build and demeanour Mrs
Ackworth is a sturdy and matronly woman; consequently
her solid stare of bitter defiance which was the immediate
reaction to my instruction that she turn round and bend
over was entirely typical. When I had earlier required her
to adopt that position, it had been while I was conducting
my detailed appraisal and criticism of her body. That
process had been thoroughly humiliating, as we both knew
it had been intended to be, but this time a more practical
purpose lay behind my request, and again it was one which
we both understood. Whether or not she really had
received similar treatment in her life, she could well
understand what was coming and would be in little doubt
that it would be as painful for her as it had been for any
of the young victims she had put through the same ordeal
in recent years. The flow of each of these thoughts could
be seen running across her face and a couple of times she
drew a deeper breath as if about to remonstrate.

Eventually, better judgement prevailed; her jaws clenched and, without a word, she turned away and bent down.
She knew that if she protested, I would have insisted and
that would only have re-emphasised that I held the power.
She rested her hands on the edges of the leather seat,
shuffled her feet a short distance apart and steadied herself
for what she knew I was about to deliver.

'Now then, Lucy, perhaps you would like to administer
the punishment today. Start with your hand and give her

a good hard twenty. You have quite small hands and so, particularly when spanking a more mature and fuller bottom like this, treat each cheek separately. You can achieve a pleasing symmetry by alternating the strokes, but twenty on each buttock as hard as you like.'

I sat as Lucy took up position to one side and then without warning slapped her victim once on each cheek in quick succession. The sound was gratifyingly loud, but showed little visible result as Lucy rested her left hand on the small of her employer's back, stretched right back and whipped her right hand down hard on the quivering pale moons that were so promisingly presented. This time I heard the sudden drawing in of breath that indicated the strokes had been a little more effective which was repeated as Lucy settled to a brisk steady rhythm and the target at last started to develop a more appealing pinkish colour.

Eventually she stopped and looked round at me, nursing her palm in her other hand. 'That's twenty on each, Mr Mortensen. Shall I do some more?' Her eyes and cheeks were aglow and her own nipples eagerly erect so that I believe she would cheerfully have tolerated further pain in her own hand for the gratification of inflicting further blows on Mrs Ackworth's full round bottom.

I stepped up to feel for myself the warmth of the broad pink patches presented before us, grasping a good handful of the woman's ample cheeks and squeezing it before taking the same on the other side. They were warm, certainly, but not greatly so, and although I myself gave her another half dozen slaps across each broad swelling, producing a much more obvious reaction and protest from our victim, I realised that she was probably not suffering nearly as much as she was pretending.

'I think we will move on to something which will have a little more effect. You may stand up, Mrs Ackworth.'

She stood slowly and turned round towards me, still bitter at needing my permission to move or stand up, still refusing to say anything. She glared at me with real hatred. Her heavy breasts swayed as she moved, and the chain which was still dangling from each thick nipple rattled in sympathy. The claws were digging in quite deeply, but I imagined the nipples themselves would be almost numb and feeling little effect.

'Lucy, I think you should remove that now.' I nodded towards Mrs Ackworth's bosom and stepped back to watch as the girl skittered up and gaily pulled at the small steel pincers. Mrs Ackworth hissed out her rage and pulled away, sucking in her breath as each tender nipple was released and the blood and feeling returned. Lucy would need to experience them soon so that she could discover for herself that the pain of attaching them is nothing compared to the agony of their removal.

'Please hand me the box, Lucy.' Mrs Ackworth's eyes followed the object as it was picked up and passed across to me. I opened the slim case and took out the tawse. This has always been a particular favourite of mine – a little over twelve inches long, almost two inches wide and in quite a heavy reddish-brown leather which I caressed between my fingers. I separated the three long fingers and slapped it gently across my palm a couple of times; even that induced a sharp sting. Lucy too was watching closely, and licked her lips in anticipation, making me wonder whether it was receiving or brandishing the implement that she envisioned. I allowed them both to continue in watchful apprehension as I fondled the leather in my hand.

'This also is an antique, although not nearly as old as that article which caught your eye the other day.' I glanced up to see Lucy blush again although she kept her eyes fixed on the thin strap. 'I picked it up,' I continued, 'in an auction of eighteenth-century Naval memorabilia. It was catalogued by some ignorant oaf as a Royal Naval bosun's starter, and indeed it is clearly English leather. However, the tooled inscription is Italian and although somewhat enigmatic, it is clearly a Christmas gift from an Italian-speaking woman to her lover, whom she addresses as 'My Lord Thunder' and entreats to be her master for all time.' I glanced up again but neither pair of eyes could be torn away from the slender object as I wrapped it easily round my hand. My explanation meant nothing; I had lost them and would have to explain. 'The reference is to Lord Horatio Nelson who, as far as is known, only ever had affairs with two Italian-speaking lovers and only one is known to have addressed him in those terms.' My audience's attention was still patently elsewhere, but I continued none the less. 'It is therefore most unlikely that this implement was ever used on any sweating seaman, but highly probable that it has been laid across the exquisite haunches of Lady Emma Hamilton during her stay in Naples or Sicily. Several sources record her enthusiasm for that particular pleasure and indeed a note in one of the recently discovered journals of Charles Greville describes his introducing her to the vice during the long summer of 1785.'

At the time, my audience showed absolutely no interest whatsoever in my account, doubtless both having their minds set more on the application of the instrument than its provenance, but I expect they remembered it later. In any case, if a girl is to be thrashed, I believe it is worth her knowing that the implement causing her so much pain has been used across the bare buttocks of the great and good.

The two naked figures were still looking bemused at my ramblings. Mrs Ackworth held her arms behind her, no doubt nursing the tenderness of her bottom as a result of the spanking she had received already and in anticipation of the beating she expected to receive soon. Lucy was still idly rubbing the sting from her right palm as she listened. Both stood in front of me, both naked, both entirely exposed to me and both with a curiously appealing innocence in the ease with which they accepted their nakedness in my presence. The contrast between them could scarcely have been greater: one just nineteen, the other more than twice that. One with fair, almost flaxen hair that hung in wild tresses and with an ethereal fluff of warm gold at the top of her thighs; the other dark with tightly controlled curls across her head and a thick impenetrable forest on her pubis that denied access with as much determination as any chaste matron could wish for. One was slim and firm, with a sleek grace that promised unequalled agility; the other full and plump, suggesting an abundance of lush extravagance. One with firm young breasts that could be held in one hand, which needed no support but craved only admiration, with little pale nipples of such purity it was hard to imagine they had ever been seen or touched or kissed; the other with confident heavy breasts that would fill a man's hands and mind with their lavish presence, breasts that swayed and rippled, topped by robust nipples that had been sampled by many lips and brazenly offered themselves for more.

What perfect counterparts: the full range of womanhood. It would have been a mean-spirited man who would not have invited the one to share the joys available in the arms of the other and a dull-witted man who did not picture the one screaming out at the hands of the other. I like to think I am neither.

'Mrs Ackworth, kindly turn round again and bend over.' The sudden start suggested that she really had thought her ordeal to be over. She stood up straight and stared me full in the eye.

'Mr Mortensen, I consider your behaviour to be utterly outrageous and unpardonable. I –'

'Mrs Ackworth,' I interrupted, 'you have required several young and inexperienced girls to strip naked for your pleasure. You have strapped them and beaten them without mercy and now you will receive the same treatment. To some degree your protests may indeed be justified, but to such extent as they are, they prove the retribution to be just. Please turn round, bend over and present your bottom for punishment.'

She took a deep breath and then turned and settled back into the same position – hands gripping the edges of the stool, legs well spaced for stability. In spite of her age and maturity, and the thicker flesh which the years had laid on, her bottom had coloured up well to its first mild spanking and promised to respond even better to the heavier treatment it was about to receive. I stood up and approached her, running my hand over her curving back and down across the round buttocks to her solid thighs below.

Back up again, running my fingertips through the valley between her buttocks so that, in spite of herself she did react and clenched up in automatic revulsion at my encroachment into so private an area. I did not press further in but continued up the length of her broad back, right up to the shoulders and then down the side, straight down to where her breasts hung free and available. I scooped one up in my open hand as she tried to twist away but I gripped the handful, pinching tightly so she could not move and so she knew that the harder she pulled, the harder I would squeeze. When she relaxed again, I relaxed, just cradled the warm heavy parcel in my palm, teasing at her tubby nipple and gently caressing the soft velvet sheen. Meanwhile, I trailed the square tip of the strap across her back and down over her bottom, tracing small patterns across her skin and sliding the narrow edge right into the crease of her bottom, nudging against the very rose of her anus. She held her breath as I pressed forward even beyond that to those thick lips which we had scarcely explored yet. She breathed again when I returned to the safer ground of her bottom and finally, with a last squeeze of her breast, released her.

'Right now, Lucy, use the strap.' I offered it across to her and she too turned it over in her hand, examining the markings, feeling the weight and the splay of the three evil fingers. 'With an implement like this you can aim the stroke right across both cheeks of the woman's bottom and although it will tend to punish the further cheek more, you can do a few that concentrate solely on the nearer cheek if you wish. Alternatively, if you are sufficiently ambidextrous, do some left-handed strokes from the other side. You should aim to get an even spread of colour and welts across the whole surface of the bottom. Even –' I could not resist the closing humiliation '– with a bottom as ample as this.'

A grunt of angry disgust sounded from the bent figure, but I ignored that and settled back to watch the scene play out. My pupil had so little experience and yet displayed such talent one would have thought she were born to the task. She did not hesitate. She took up position at the side of her victim, laid the leather across the centre of her target, shuffled her feet to perfect the distance, swung the strap back and brought it down with the firm determination of a professional. The effect was immediate.

The smack of leather across the broad cheeks rang out like a shot. It was drowned instantly by a squeal from Mrs Ackworth like a piglet being butchered and the woman leapt up as if she had been electrocuted. Her hands whipped back to cradle her heavy buttocks and she spun round to glare at her tormentor in silent, blinking fury. She did not speak, but her breath rasped out as she struggled to restrain her protests, her chest and flushed breasts heaving with the effort of retaining her dignity. Her hands continued slowly massaging the soft flesh of her bottom and she stared at Lucy in defiance. After a few seconds Lucy weakened and looked across at me, wordlessly appealing to me for support. I was disappointed in this, for the girl had to exert her own discipline over her charges. I shrugged my shoulders and gestured to her to continue.

Lucy blushed and swallowed nervously. She could never have imagined just one hour ago that she would ever be in such a position of power over her employer, but she needed to learn to adapt to such changes. She glanced over to me once more then pulled herself up straight to return the woman's stare.

'Bend down again, Mrs Ackworth. I have not finished.'

Good. Extremely good. The girl was learning well, but the tempest of black fury that swept across the woman's face warned of a challenge that might have broken her. My help was needed after all.

'Please do not waste time, Mrs Ackworth. Lucy is acting on my instructions and she will stop when I instruct her to do so. Until then, please do as she tells you.'

She blinked, and I do believe that it was not all show – there genuinely were tears which she was struggling to hold back and she had shivered through a couple more deep breaths before she finally turned away and bent down, eventually removing her protective hands and uncovering her bottom once more. The cheeks were now crossed by a trio of close red tracks which had landed straight across the fullest, softest, most tender part of her body and already were rising. It was so entreating a picture that I reached out to feel them, running my fingers along the crisp edges and round the neat curved ends. The stroke had clearly been extremely effective but, as I had told them, this implement has always been one of my favourites.

Lucy took up her position again and Mrs Ackworth spread her fingers and gripped the rolled leather edge of the stool. She flinched as the leather was lain across the first line of weals and pulled away when she felt it lifted off. Perhaps Lucy had frightened herself with the reaction to her first attempt because this second stroke was much lighter and with a hiss through clenched teeth, Mrs Ackworth managed to retain her position.

For the next one, Lucy let herself go again, measuring the distance carefully, swinging the strap right back over her shoulder before bringing it down with eager determination on the broad expanse of pale skin. Another squeal was torn from the woman's lips, and she shot up straight, her hands reaching back to nurse the injuries. She didn't turn to face us, but her head was bowed and we could hear the deep steady breaths being drawn in and out as she shifted her weight from one foot to the other, determined to maintain her self-control. I allowed her a few seconds and then, of her own accord, she bent back into position. It was time for a little change before Lucy continued.

I stood up beside her again and ran my hand over her bottom. The skin was unmistakably hotter and each of the raised weals clear and rough under my fingers. I caressed each of them gently and then allowed my other hand to slip down again to the hanging breasts. I found the nipples still full and hard and the sigh that escaped when I squeezed as if milking her seemed more like pleasure than protest. Then I moved further down, across her stomach to the thick tangle of hair and through that into the soft, warm and moist crease between her legs.

I had not bothered to explore or even examine her sex when she was bent over earlier, but now that I could dig my fingers deep into the warm welcoming folds, I found as rich and lush an arena as any man could have hoped for. She was already thoroughly moist and as I worked my fingers far inside her, the thick syrup flowed with all the impatient generosity of a teenager. Further up, I pinched her stout clitoris between my fingertips and felt her whole frame shudder as she ground herself further into my hand. Having balanced the pain of the beating with the pleasure of a caress, it was time to return to the punishment.

'Continue, please, Lucy. Three more, I think.' A slight whimper broke from our victim's lips so I quickly corrected myself. 'No, better make it six more.' My remark fell into silence as Lucy stepped up to her place again.

These last strokes fell in a steady, even rhythm. The crack of each echoed round the quiet room and was answered immediately by a squeal from Mrs Ackworth. She could not stay silent and she could not stay bent over. After each stroke, she leapt up, clasping her injured cheeks in her hands and gasping through her teeth as she struggled to keep her composure. Her eyes were silently blinking back the tears; she stood on one leg and shook the other as if trying to rid herself of the pain, then the other leg, then back again. Finally, anxious to avoid the humiliation of any further instructions, she bent down again, her hands reluctantly peeled away from the reddened surface of her bottom to return to the leather stool where she waited for the next stroke. Lucy tried to let the minutes drag, and between each stroke laid the strap again across the proud target and played it up and down the surface. However, she was too young and too impatient to do the moment justice, too eager to see the gratifying reaction when each blow landed on the round red cheeks of Mrs Ackworth's bottom. As the strap whistled through the air, the full buttocks compressed in a web of little wrinkles as they were clenched tight against the imminent agony, her knees straightened to try to haul her bottom as far away from injury as she could, and then the stroke landed.

For all her pride and arrogance, for all her bitterness towards the young girl who was doing only as I had instructed her, for all the cruelty she had shown to so many others, I could not help but admire the courage and resilience of the woman as the beating finally concluded. She had accepted the shame of being stripped entirely naked, of being most soundly whipped by one of her most junior employees, and had tolerated a vicious thrashing across skin that, I was now convinced, had never suffered the like. She had previously displayed a keen determination in inflicting the hardest of punishments and now showed an equal fortitude in receiving them. When the final stroke landed she turned to face me again, conscious of her nakedness, and accepting my involuntary examination of her figure. She made no coy moves to conceal her ample breasts or rounded belly nor any secret of nursing the tortured cheeks of her bottom. Instead, she turned a tear-streaked face to me, displaying cheeks flushed with what might have been passion but might as easily have been humiliation, and defied me to find fault with her behaviour. She took a breath and composed herself to ensure her words would come out cleanly.

'Are you satisfied now, Mr Mortensen?'

I am not so churlish as to belittle her achievement. 'Yes, Mrs Ackworth, you have acquitted yourself very well. I think we may finish for the day.'

It was Lucy though who seemed unwilling to stop so soon. She was still standing at her post, running the long tails of the tawse through her fingers, and although she was admiring the brutal array of stripes she had created, her enthusiasm was not yet satisfied.

'Please, Mr Mortensen, couldn't I cane her?' My pupil certainly did not lack ambition but although pleased at her enthusiasm, I thought it better to wait a while for that.

'I think not. The cane is a cruel instrument, Lucy, and if not skilfully used, can cause serious, even permanent damage. That is not our intention and I think Mrs Ackworth has suffered quite enough for one day. Maybe when you have experienced the cane from the receiving end, you will be better prepared to administer it.'

I could have lived with Lucy's disappointment, even the worry that creased her forehead at the reference to her receiving the cane. I could have lived with Mrs Ackworth's obvious relief at her escape. I could not live with her smug grin and the excited glance across to the girl as she considered the possibility of exacting her revenge. That was too much and I needed to take her down again, but there is more than one way to skin a cat. I turned back to Lucy.

'Perhaps instead you could settle yourself on the stool and face me.'

She appeared apprehensive as she took up the position, and although relief washed over Mrs Ackworth's face when she realised she was not to be sent over the stool again herself, she was perhaps beginning to know me too well to be entirely sanguine. Lucy sat with her legs crossed and her hands clasped neatly in her lap.

'Put your hands behind you and open your legs wide, as wide as you can.' She licked her lips nervously as she slowly allowed her legs to fall apart and the crease of her vulva appeared, stuck together at first and then slowly peeled open: shiny, sticky, eager. She blushed at the revelation.

Mrs Ackworth, for all her affected indifference, stared at the open crease and the moist treasure inside. I turned to her.

'There you are, Mrs Ackworth. For you. You may drink at the fountain of youth.'

'I beg your pardon?'

They both turned to me, equally perplexed and then equally appalled as they began to understand my intention. 'Do not pretend, Mrs Ackworth. Do you really ask me to believe that your punishments of these girls has never ended with you calling your young victim to kneel between your thighs? Well, today the position is reversed. It is Lucy who sits and waits, and you who will kneel between her thighs and use your tongue to bring her to orgasm.'

'I will do no such thing, Mr Mortensen.'

'It is not a request, Mrs Ackworth. It is an instruction.'

She stared at me again, her hands still working absent-mindedly at her bottom, but her resolution was a fraction weaker. 'I refuse.'

I shrugged. 'Then you have suffered the beating for nothing, for it seems that your inexcusable treatment of the young ladies in your charge must become public knowledge after all.'

She stared frantically from my face to Lucy's and down to the open crease waiting so close beside her. 'How am I to maintain discipline among my employees if this becomes known!' Her tone had risen almost to an entreaty.

'It will not become known, Mrs Ackworth. A great deal passes within these walls that is never known outside them. Only the three of us will know of this incident and since I have no intention of broadcasting it and Lucy can imagine only too clearly what her punishment would be if she were to do so, I think you can rest quite confident that your secret will be maintained. Come along now.'

Mrs Ackworth stared at me and at Lucy, then down at the open crease between the girl's legs. She hobbled forward, her palms still cautiously massaging her bottom, and finally leant down in front of the girl. As she shuffled up closer, Lucy automatically closed her legs so that the woman had to reach up and press her thighs open again. I saw their eyes meet briefly, reluctance on both sides but on the one side coupled with resentment and on the other with desire. Lucy knew that for all the embarrassment at being so exposed and for all the awkwardness of having her superior kneeling at her feet, preparing to bestow that most intimate of all caresses, the outcome would be deeply satisfying. On the other side, Mrs Ackworth was humiliated beyond bearing at being forced into so menial a position between the legs of her junior staff, and yet she had already tacitly admitted to me her attraction to her own sex, and the girl now sitting in front of her was as gorgeous and tempting as any she could have known. Only a profligate would have hurried them when so much fruit lay in watching the conflict being played out.

Lucy's hands were running almost unconsciously down the insides of her thighs, sweeping up almost to her vulva and then back down. It was a curiously hypnotic and commanding gesture as she waited for Mrs Ackworth to obey. The open crease of her sex shone as ripe and luscious as it had ever been and although I was almost certain that she had never previously had any experience with her own sex, she showed not the slightest trace of reluctance now. Whether this was the discovery of a natural leaning towards other women or whether she was learning more cosmopolitan tastes, I did not at that stage consider. Neither of them spoke, neither moved (beyond Lucy's slow caress of her own legs) until finally, with one last anguished glance back at me, Mrs Ackworth inched forward the last little distance, one hand rested on the girl's pale thigh, the other reached out to frame her open crease and then the head dipped down hiding my view completely as Lucy sighed a long slow moan of welcome.

As Mrs Ackworth leant forward, her broad buttocks lifted up and were now even better displayed. A wide crimson band across the central curve showed where Lucy had so consistently applied stroke after stroke. The plump thighs were parted, allowing a straggle of untended black hairs to poke through and allowing me glimpses of the loose, sloppy lips of her vulva. For all the undeniable delight of a girl such as Lucy, a girl in the finest bloom of youth, one cannot deny the lush glory in the ripe generosity of a figure like Mrs Ackworth's, a woman now in the full abundance of maturity whose ease and confidence would gladden any heart. In a few short years, that ample maturity would have sagged into middle-aged decline, but for this day, in this summer, she was a woman to turn heads. I settled back to enjoy the contrast.

Lucy had brought her feet up on to either side of the stool and was now gripping her ankles, pulling herself even more open to receive the first kisses, licks and caresses from the woman at her feet. Her little breasts quivered as she cherished the attention, while she stared wide-eyed down at the head bobbing so unexpectedly and yet so rewardingly between her thighs.

In spite of her initial resistance, once she had accepted the inevitable, Mrs Ackworth warmed to her task. Her open palms had pushed their way right up to the top of

Lucy's thighs where the thumbs could reach in and touch the podgy lips while her tongue, after a few tentative light sweeps along the full length of the open crease, gradually started to centre on the little swollen clitoris, running tight circles all around it and then stopping to flick impatiently at the underside of the floppy hood. Lucy pulled her legs back even further, opening herself as completely as possible to the probing tongue. She was staring down at the head bobbing so obediently at her crotch, but then she caught my eye across the broad white plain of Mrs Ackworth's back and shone a grin of such capricious joy that I could barely control my own laughter. Yet as quickly as her grin appeared, it vanished, to be replaced by rapt concentration on the erupting intensity of the feelings induced by the unfamiliar caress.

One of Mrs Ackworth's hands had now fallen away from Lucy's vulva to take up duty at her own and I was treated to the view of her fingers regularly reaching through between her fleshy thighs to rake at her own lips and clitoris. I should have stopped her; she was there for Lucy's pleasure not her own, but I could not recall ever seeing so mature and well built a woman in the throes of masturbation, so I was moved to let her continue.

Yet Lucy's pleasure was growing the faster. As the head dug deeper between her legs, she let out a long groan and her own head fell back, eyes tight shut as she squeezed every scrap of pleasure from the attention being paid her. Her legs were quivering, her feet kicking up and down as she battled to contain the ecstasy swelling up within. When Mrs Ackworth finally abandoned her own craving and resumed her full, two-handed attention on Lucy, the girl was lost. She cried out, whimpered and groaned again and then hauled Mrs Ackworth's head tighter into her sex, clamped her thighs back round her and shuddered out a single wringing wail.

Mrs Ackworth sat back on her heels and then pulled herself upright. She seemed to have forgotten to be ashamed of her nakedness in front of the two of us as she turned bitterly towards me, absentmindedly wiping the back of her hand across her shining mouth.

'Have you seen enough now, Mr Mortensen, or do you have some other bizarre perversion in mind?'

Given all I knew and had witnessed, I felt inclined to draw parallels between pots and kettles, but let that pass. 'Thank you, Mrs Ackworth. That will be quite enough. Please get dressed and feel free to go home. You may, of course, take the video tapes with you.'

She snorted her disgust, gathered up her clothes and I heard her stalking down to the cloakroom to get dressed in privacy. When she re-emerged no more than five minutes later, she was washed, brushed and immaculately presented in every detail. A pillar of conservative respectability, nobody could have guessed the scene in which she had just participated on my drawing-room floor. With only the most superficial inspection, she gathered up the pile of video tapes and, with a last snarl at Lucy, who still squatted naked on the footstool, she turned and strode out. A dangerous woman, I remember thinking, one I would do well to watch, particularly if she tried watching any of her precious tapes.

11

Thursday

I forgot that resolution and didn't watch her, but I should have done. In fact I should have paid more attention and thought of it earlier, but it didn't really occur to me until the middle of the following day that Lucy would have to return to work where she would encounter Mrs Ackworth without my being present to offer protection. The initial contact and greeting would be strained on both sides, but I imagined the resentment growing in Mrs Ackworth's mind all afternoon. I could picture the two of them moving in silence round the shop, each engaged on her own duties and trying to avoid the other as much as could possibly be managed. Yet it was a small building offering little room for retreat. They would circle round one another, glancing across when each thought the other was not watching, and they would both remember what they had suffered and demanded. But ultimately the shop was Mrs Ackworth's territory, and she was the one with the greatest ground for resentment. As the hours passed, she would be quietly seething while she watched Lucy flitting about the shop and by the end of her shift, when Lucy could be spared from waitress duties, I did not put it past Mrs Ackworth to exact a fearsome revenge. Initially, I thought I should let her fight her own battles, but this was one that I had brought on her, so perhaps I owed her something. Then Alan turned up, said nothing about her, nothing about last Tuesday, and his tactful silence reminded me of my responsibilities. I decided to go down and make sure I was on hand to protect my ward from any harm. She suddenly seemed much more vulnerable than I had intended.

I trudged down through a dismal afternoon towards the Castlegate Tearooms and pushed open the door. It was entirely empty save for one middle-aged couple sitting forlornly silent in the front bay as they struggled to enjoy their day out. The log fire was burning but showed little enthusiasm for so meagre an audience and it was a joy, as the jingle of the shop bell died away, to see a little figure come darting through the kitchen door. However it was not Lucy, but Sam. She recognised me immediately from our chat previously, for she hesitated a moment, but then continued with her message.

'I'm sorry, sir, we are just clo . . .'

And then Mrs Ackworth loomed into sight behind her. 'Ah! Mr Mortensen! What a surprise!'

She pushed past the waitress and took up position behind the counter, her hands firmly gripping the edge, and her smile holding more than a trace of glee that we now met on her home ground, that I had been forced to come to her. 'Have you come for some tea or to see your little friend?'

It was stupid of me, but I admit I was not prepared for this. I had anticipated finding just Lucy or possibly both of them; I had not anticipated finding Mrs Ackworth on her own.

'Both, to be honest.'

She still smiled smugly. 'Well, as we weren't very busy, I allowed her to have a little time off. She is through in the sitting room with my sister. Please go and join them if you like.' She nodded towards the back of the shop where a door proudly designated 'Private' lurked in the shadow. 'The door straight ahead is the sitting room; you'll find her in there, I expect.'

Her uncertainty was undoubtedly a sham; I am sure she knew exactly where Lucy was waiting. The passage leading away from the back of the restaurant was in darkness but light flowed round the edge of a half-open door at the end. I pushed it open.

153

Lucy was at the far end of the room, perched up on a deep red velvet chaise longue, and entirely naked. Her feet were drawn up on the seat in front of her, her wrists crossed in front of her ankles, her fingers entwined with her toes as she stared mournfully down at the seat beside her where all her clothes lay in a discarded heap. Her shoes stood neatly side by side on the floor in front of her, but that was as far as the calm order extended. All the rest of her clothes were piled in a frantic disarray which presented such undeniable evidence of a frightened scramble to obey, harassed by a master impatient to see the victim stripped and available. She presented a gloriously eloquent picture, her nakedness somehow emphasised by the clothes being so close at hand, and yet she was forbidden to wear them. Moreover, her fear and apprehension were unmistakably revealed by the terrified way she had tried to roll herself in a ball of protective modesty. I don't remember ever seeing her look so enchanting. She suddenly became aware of my presence and looked round, initially startled, then embarrassed and finally ashamed.

'I'm sorry, Mr Mortensen.' This was guilt almost as if I had caught her in an act of unfaithfulness, when in fact it was me whose actions had led her to this plight. We were interrupted before I could reply.

'Ah! You are the gentleman of whom I have been hearing.' I was unprepared for the face of the woman who peered round at me, for she was patently not just Mrs Ackworth's sister, but her twin. She was not entirely identical to the virago I had passed out in the tearoom, but she had the same colouring of skin and hair, the same tone of voice and similar, if a little lighter, build. The leaner version looked no more kindly. Her witch-like face squinted round from a high-backed two-seater settee directly in front of me and she introduced herself as Margaret Kewell; we shook hands with a ridiculous formality under the gaze of the little naked figure at the end.

'I believe,' Mrs Kewell continued as she settled back in her seat, 'that my sister will be joining us as soon as she has got rid of a tiresome couple who are dawdling in the tearoom. In the meantime, I have had the girl strip although I have not examined her as yet.' For a second she stared down towards the subject of her comment. 'These things are often better done in the presence of a witness.'

The ambiguity of her remark was not lost on any of us, but the entirely casual tone suggested that she was at least as capable as her sister and possibly more so. It even suggested that the two had acted in concert before and I had a picture of them some 30 years ago when, as schoolchildren, the unbreakable power of their alliance would have ruled the playground with their sadistic private games.

'Please sit while we wait for my sister.'

I hesitated and glanced round the cluttered room. Almost Victorian in its fussiness, over furnished, over decorated, over tidied, like a seaside bed and breakfast, it was a room in which I could picture the two sisters would be entirely at home and yet where I already felt myself an intruder. Lucy too looked out of place. She would have been incongruous even if she had been fully dressed, but was quite bizarre perched naked and ashamed on so ornate a piece of furniture.

I had come to ensure that Lucy would be spared any retribution for yesterday, but clearly I had already failed. Not only was I too late, I now found that the retribution I had feared from Mrs Ackworth would be delivered not by her alone but also by another woman whose initial comments implied greater experience and promised even harsher vengeance.

Yet I had responsibilities towards Lucy, and when she turned her deep anguished eyes on me, silently appealing for the help that only I could give, I understood the full extent of the sisters' vengeance. That she had already been stripped naked was a clear indication of the form that they intended their revenge to take and Lucy's expression suggested that she also understood, had perhaps even had explained to her, what to expect at their hands. As the full picture became clear and I began to visualise what may be in store, I melted entirely. In the face of such temptation, I could resist nothing. I took the proffered wing-back chair and turned to Mrs Kewell with a smile. 'Will she be long, your sister?'

In fact she was not long. We heard the muffled sounds of the front door being closed and bolted and then Mrs Ackworth's busy voice giving a succession of crisp instructions to the girl who was being left to clear up. Finally her footsteps came clicking down the stone floor of the passage to where we were all waiting.

'Margaret!' she protested as she closed the door behind her. 'I do hope you haven't started without me!'

'I got bored, so I had her undress, but that is all. I haven't laid a finger, or anything else, on her.'

'Excellent! Well, come here, child, and we may as well begin.' She took a place next to her sister on the short settee. 'Have you decided to stay and watch, Mr Mortensen?'

'I will stay to ensure fair play.' I lightly but significantly changed the emphasis of her question and nodded with a polite smile that would not reduce the strength of my reply.

'Fine, but you must appreciate that today we are on my court, so we play by my rules. As you so succinctly put it yesterday, you may stay or you may leave, but there is no other choice.'

'I understand, Mrs Ackworth. You may count on my constancy.' I addressed the last remark to the whole room, but smiled at Lucy as I spoke and if Mrs Ackworth misunderstood me, that was up to her. However, I had promised Lucy at the start of her visits to me that one barrier would not be crossed, and I intended to stay to ensure that, whatever happened, it was not.

'Very good. Now, come over here, girl.'

Lucy dragged herself uncertainly to her feet. In spite of her nakedness, the pose that she had taken up previously had succeeded in concealing her more intimate parts completely, but as she got to her feet, we were treated, and she knew that we were being treated, to exposure of her breasts, her pubic bush and even, as she manoeuvred her legs out in front of her, a fleeting glimpse of the little lips tucked within. She crossed towards the two women sitting so cosily side by side, came up in front of them and stopped. Her ankles automatically crossed over one another to close up any possible access or probing towards her vulva, and she held her hands up under her chin, her little arms concealing her breasts, her writhing fingers betraying her fear.

Mrs Kewell beckoned her up closer and closer until she was standing well within an arm's reach, but I did not doubt that it would be Mrs Kewell's arms that would do the reaching.

'Arms behind you, girl, and turn around.'

Lucy turned her back to us and reached back, her hands clasped ineffectively over her little round buttocks. Mrs Kewell's bony fingers grasped her wrists and pushed them up to the small of her back. 'There. Stay like that.'

Then that same bony hand slithered down Lucy's skin to rest on the smooth curve of her bottom where the fingers opened like a claw to enfold a roll of skin and then closed in a vicious pinch. I heard Lucy suck in her breath and although she resisted any greater protest, it was enough for the two sisters to know they had opened their score. Mrs Kewell laughed, an almost girlish giggle, and looked round at her ally with pride before lifting her hand away and planting it back with a ringing slap that broke the quiet of the afternoon.

'Quite a little treasure, you've found for me, Celia, dear. You have done well. I think we'll have her on the settee, here.'

The two women stood up and Mrs Ackworth tidied the couple of small coloured cushions. She glanced across at me once, but it was to make sure I was taking all this in, not out of concern at my reaction.

'There,' continued Mrs Kewell softly, almost emotionless confidence strengthening every word. 'Lie down here on your back, put your arms up above your head and let's have a look at you.'

They stood waiting, watching her, while Lucy stared down at the expanse of dull striped fabric that they had cleared in readiness for her.

'What are you going to do?' Lucy still held her hands clasped under her chin, but it seemed such an inadequate protection of so sweet and vulnerable a body when faced with such assured determination.

'There's no need to be shy, dear. I'm sure you don't have anything that we haven't seen before.'

Lucy took a single step forward, then a second, and paused again before she finally turned and sat down where they had indicated. She swivelled round, lifted her feet up beside her and slowly uncoiled until she was spread almost flat except for her legs crossed protectively one over the other. One arm reached across to shield her breasts, the other to guard her vulva as she turned her head to look at us.

Mrs Kewell licked her lips, her bright eyes following every movement that Lucy made, like a cat toying with a mouse it knows it has already defeated.

'You heard what I said, child. Hands up behind your head.'

Lucy glanced nervously at both the women – she seemed to have completely forgotten about me – and lifted her hands back behind her head. Her fingers twisted together nervously but gradually, as she became more accustomed, or perhaps simply more resigned, to the pose she had been required to assume and the way it exposed her so entirely, and her arms dropped back on to the arm of the settee.

'Now your legs. Straight out, and side by side.'

She stretched them out, and her face coloured a deeper pink as she accepted the inevitability of this revelation of her lips.

Satisfied at last, the two sisters glanced over at each other, an almost childishly mischievous grin on their faces as they climbed deeper into their private conspiracy. Mrs Kewell continued to take the lead.

She sat beside Lucy, and with all the casualness and boldness of a doctor engaged in legitimate duty, reached out to Lucy's little breast. She ran her open palm up the smooth mound, reaching round with her fingers to gather it all into a point and there, at the delicate pink centre, she pinched the girl's nipple between forefinger and thumb until I saw silent tears starting to come to Lucy's eyes. I was not the only one to see them, for I realised that both the women were also watching and that they would not be satisfied until the tears had appeared. Although she was shaking, every muscle in her arms quivering in the agony of staying still, Lucy said nothing while one small tear slid silently down the side of her face. Only then did Mrs Kewell release the nipple, although she stayed to rub at the breast in a way that could have been a relieving massage but could as easily have been a selfish caress. Swiftly, Lucy brought one hand down to wipe away the tear before obediently clasping her hands together again.

As soon as she was back in position, Mrs Kewell moved on to the other breast, repeating exactly the steady encirclement, the grasping squeeze and final pinch that pressed steadily tighter until, this time with a strangled cry, another rewarding tear welled out of the corner of Lucy's eye and ran down on to their settee.

Mrs Kewell looked round to her sister. 'She's very sensitive, you know. I was hardly applying any pressure at all.' She stood up. 'Here, you try.'

Mrs Ackworth took her sister's place on the settee beside their prey, but did not exactly copy her actions. Instead, she reached out and, with her podgy hands feeling across the whole surface of both Lucy's breasts in an action which was clearly for her own pleasure, grinned at Lucy's expression of loathing. Inevitably, the repeated sweeping of her fingers caused the nipples to rise and on noting this, the woman pounced. She reached for them both, grasping as her sister had done between finger and thumb, but squeezing, twisting and pulling at the tender points until she in turn was rewarded by a pathetic sob and tears wrung from Lucy's eyes.

At this Mrs Ackworth released her and sat back. With a callous slap across first one breast and then the other, she relinquished her place on the settee.

'Yes, she does seem very sensitive. Unless she's just a cry-baby.' They both laughed as Lucy turned her head away.

Mrs Kewell returned to the settee but, inevitably, took up a place further down, level with Lucy's knees.

'Now then, child, let's see what you have down here for me to play with.'

Lucy looked from one woman to the other, the dread written clearly across her face, yet as Mrs Kewell settled down, I saw Lucy fractionally lift her hips, and when she dropped back on to the settee, her thighs had opened fractionally. Even faced with the next ordeal and with the last barely over, she could not resist making herself just a little more available for the approaching humiliation.

The gesture, whether resignation, acquiescence or invitation, was not lost on Mrs Kewell, but it was not enough. She was already forcing her hand down between the girl's thighs and sliding it up towards her vulva. She pushed the legs apart, bending the nearer leg up and pulling it over on to her lap and pushing the other against the back of the settee, but she did not seem to be meeting any resistance from Lucy to this shameless arrangement of her limbs. Finally Mrs Kewell had complete access to Lucy's sex, opened and available right in front of her, and she sat back to take in the spectacle.

'Well, now, you're a very lippy little thing, aren't you? Do come and see, Celia. She is quite remarkably well developed for one so young. See?'

I could see too. I could see that looking alone was not enough and already Mrs Kewell's fingers were moving in, gripping the whole delightful bundle of Lucy's ample vulva in her hand and pulling at the inner lips, stretching them down as she went. Mrs Ackworth came round to peer over her shoulder.

'So she is, dear. She's just like that girl you had working for you at the nursing home. What was her name, now? Do you remember? You caught her sneaking in with some young man. She was supposed to be working a night-shift and we had to punish her severely. What was her name, now?'

Mrs Kewell made no answer but continued toying with Lucy's lips: pulling at them, stroking them between her fingertips and rolling them from side to side. She squeezed the heavy folds together and stretched them out from the light fringe of golden hair. She carefully peeled them apart and lay them open like the wings of a butterfly. Inevitably, Lucy could not withstand this for long without its effect becoming visible, and as the lips were neatly pressed open and the soft hood pulled back to bare the shiny pink nib of her clitoris, a single drop of moisture appeared at the bottom of the little slit.

'Oh my goodness!' Mrs Ackworth's tone of disgust was commendably convincing. 'Look at that, Margaret. The girl is entirely shameless. She seems to be taking some sort of perverted pleasure!' As if the hypocrisy of her words were not enough, a perfectly manicured fingernail reached out to scoop up the incriminating drop and raised it for more careful scrutiny. The two heads bowed over the disreputable evidence, tut-tutting over its existence but finally smearing it between greedy fingertips. However, by the time they had finished their examination, another drop had arrived to nestle between the tips of her lips and be greeted by further accusations.

Although they had, temporarily at least, stopped their intrusive groping of her vulva, Lucy's eyes had begun to waver and her hands, still dutifully clasped above her head, were wringing together in vain attempts to withstand the feelings being forced on her by the two women.

Mrs Kewell stood up at last. 'Shall we continue, dear? Such shameful conduct certainly deserves the belt you intended.' Lucy shuddered at the words, but again her hips lifted minutely in another silent invitation and the drop trickled down towards her bottom.

'Not quite yet, dear,' Mrs Ackworth answered. 'Wait a moment.'

We all watched her leave, the expressions on the other two faces suggesting they had no better idea than me of her purpose, and we all waited for her to return. She did not take long.

'There. I don't have any of those obscene little clips like Mr Mortensen's, but I'm sure these will be just as effective.' She showed Lucy the two wooden clothes pegs that she now held in her hand. 'Sit up, girl, and let's see how you like this.'

Lucy was too slow for her – how quickly would any girl move to present herself in a position for her breasts to be tormented in such a way? – and Mrs Ackworth grabbed her wrist and pulled her upright.

'Now then, child, I'm sure you will remember how this is done.' The woman's stubby fingers reached for the nipple and closed round it as if picking at a delicate fruit, but they squeezed tighter than a delicate fruit should be squeezed and they pulled the little pink tip right out before releasing it and enclosing it again further back. For several seconds she repeated the same milking movement, urging the little nipple out to its fullest erection although this would evidently be paltry by contrast with Mrs Ackworth's own ripe teats which I so vividly recollected being similarly treated just yesterday.

Lucy had brought her own hand up to shield the other breast and stared into the woman's eyes as the process continued. The nipple was now undoubtedly as erect as it ever would be, but still she did not stop and the effect was so clear on Lucy that soon she started herself caressing her other breast. This was too much for Mrs Ackworth.

'Stop that at once, you depraved child!' She slapped Lucy's hand away.

Then she took up the first peg, pinched the nipple right out again and held the wooden jaws open over the tiny pink peak.

'This will hurt, you'll find, but it's no more than you deserve.' With that she released the jaws. The cry from Lucy was immediate and although she clenched her fists to give herself strength, squeezing until her knuckles were white, it was not enough. Tears were forming in her eyes and when she blinked rapidly and turned her head away, desperate to hide her suffering, the two sisters were jubilant.

'There! I told you!' Mrs Ackworth paused for a moment to bathe in her triumph and then turned to Lucy's other breast, where the nipple, already erect from Lucy's own caress, was soon tightly pinched between the woman's fingers before she started the same hypnotic milking to draw the nipple right out.

She was quicker this time, eager perhaps to see the effect of the second peg, and quickly brought it up into position, allowing Lucy only a second or two of fear before she let it spring shut.

Again Lucy cried out, a succession of plaintive cries and protests that almost melted me, and when she seemed at last to remember my presence, she turned to me with such pleading on her face and in her voice that I almost weakened. Almost.

'Now then,' continued Mrs Ackworth, 'let's turn you over, girl. I shall be interested to see how you manage with the same investigation.' She pulled at Lucy's further arm, twisting her round, and as the girl started to turn away took a final chance to run her hands across her breasts, dragging at the pegs and making Lucy cry out again. Her misery was met with a laugh.

Between them the two women manoeuvred her round until she was on hands and knees on the settee, then pressed her down on to her elbows, pushed one leg hard against the back of the settee and dragged the other over to the edge.

'There! That's better!' Even so, Mrs Ackworth pulled at the small round cheeks, prising them apart with an eagerness that was so reminiscent of the scene yesterday when she had herself suffered similarly. However, the target this time could scarcely be more different. Where Mrs Ackworth had displayed a full round bottom, soft, fleshy, fat and dimpled, Lucy was so firm and compact that the probing fingers made little impression.

'So, my dear, how do you like this now?' She scratched one long painted fingernail across the little puckered star, causing Lucy to pull away immediately. 'Such a pretty little bottom too, and entirely virgin unless I am much mistaken.' She circled round again, purposefully drawing out her examination and bringing the tip of her nail back to press just a fraction harder on the very centre of the cluster of wrinkles. The entrance closed tighter and Lucy tried to pull even further away, but she had nowhere further to go.

'No admittance here, my dear?' The women were huddled together like schoolgirls, practically giggling as they inspected their victim. 'Not to the foul penis of some rough yobbo, perhaps, but not even a curious finger?' They laughed again, and the fingernail traced a path down from her bottom towards the pinker entry, circled and scraped back again.

'Not so much fun this way, is it?' The single scarlet nail rasped like some feral claw up the stretched crack of her bottom until the valley stopped and there it lingered and circled and finally returned, pausing again to trace round the edges of the sensitive little rose that it kept threatening to breach.

The sudden rap on the door took me entirely by surprise, I was so engrossed in the spectacle. Lucy and the two women also started up and the sisters exchanged a glance charged with guilt. Even so, Mrs Ackworth called out to our visitor to enter.

The young waitress, Sam, craned nervously round the door, was relieved to find Mrs Ackworth and started to speak before taking in the rest of the scene.

'I'm finished, Mrs Ackworth, so can I . . .?' Her request died away as she absorbed the vision and eventually she simply stood with her jaw working up and down as she stared in silent horror.

I could hardly blame her, for the scene could have come straight from the Marquis de Sade. The two women, fully dressed, were gathered round their naked victim whose obscene posture was unambiguously devised to reveal her as intimately as possible. From her position at the door Sam would have seen not only the wet evidence of arousal between Lucy's wide-spread thighs, but also the grotesque clothes pegs hanging from her nipples. The two women

164

started round guiltily at the interruption, each with a hand resting possessively on their victim's upturned bottom, each undeniably interrupted in the middle of evil.

Eventually Mrs Ackworth straightened up. 'Very good, Sam, then you may go. Please ensure the kitchen door is bolted and that the front door locks behind you.'

'Yes, Mrs Ackworth.' The girl exchanged a last tortured glance with her friend and slithered back round the door. The two women turned their attention back to Lucy; the nail resumed its cruel path across her skin, keeping on returning to circle the real target, like a vulture round its dying prey, before spiralling away again leaving a thin white scratch in its wake.

Eventually, with a last spiteful jab of her nail at the taut stretch of skin between her vagina and bottom, Mrs Ackworth sighed and pushed Lucy away. 'Now then, perhaps it's time for you to sample the punishment you were so eager to give out yourself. Margaret? Why don't you sit down and hold her across your lap? That way I can be sure she won't move while she is receiving her punishment.'

Lucy struggled slowly to her feet, trying not to knock or disturb the two vicious pegs in any way which would increase her pain, but they swung freely from her nipples and every movement she made produced another pained breath. She stood in front of the women, her teeth chewing at her lip and delicately cradling her breasts in her hands to support the weight of the two pegs.

Mrs Ackworth now understood about these and with a quick 'That'll do for them' she reached up to the pegs. Lucy screamed, her little hands flying up to protect herself, but it was too late. Mrs Ackworth had already snatched them away, barely bothering to press open the jaws before dragging them over the tender nipples. The two sisters exchanged a smug conspiratorial glance and sat back to enjoy the sight of Lucy's agonised twisting as the feeling returned to such delicate nerves and she finally gave in to the sobs of pain that she had managed to hold back before. That glance between the women made me suspicious; they had known the pain that removal of the pegs would cause and I began to wonder whether their claims of ignorance were as genuine as they had pretended.

Lucy barely moved beyond swaying gently but her little body shook with every sniff as she tried to hold back the tears, and her hands nursed the angry red indentations where the jaws had bitten in so deep. Mrs Kewell stepped up and rested her hand lightly on Lucy's shoulder, squeezed gently and finally slithered down her arm, dragging it away as she took a seat squarely in the centre of the settee. The hand stayed firmly wrapped round Lucy's wrist and she pulled the girl towards her, across her and down over her knees. Lucy searched forlornly round the room as she was toppled across the waiting lap and reached out in front to support herself. Mrs Kewell lay her arm across the slender waist and tucked her tighter into her lap.

'That will do, I think, Celia. She will not be moving from here.'

'Excellent.' Mrs Ackworth drew over an upright chair, placed it squarely in front of her sister and, with Lucy stretched out between them, she settled herself down comfortably. Her open palm came to rest automatically on the girl's bottom, where it circled slowly, jealously possessive. The vulture could bide its time. Lucy buried her face in her arms and we all waited.

The smacks, when they came, were steady, solid and earnest. They resounded round the room in a measured rhythm interspersed by cries and pleas from Lucy that went entirely unacknowledged as well as unheeded. The course was broken every few minutes as Mrs Ackworth stopped to run her hand in smooth avaricious sweeps across the surface of the upturned bottom, and each time she did so, her sister joined in the assessment of the effect they were having.

I could gauge the effect quite clearly from where I was sitting. Lucy had stopped protesting and sunk into a resigned acceptance of her fate although a trail of low cries still seeped out through her thick curtain of hair. Her entire bottom was now a uniform deep pink which I imagine was satisfyingly warm to the touch, and extended down to the backs of her thighs where Mrs Ackworth had also aimed several cruel slaps.

The spanking resumed, both sisters taking part now and striking alternately at both tender cheeks until the pleasure was overcome by the temptation to stroke again and they stopped to enjoy a succession of further caresses under the pretence of objective examination.

Finally they decided that was enough and Lucy was released and allowed to stand up, where she faced us, both hands slowly massaging her bottom. I started to get up myself, ready to take the girl home, when Mrs Ackworth spoke again.

'Now then, over the settee with you and we can continue.' She manoeuvred Lucy round until she was bent over the end of the settee. The upholstered arm pushed between Lucy's thighs, forcing her legs apart either side of it and she was pressed down until her back was horizontal and her head was resting on the back. Mrs Ackworth lay one hand on the girl's shoulders to hold her in place.

'I do not go in for all these bizarre instruments such as Mr Mortensen employs –' Both women turned to stare accusingly at me '– but I have always found a stout leather belt to be an extremely effective instrument, and I do believe that you will soon agree with me. Margaret, dear, would you keep the girl in position?'

Mrs Kewell hurried up to take her sister's place, similarly keeping a commanding hand on Lucy's back while Mrs Ackworth scuttled out and returned after a few seconds – the object was obviously kept close at hand – with a shining black leather belt a good two inches wide. It clearly was not new, although I guessed it to have been many years since it had last supported any clothing, yet the familiarity with which its owner fondled it in her fingers showed it to be a known and familiar friend. Lucy's eyes followed in wide horror but I was actually relieved at the sight. Although something thinner would have looked less intimidating, it would have carried a more vicious and painful sting than this broader strap.

On the other hand, being less severe meant that it could be used for longer periods without inflicting an unacceptable level of injury.

Mrs Ackworth took up position first. She doubled over the belt and stood to Lucy's side, her left hand resting briefly on the girl's back and slowly sliding down across her cheeks. Her palm roamed over the reddened surface before returning to the top again and instead she placed the belt carefully in the centre of the girl's bottom, determining exactly where she would strike, and letting Lucy know exactly what was going to happen.

Mrs Kewell licked her lips in expectation. Both her hands rested on Lucy's back to prevent any possibility of her leaping up, but as the belt was tapped lightly against its target, I saw one hand slither down and reach for one of the small hanging breasts. Her fingers scooped it up and cradled it, the thumb brushing across the proud pink nipple, and then she reached further through for the other one, fondled that a moment and then stopped, waiting, but still clutching her soft round prize.

Mrs Ackworth lifted back the belt and started to whip her. The first stroke landed with a resounding smack across the centre of its target and Lucy barely flinched. The second and the third were similarly received without protest but after that Mrs Ackworth paused. She again fondled the target a moment, then set her feet squarely on the floor and brought down the fourth with much greater determination. At this Lucy flinched and a little cry escaped from her lips. The women exchanged a glance, a satisfied smile, and Mrs Ackworth settled to her work. The strokes fell in a slow measured rhythm, at a pace which remained unaffected when Lucy's resistance began to crumble and the gasps became cries and the cries became sobs as the weals appeared in a wide band across the centre of her bottom. I was not counting, but she must have done at least twenty before she stopped, swapped the belt to the other hand and reached down to smooth away the dark ridges she had just created. Her fingertips traced delicately and adoringly along each line before running her open palm in broad sweeps that took in the whole surface, straying down as far as her thighs and, on the return, creeping into the half-open crease between her buttocks.

Mrs Kewell was watching every move attentively, one hand still stretched underneath to toy with Lucy's breasts, pulling at her nipples and stretching them out, but the other hand weaving impatient little circles across her back, itching to take over the belt.

'My turn?' Her tone was as innocent as if they were sharing a dolly, but perhaps this was the way they had done just that.

They swapped places. For a few moments Lucy was allowed to stand up and rub gingerly at her bottom before Mrs Ackworth's hands forced her back down over the arm and pulled her legs open. Maybe she had seen what her sister had been doing, maybe this was a normal part of their play, but as soon as Mrs Ackworth had taken her place at Lucy's side, she too reached down underneath to grasp avariciously for a breast and pinch at the defenceless nipples that hung so easily within her reach.

Mrs Kewell took up the belt, carefully measured her stroke on Lucy's bottom and then started with no less determination than her sister. The strokes were faster but also harder and after a dozen or so on the glowing bottom, she deliberately directed a volley of three right across the back of Lucy's thighs. Lucy squealed at every blow, wriggling and twisting, turning her hips from side to side to try to deflect the flying strap, twining her legs together as far as the settee arm would permit and soon crying out in a rising pitch of protests. In spite of all this, there seemed little real conviction in her attempts. She was not really trying to pull away from Mrs Ackworth's groping hands nor did she seriously try to get up from the humiliating position in which she had first been placed. By the time Mrs Kewell stopped, Lucy's whole body was quivering. Her thighs were working against each other, rubbing against the arm of the chair, but the whimpers from her throat were too low and rasping to be pain.

Mrs Kewell stepped back to survey her work. Between the volley of spanking Lucy had received first and the vicious whipping from the belt, the whole of her bottom was entirely red. She was still being held down by Mrs Ackworth, although it is questionable whether this was to prevent the girl evading further punishment or to keep her breasts within easy reach of the continuing caresses.

Mrs Kewell followed her sister's example and reached out to touch the tender skin displayed in front of her in what was doubtless meant to appear a tactile assessment but in reality was a self-indulgent caress. Her hand meandered over the whole area of the girl's bottom and along each of the weals, tracing the path of each and then working down to her thighs, to the single livid flash that was emblazoned across them. From here she moved up but so casually, almost accidentally, that she could really plead innocence when her fingers curled round the inner surface of the thigh and crept inevitably into contact with the hanging lips. She stopped.

'Good grief! Turn round, girl.'

Lucy stood up and turned as instructed but Mrs Kewell pushed her back until she was just sitting on the arm of the settee. Her face was streaked with tears, and she sniffed noisily as she wiped her eyes with her fingers, but she was also flushed, and her left hand dropped automatically to her belly where it modestly covered her pubic hair and immodestly curled under to cradle her vulva.

'For heaven's sake, stop fiddling with yourself, girl.' Lucy reluctantly dragged away her hand. 'Now, move your feet apart and let me see if my suspicions are correct.'

Lucy shuffled her feet apart and paused. Then she glanced round at the two women and – briefly – at me before staring down at the floor. Without looking up, she moved her feet even further apart, lay her hands on the arm of the settee behind her and leant back. She was displayed absolutely.

The two sisters slid round in front of her, their heads close together as they jostled each other for position so that it was impossible to tell whose hair was which as they peered down at the sight being so freely offered: the flushed face, bare breasts, erect nipples, heaving chest, matted curls and at last the open crease, with its hanging lips shining in the shame of Lucy's arousal. Gingerly Mrs Kewell reached forward again until her finger was just touching the top of Lucy's crease, where the straggles of tawny hair allowed glimpses through to the skin beyond. The top of her fold, the entrancing little point where the stomach first dimpled down, was visible to us all and there Mrs Kewell placed her finger. She slid it a little further down the open crease and Lucy sighed and turned her head away but made no move to oppose the imminent progression of that slowly advancing finger. It reached the first little ridge, the soft wrapping of the clitoris, and Lucy sighed again as the finger pressed deeper and paused a moment and then squirmed, drawing tiny circles, in that one single place.

Mrs Ackworth was not prepared to continue long as a mere spectator and her hand reached up towards Lucy's breasts, enveloping one entirely and squeezing each in turn with her fingers as if testing their ripeness. Apparently satisfied, she focused on the nipples, rubbing her hand straight across the girl's chest but gripping each pink tip briefly in her fingertips as she passed.

The effect of Mrs Kewell's attention between Lucy's legs was rapidly becoming obvious. Although she continued toying with her clitoris, pinching at the surrounding lips and hood and sometimes working her fingertips right under the hood to stroke the swollen little nib directly, from time to time she reached further down, pushing her fingers along the valley between her lips. Ridiculously, neither of the women ever lost her air of haughty disdain as they stood feverishly masturbating the girl and when, eventually, Mrs Kewell withdrew her hand to find it was entirely coated in the juice of her prey's arousal, they both examined the finding in disgust. They immediately scolded Lucy for her lack of restraint as if this was entirely of her doing and they had played no part. However, once the point had been made, and Lucy had been required to apologise to each of them and even – to her utter disgust – to lick clean the incriminating evidence of her own stimulation off the proffered hand, they quickly returned to their caresses.

Lucy had almost sunk down on the arm of the settee by now, her thighs parting wider and wider of their own accord. Her eyes were tight shut and her face turned away in shame, but the two women obviously did not intend to stop just yet. To have done so now, leaving her aroused but unsatisfied, might have held a certain perverse cruelty which would doubtless have been pleasing to both of them, but if their task was not completed, neither was their victim's humiliation. That could only be brought to fruition by forcing her to lose all self-control, all self-respect and all dignity as she succumbed to an orgasm in front of us all.

The moment was clearly not far off. Mrs Ackworth had now brought both hands up to maul at Lucy's small breasts and after vigorously squeezing and pulling at them in open-mouthed greed, the woman finally gave in to her own desire and sank her mouth down on to the nearer nipple with as noisy an enthusiasm as any baby. Mrs Kewell seemed equally absorbed in her toy. Satisfied that she could make it seep liberally, she now concentrated again on the clitoris. She even sat next to Lucy so as to bring both hands to play in opening the girl's lips up wide, pulling the little swollen flaps out to their maximum extent and then returning again to a fierce circular kneading of the little bud of her clitoris. Lucy could still not bear to watch what was being done to her, as if somehow deflecting her gaze would deflect the blame, but her hands were visibly gripping tighter at the settee behind her and her cries were growing louder, more insistent and more pleading. Her thighs quivered in the intensity and her mouth fell open in panting entreaty for more of what they would not hold back in any case. Finally, with a single strangled groan, the quivering suddenly stopped, she stretched up on her tiptoes, and then she simply collapsed, shuddering, calling on God and her mother for help or forgiveness or reward. The sisters immediately removed their hands, staring in contempt while Lucy crumpled into a heap in front of them.

Dismissing her at last, the two women sank into a torpor of smug tranquillity as Lucy calmed down and hurried up to the other end of the room to collect her clothes. However, after a few moments, Mrs Kewell held up her hands, sniffed disgustedly as if she had been handling something unpleasant and ostentatiously wiped her fingers on a tissue.

Lucy dressed in almost complete silence. The two women watched carefully, chivvying when they thought she could have been quicker with her blouse buttons, and finally Mrs Ackworth stood up to let us both out of the little front door. At the doorway she turned to us, her eyes gleaming with smug satisfaction and suddenly reached up to grip Lucy's chin.

She pulled the girl's head round until they were completely face to face, tilting the head back and then pushing up her thumb and smearing it crudely across Lucy's mouth.

'I still have one debt left to collect, child, and you need not think that I will forget that.'

Then she released the girl and practically shoved her out into the afternoon sun. I heard the locks being fastened behind us and for a second, inevitably, considered what might be the next stage of the scenario that would be enacted the other side of the door: sisters maybe, but their relationship was obviously a little out of the ordinary and, in common I suppose with many men, pairs of twins have always held a fascination which was not greatly dampened by their more advanced years.

We trudged up towards the cross again just as we had done a day or two earlier, each lost in our own thoughts. At the crossroads, we paused and Lucy turned shamefacedly to me.

'I am sorry, Mr Mortensen. I didn't mean to do that. I didn't think it would happen like that.'

It was unclear then whether she meant allowing herself to be so completely at the two sisters' mercy or demeaning herself by wallowing in so fervent an orgasm at their hands. I should have let it pass, but I could not do so entirely. I put my arm round her shoulder and gave her a little hug.

173

'Don't be silly, my dear, it was quite wonderful. How does it feel?'

She jiggled her hips as if gauging the effect.

'My bottom feels hot, but not exactly sore. It's quite warm, but comfortable, like sitting too close to the fire on a cold day. Rather pleasant really.'

I was proud of how far we had come. 'Now then. Do you remember that I am having a dinner party tomorrow evening? Do you think you can stay for that and be my hostess? I would be so pleased if you can.'

She grinned.

12

Friday

I have always been conscious of the majesty that dining room; its perfect stillness and dignity hold a strangely mystical quality that I could never identify. It is in the oldest part of the house and retains much of the original oak framing and panelling, but there is more than that. It always seemed to hold an aura of quiet solemnity like an ancient courtroom and I had felt its power even before Duncan McQuillan had read me the diary of that day and the events which had once unfolded beneath its sombre walls. Having heard this, I could not help but wonder what other scenes might have been played out on its worn flagstone floor, in the glow of its flickering fire, across the looming bulk of the massive elm dining table whose great top could easily carry one or more quivering victims.

I was considering Duncan's account, imagining the young Anne Markham, trying to sense what she must have felt that evening as she was stripped in front of all those men and learnt the ordeal that she faced, when my reverie was broken by the bell announcing Lucy's arrival. She charged straight in, waving a letter at me.

'Here you are! Mr McThingy, you know, the bloke from the castle museum, he brought it over and asked me to give it to you.'

She was clutching a holdall which, she explained, contained her dress, shoes and make-up for later, but she tossed this down in the hall and, entirely ignoring our usual arrival ceremony, rushed into the kitchen full of questions and excitement. I know that this was to be her first real dinner party and that she was impatient to be getting on, but she was too impatient, suspiciously impatient, too eager to talk about the guests and the wine and the table settings.

Eventually I managed to rein her in and remind her of my instruction regarding her clothing while in my house. She apologised, a little guiltily, but then behaved as if she were at home, tearing at her clothes with such careless abandon that I had to intervene again. However familiar the vintage, a claret is still to be relished, not gulped like a supermarket lager. I made her stop entirely for a moment, then continue more appropriately, laying each garment out with proper respect so that I could savour the ritual of her steady revelation, a ritual that I was all too aware would be repeated few times more. When, all but naked at last, she stood in front of me to await the customary completion of the process, she was still distracted, her thoughts clearly directed towards the evening. I took her knickers down and raised them to my face, but she was starting to grow accustomed even to this invasion of her privacy and no longer showed the profound dread nor the compelling anxiety that had been her first reaction.

It was time to set up another hurdle along her path.

I held the knickers in place, savouring her scent, considering the options. 'Move your legs apart, please.'

The unexpected command took her by surprise, hauling her attention back to the present. She cautiously shuffled her feet some twelve inches apart.

'A touch further, please.'

When it was enough, I finally reached forward and touched her between her legs. She recoiled instantly at so close and intimate a caress, pulling away from me as shocked as if I had been a complete stranger, molesting her on a train.

I said nothing, but no words were needed. She glanced up at me from beneath lowered brows, contrition painted across her face and quickly returned to her place.

'I'm sorry, Mr Mortensen. I just wasn't expecting that.'

I pushed my hand out again, slowly so she could anticipate every detail and prepare for the moment when finally I would touch the most intimate part of her body. Her eyes followed my hand and, as it came ever closer, she shuffled her feet apart yet again to allow me even easier access. I touched the warm skin on the inside of her thigh and slid up to the gentle swelling of her lips at the top and then eased between them. The groove was soft as velvet, her delicate inner lips puckered and relaxed like a sleeping kitten, warm to the touch and just slightly moist with that perfect fragrant dampness that comes from only one place. I slowly ran my hand the full length of her crease and back again, not pressing, but allowing the full fluffy lips to caress my hand with the lightness of a butterfly.

Despite the gentleness of the touch, my fingers came away with an exquisite sheen whose perfume I savoured while Lucy blushed crimson and stood staring demurely down at the floor while she waited to be allowed to go. It was still all too innocent.

'Is there something you have to tell me, Lucy?' I twisted my hand in the light, admiring the sheen from all sides as she prepared her response. She kicked from one foot to the other.

'No, not really.' The light innocence of her reply would have deceived a saint. I am no saint.

'Is Mrs Kewell still staying with her sister?'

'No, I think she's gone home again.' Blasé, too blasé, and Lucy would certainly have known or not known. The pretence of uncertainty and unconcern were unconvincing.

'And young Sam – did you see her today? How is she?'

'Oh, fine.'

'Not curious about yesterday?'

'Well, yes. A bit, but I put her off.'

'I understand.' I did understand. If she didn't want to tell me now, I would not insist now. I could find better times for that so I let the topic drop and we returned instead to the kitchen, where she bustled about preparing a salad. I gave her an apron, and it was a delight to see the respectable and altogether unremarkable front view, demurely encased in thick red and white striped cotton, only for her to turn away and display the sweet round cheeks of her bottom, entirely bare but still faintly marked with the signs of yesterday's beating. The uniform may not have reached the standards of the Health and Safety Inspectorate, but it pleased me enormously.

Once the job was done, she immediately took off the apron again and stepped naked out on to the terrace. Accustomed to nakedness now, the confidence and contentment she displayed seemed so serene that as she wandered down among the trees, scattering bread crusts for the birds, she could have been a wood nymph from another time.

When she returned, I started her on arranging the dining room: laying the table, spreading out the dishes, the cloths, the napkins and the candles. I went in once and found her thoughtfully stroking the smooth dark surface of the wood, her pale naked figure almost spectral in the late afternoon gloom. She started round when she heard me but her fingers continued gliding across the surface.

'Is this the same table?'

'Almost definitely. It is certainly sixteenth or early seventeenth century and must have been constructed actually in this room, because you can see it is far too large to fit through the door.'

She stayed there, stroking thoughtfully at the table. 'I wonder how she felt.'

When the table was laid and ready, the curtains drawn and the candles lit, the whole room glowed with a timeless warmth. I left her there and returned to my cooking but she soon appeared behind me, repeatedly trying, but always failing, to work up the courage to ask whether I was going to allow her to dress before the guests arrived. Finally she took refuge in probing into their background.

I had invited two other couples: Graham and Judith Worthing and Mark and Kathy Stenning. Graham Worthing, who was now the managing director of the insurance company for which Lucy's fiancé worked, I had

178

met when we found ourselves bidding against each other at an auction of erotic prints over 30 years ago, and we became friends through our shared interest. He was then divorced but after a long period of extremely social and pleasurable bachelorhood, he had married again within the last couple of years. His new wife, Judith, was about 40, a good fifteen years younger than him, and I scarcely knew her at all. Both at their wedding and the few times we had met subsequently, she seemed quite aloof and frosty. This was entirely in keeping with her professional situation, for she was a commercial solicitor of some standing, but she had seemed an odd choice for Graham. However, when I made a vague reference to my curiosity at his choice he said I should not be so easily taken in by appearances.

Mark and Kathy Stenning were a good bit younger, both around 30. They had recently taken over a company that I had dealt with for many years which specialised in locating rare books and was about to branch out into the republication of classics. Mark had asked if I was interested in undertaking a new translation of *The Decameron*, something I felt to be long overdue, and things led on from there. Although their range was wider than historical erotica, I had gained the impression from my first few dealings with Mark that this was a subject that particularly interested him. His wife Kathy I did not know so well, having met her less than half a dozen times. However, I had gained the distinct impression that she disapproved of me.

As I gave Lucy all the background information on what would be a select gathering, but one at which she could be properly presented and introduced, I was aware of her continually glancing up at the clock. With each minute that passed, she grew increasingly anxious and at each new errand that sent her darting still entirely naked round the house, she fretted yet more. Finally, when the guests were due at any moment, I relented and allowed her to go upstairs to dress and get herself ready. She returned looking magnificent in a rich burgundy velour dress that we had bought together in Oxford Street that Tuesday. It was long enough to reach to her knees and at the front had a modest high neckline which gave no hint that the back consisted of no more than a web of thin straps. These left the skin of her back entirely visible so had the advantage that she could not possibly wear a bra beneath it, while any weals would be tantalisingly displayed. I had liked it at once and although she lacked the weals which would have finished it off, it suited her perfectly. That is not to say that I would want to see her dressed like that too often; enchanting though she was, I do not believe that I could ever have become accustomed to the sight of her walking around my house with clothes on. Somehow, it looked out of place.

Lucy enjoyed playing hostess so once the guests were assembled, I let her lead them through to the dining room, while I popped into the study on the way. I found them all settling cheerfully at the table but they looked up as I joined them, and every voice stopped, every smile froze when they saw the object I had brought in with me: a cane, medium weight and mid-length, which I lay on the sideboard behind my chair before I sat down. I had arranged the seating with Lucy directly opposite me and the men either side of her and the two women on either side of me. From her seat, Lucy watched intently, turned pale but said nothing. She did not dare ask whether this was for her or someone else, feared the worst and probably suspected I would not tell her in any case.

Although her patience was commendable, and the uncertainty would keep her on edge throughout the evening, I have always believed that these events are improved by being allowed to mature in a marinade of anticipation.

'Lucy, I should explain about this cane. After dinner, I want you to get up on the table and then I am going to beat you.'

She said nothing, just stared down at her plate through the silence that blanketed the guests seated round the table. The polite chatter and arrangement of glasses and cutlery stopped as if switched off, for none of them had been given any inkling of this. After a moment's silence I shook my napkin out over my lap and continued, talking to Lucy as if I were totally unaware of the other four listening so intently. 'Shall I tell you why?'

The 'yes' was almost inaudible.

'Because I want to. That is all. Now, perhaps you could fetch the soup?'

'All right.' This was brave enough, but when she looked up at me – her lips trembling, her great round eyes already red, already moist – I yearned to take her up and hug her. 'Couldn't you . . . Could I speak to you privately? Please?'

I could have refused – maybe a stricter master would have done so – but she had never made such a request before and I had given her no chance to discuss the punishment in private before the guests arrived. 'Excuse us for one moment, would you?' I said, and led her out to my study.

She carefully closed the door so that our voices could not be heard by the other guests.

'Please! Not that, Mr Mortensen. I really don't want all those people to see me with nothing on, specially not bending over like that. If you really have to do that to me, couldn't we wait until they've gone? Please?'

'Nonsense, Lucy. Where would be the challenge in that? This will be like that evening at the ballet. You'll be able to show how far you've come, what you can do that they can't. How many of those people sitting out there do you think could face something like this? Not one. Instead they'll all be watching you, admiring you, jealous of your strength and your courage and knowing that they can never be in your place. Besides, I'm not going to cane you just yet; we'll wait until dinner's over for that.'

She considered my words for a moment. 'Will the others want to cane me too?'

'Oh, yes, I should think so.'

'Oh.' The response was painfully sad, pathetically resigned.

'I don't think I'll let them though. I do rather want to do it myself.'

She glanced up at me then, pride and loyalty shining in her little face as if somewhere, in the midst of my treachery, she had found faith. 'How many will you do?'

Her loyalty deserved a reward. 'I'll let you decide. You know what you can stand, so I'll go on until you ask me to stop. Count each stroke out for me, and when you say stop, I'll stop.'

She considered the implications of this, her hand straying back to brush absentmindedly down the curve of her bottom, a curve now so pale and unsullied but which would soon be changed to something so horribly different. 'Could I say stop now? Before you've even started?'

'Yes, if you want to.' I watched the contortions in her face as this information was absorbed, the options it presented and the consequences. She was better than that.

'Will it hurt?'

'Yes.'

'A lot?'

'Oh, yes.'

She paused again for a few seconds. 'All right, then.' She took my hand to lead me back to the dining room before she herself scuttled through to the kitchen.

I wish I could know what had passed during our absence, but the voices stopped the instant I pushed open the door, and immediately resumed more loudly to atone for the silence. As I returned to my chair, I caught a glance flying between Graham Worthing and his wife but was too late to gauge the meaning. However, Graham turned to me, twisting thoughtfully at the stem of his wine glass.

'Alex, would I be right in thinking that Lucy is in some way connected with the young man that we spoke about a week or so ago?'

I smiled at his deduction. 'Indeed she is.' Judith frowned at the question, tilted her head to me and smiled, but I merely smiled back. If she had a question to raise, she would have to put it explicitly. The other two craned forward.

'So this is part of your deal?' Graham continued.

'No, not really. I did not make it conditional on this, or anything else. She comes because she wants to.'

At that moment we were interrupted by Lucy returning from the kitchen, the tureen hugged to her breasts as she walked quietly down the room, past the sideboard, and set the soup down in front of me.

'So,' Graham continued, I think to cover the embarrassed silence which had greeted her return more than from any real interest, 'what do you do, Lucy, when you are not visiting Alex?'

'I work at the Castlegate Tearooms.'

So the conversation continued, on the castle, its history, other stories, other histories and nothing of too much consequence nor too controversial, while the soup was finished and Lucy cleared that and fetched the salmon. Each time she came into the room or went out, she passed the sideboard and the cane lying ominously waiting for her. Nobody mentioned it. We all continued as if there was nothing the least unusual about the evening; as if no cane was lying in wait on the sideboard; as if I had not made the announcement about her fate, an announcement that they were all pretending so politely to have forgotten.

I waited until I was serving the salmon before returning to the topic Lucy had tried so hard to parry earlier in the evening.

'Now, Lucy,' I remarked casually, 'you were going to tell me about your day.'

She stared at me but said nothing.

'You were telling me that Sam had been asking questions. Sam, I should explain –' And I turned to the rest of the company '– also works at the Castlegate tea shop.'

'Well, it's nothing really,' Lucy began. 'Only Sam and I often used to go into town together after we finished work but now I always leave promptly and come straight here so we don't get time. She was just wondering why, that's all.' She quickly started offering vegetables round the table.

'I'm sure that isn't all, is it, Lucy? Didn't she ask about what had been going on yesterday?'

'Yes,' she mumbled into her plate.

'So did you explain?'

'I had to.'

'Then you could perhaps explain to us, because I'm sure the others would be interested.'

Lucy swallowed and hunched herself into as small a ball as she could contrive as she prepared to disgrace herself. 'She – I mean, Sam – came in yesterday into Mrs Ackworth's sitting room and found Mrs Ackworth spanking me.'

So thin and imprecise an account needed to be fleshed out. I leant forward. 'To be precise, not only Mrs Ackworth but her sister as well.'

'Yes.'

'And – because I do think we should be precise about this – you were entirely naked at the time, were you not?'

'Yes.'

'And Mrs Ackworth was not only spanking you; she had placed clips on your nipples.'

'Yes.'

I could have continued, was tempted to drag her down a spiral of steadily more intimate revelations, but strongly suspected riper fruit were waiting to be picked. 'And how was Mrs Ackworth today? Did you see her?'

Lucy nodded.

'And what did she have to say to you? Presumably she made some reference to yesterday's events.'

We waited. Lucy gazed round the table: at the abandoned plates, forgotten glasses, uneaten food, at the men on either side of her, the two women facing her, all sitting in silent concentration as they waited for her to continue. Waiting for her and her alone.

'She asked me to go and see her in her room.'

'And?'

She hesitated, turned bright crimson and stared at her placemat. 'Please, Mr Mortensen. It's very personal and very embarrassing. I don't want everyone to know about it.'

This rather went without saying; I would hardly have asked her to go into detail if it had not been so. 'Nonsense, my dear. Was this something you volunteered to do?'

'Oh, no! Not at all. Honestly!'

'Well, then, what blame can be attached to you if you were not a willing participant? If it was something forced on you? I am sure we will all be most sympathetic.'

'But it's so embarrassing!'

'Please don't argue, Lucy. Tell me what happened.'

She glanced round the circle again, searching for courage, so I repeated the question. 'So why did she want to see you?'

'She wanted me to . . . kiss her, and lick her, you know, between her legs.'

'Ah!' Mine was not the only exclamation, but I was perhaps the least surprised. After all, Mrs Ackworth had practically threatened as much when we were leaving yesterday. 'What a shame I missed that; I would very much have liked to have witnessed it.' I picked up my knife and fork and the others finally followed my example. 'So, tell me all about it. Describe the scene. And Lucy?'

'Yes, Mr Mortensen?'

'Don't leave anything out.'

She paused a moment to consider her choices then finally took a breath and began.

'When I arrived this morning, Sam was already there. Apparently Mrs Ackworth had phoned her last night and asked her to come in again because she said I would be too busy with other duties. Sam didn't know what she meant but she sort of guessed it was something to do with what had been happening yesterday. Anyway, as soon as I got there, Mrs Ackworth took me through into the sitting room and told me to take my clothes off again. Then, when I'd done that, she made me turn round to see whether there were still any marks on my bottom . . .'

'And were there?'

'I think there must have been, because she spent quite a long time looking at it.'

'You had better show us.'

'What, here? Now?'

'Yes, of course.'

'But . . .' But she had already run out of 'but's; she had exhausted all the objections and all her appeals had been refused. Delicately she lay down her knife and fork and stood up, sending a single accusing glance across at me before turning her back on us all. The fine material of the full dress was hauled up in armfuls until the white cotton of her knickers appeared, stretched tight across her round bottom. She eased her knickers down to an untidy roll across the top of her thighs, hoisted the dress up again and then stood silently waiting until she should be given permission to cover herself again.

The marks were still there, admittedly faded from yesterday's livid weals but unmistakable and unmissable and as fine an adornment as any girl could require. The circle of guests fell into stiff silence as each considered the marks and each envisaged, from his or her own perspective of flagellant or victim, the solemn ritual during which they had been created. Both the women stirred uneasily in their seats, whether at the unexpected exposure or a memory that the stripes induced. I could not guess but it was a promising sign.

'Thank you, Lucy. Please continue.'

In complete silence, she pulled her knickers up again, allowed the dress to tumble back into place, brushed it down (with a care that seemed a trifle exaggerated) and finally returned to her chair. She glanced round at all the eyes which had so closely followed her every move, and bowed her head, the picture of humility. Yet it seemed that the little smile she was trying to suppress was more of pride than shame. At nineteen, did we not all relish being the centre of such scandalised attention?

'Well, then she made me bend over again, and I thought at first she was going to hit me some more and I did ask her not to, but instead she started stroking the marks and all round them and then she was just, well, she was just sort of feeling me, I suppose. There didn't seem to be any reason for it, she just started feeling my bottom, but her hand kept going lower and lower until she was feeling right down between my legs, along my private parts.'

The story tailed off into silence.

'Do you mean she was . . .' Kathy started but faltered herself. 'She was playing with you?'

'Yes, I suppose so.'

'Masturbating you?'

'Yes.'

'But why did you let her?' Kathy seemed to have forgotten that the rest of us existed.

'I don't know.' Even Lucy must have known this was a pathetic response and it hung in silence before Kathy urged her on.

'What happened next?'

'She said that I was all wet down there and that I was disgusting.'

'And were you? Wet, I mean?'

'Yes, I think so. I mean, she had been rubbing me.'

'Oh, for heaven's sake!' Kathy's exasperation was unhidden. 'Not for very long!'

'It doesn't always take me very long.' The quietness of Lucy's whispered confession gave it a credence that a greater volume would have lost, but in the stillness that followed, who could have failed to picture the scene she had described, picture the specifics, picture the girl who now sat blushing before us, but picture her as she had been then: naked, bent over and being fingered until she was wet? I doubt if I was the only one for whom this account had raised another question.

'Are you wet now, Lucy? Telling us about it?'

'Yes.'

I let the admission hang in the room for a few minutes before telling her to continue.

'Well, then she stood up and she . . . she . . .' Lucy's voice faltered and then she took a single deep breath and launched back into her tale. 'She just stood up and took her skirt off and then her tights and knickers and sat down again. Then she told me to kneel down in front of her and . . .'

This time I did not need to make her continue. Checking the other four people sitting around me, the reactions were unmistakable as our imaginations completed the details of a picture that Lucy could not bring herself to describe. The two women in particular looked to be completely immersed in the scene and Kathy was still searching for words.

'Did you do it?'

'Yes. I had to.'

'I mean . . .' Kathy was determined to find out, but reluctant to appear too indelicate. 'I mean all the way?'

Lucy just nodded. It was still not enough.

'She . . . you know, came?'

Lucy nodded again.

'Christ!' Kathy stared at her in bewilderment. 'I just don't understand it. No way would I do that to another woman. It's just too gross. I mean, why? Is she a dyke?'

'Well, to be fair –' I volunteered the extra information because I knew that Lucy would not '– Mrs Ackworth had been required to do the same for Lucy a day or two ago.'

'What?' Kathy stared round at me, and across at Lucy as she digested the details. For a moment she looked as if she would argue again, but then she glanced round at the rest of the company, none of whom had reacted so vehemently to the tale. I caught Graham's eye and knew he was thinking the same as me: she doth protest too much. Maybe we were right, because Mark stepped in and hurriedly changed the subject by asking about the house, a topic which proved safe enough for everyone to stay with and one to which, once everyone had finished their salmon, I could in all innocence return.

'I discovered an interesting piece of history about this house last week – indeed, about this room, this very table. Lucy, could you fetch that letter Duncan McQuillan gave you? Perhaps you would read it out.'

And then, gathered round that ancient table in the feeble light of half a dozen candles, I listened again to the extract from Cecily Markham's diary and I lived again through the vivid intensity of that ghastly tale. The instant Lucy started to read, the strength of the account grabbed the four who had never heard it so that as they listened in the room where it had actually happened, gathered round the same table, the table on which the girl had been stripped and humiliated and whipped, the soft quivering voice lent the words an intimacy and a power that gave new life to her ordeal across 400 years.

At the end, nobody spoke. Lucy carefully refolded the letter and, as the silence stretched out, started to gather up the plates. When she stood up to take them out, I stopped her.

'I think, Lucy, it's time for a change of view.' She stopped and dropped back down on to her chair, uncertain where I was leading. 'Please stand next to Graham.'

Obediently she moved round to the end of the table beside him, where she waited, her hands clasped in front of her. Graham glanced at her, intrigued, and then at me.

'Now, Graham, would you be so kind as to help Lucy out of her dress?'

Immediately she stepped back out of his reach and looked slowly round the assembly, at the circle of eyes which waited for her to respond or argue or obey but she did none of those things. Instead she stood with her hands clasped together, her legs working nervously as she absorbed their scrutiny, glancing fleetingly towards the cane on the sideboard behind me. Her voice came as little more than whisper.

'Are you going to cane me now?'

'No, not yet. I would just like you to be naked for the rest of the evening, that's all.'

She swallowed, looked round at everyone again, trying to see who was on her side and who was on mine. I tried too, but the reactions were not entirely clear. Naturally enough, both the men looked to be keen, but the two women were harder to fathom. Judith had turned away, yet those long fingers toying incessantly with her place setting suggested impatience more than disapproval. Kathy, on the other hand, was staring. The disbelief was painted across her face as she looked to Mark, to Lucy, to me, to anyone who would say something to make sense of her surroundings. She did not appear shocked, not scandalised, simply utterly bewildered at so calm an acceptance of a suggestion so far outside her own experience.

Whatever response Lucy received, whatever allegiances she deduced, she finally returned to the place beside Graham, meekly turned her back to him and allowed him to untie the thin straps which held the dress in place. After an agony of fumbling, they came undone and the top of the dress fell away, exposing her back entirely. She turned round again, clutching the front of the dress up under her chin, and only when she was fully facing us all did she allow him to tug it free of her grasp and pull it down first to reveal her breasts, proud and swollen, and then after pausing a moment to let us take that in, he pushed it down her body and she stepped right out of it. I let her wait for a moment in the skimpy knickers and hold-up stockings.

'Thank you. Now, Lucy, please take off your shoes and go round to Judith.' I was watching for Judith's reaction and caught the surprise, the quickly suppressed glee and the resumption of a stern, blank front. Lucy was no such actress. The dismay was painted clearly across her face and she stood there, her dress clutched in one hand, her nipples erect and quivering with each terrified breath while she considered the shame which now awaited her. Finally she gave in, her rebellion quashed by the silence of her audience and the patient confidence shining on Judith's face. She squatted down to slip off the shoes and then padded round to the other side of the table.

'Judith? Perhaps you would help her with the stockings.' Lucy shuffled forward to place herself more readily within the woman's reach and meekly presented each leg in turn for the stocking to be rolled down. As I had expected, Judith showed no qualms when her hands brushed against skin, happily savouring the caress of thighs and calves, taking her time and clearly enjoying to the full the opportunity given to her. For her part, Lucy made no attempt to pull away, even when Judith started on the second stocking, scrabbling for the elastic braid on the delicate skin inside Lucy's thigh. Even there, she did not shrink from the touch. At last the stockings were dangled from outstretched fingers and Lucy muttered thanks as she shyly picked them away.

'Wonderful. Thank you.' Lucy knew what would come next. Many times during our short acquaintance, although admittedly never in such public circumstances, I had called her to my side so that I could complete her undressing. Now she did not even wait to be instructed but came meekly to my side awaiting the inevitable and I let her stand there a little longer as I turned to the others, waiting expectantly for the final revelation.

'For reasons I don't need to explain, Lucy has been coming to visit me for a week or so now, and whenever she comes here, I like to have her naked. I just find something quite glorious in the sight of her flitting about my house with nothing on. Usually I also like to remove the last garment myself but, this evening, I think it should be Kathy's privilege.'

As I had hoped, this shocked both of them and for a moment neither moved while they stared at each other across the width of the table. This would be the greatest test and I recognised the risk I was taking. Kathy was already floundering out of her depth, confused by what had happened and what was promised for later. She was already uneasy, probably staying in her place only because nobody had set the example to leave. Faced with this she might find the strength, or at least the pride, to walk out.

On the other hand she might not. If curiosity, or an unwillingness to be seen to fail where Judith had already succeeded or even – best of all – desire kept her here now, I was confident she would stay to the end. She did not move at first but continued to gaze across at Lucy, turned once for support to Mark, but his eyes were gleaming with an excitement that his nonchalant shrug belied. Finally her gaze dropped to the table, I breathed again and Lucy took the last few steps to stand in front of her.

I didn't say anything. She could be in no doubt what was intended of her, so I waited, savouring the reluctance as she reached out, picked carefully at the elastic waistband and then briskly pulled the little knickers down at last to reveal Lucy to the whole company, entirely naked.

Nobody spoke at first. Kathy made a fuss of folding the skimpy knickers while Lucy's immediate reaction was to lift her hands over her breasts and pubis, although once

191

she had done so, she saw the error. When she had just been stripped for them all to see, and they were all sitting watching her, the pathetically inadequate covering offered by her hands was quite pointless and ridiculous. She let her arms fall to her sides again. I looked a question round the guests, taking care to include all four in my invitation.

'Very pretty indeed!' Unsurprisingly, Mark was first to comment but Judith was not far behind. Graham is perhaps too much of a gentleman and Kathy too confused for either of them to express a view.

'Thank you, Lucy. Now perhaps you would clear this and fetch the dessert.'

It was such joy again to have her working away without a stitch on her body. The other four were entirely engrossed in the novelty as she moved round the room, reached across in front of them and, I did rather feel, even flaunted herself a little. Still, she was perhaps entitled to do so: a beauty so rare and perfect merits display. Judith took as much interest in the display as both her husband and Mark, but Kathy sat bashfully still, trying not to watch the naked figure darting round her, although occasional glances betrayed her.

The dessert course passed quietly, what little conversation there was being kept alive by Judith and the men while both younger women remained discreetly quiet, sounding strained and artificial on the few occasions when they did speak. Finally this course too was cleared and we sat with our cheese and grapes until I realised that the conversation was slowly dying away entirely as each of the guests remembered the promise I had made for the end of the meal. Each in turn put down their knife and dropped into silence until only Lucy was still playing with the last few grapes and pushing a small cube of cheese around her plate. She seemed at first unaware of the silence and attention, but suddenly glanced up from under her eyebrows at the ring of waiting faces. She faltered, her movements frozen, before slowly putting down her own knife. From my position opposite her, I could see her pale little nipples start to pucker in fear. She looked up at me.

'Shall I clear the table, Mr Mortensen?' Her eyes stayed firmly fixed on me, fighting the urge to glance behind me at the waiting cane.

'Yes, that would be a good idea.'

We watched in silence the stretching of her naked limbs as she moved round the table, reaching for the few remaining pieces, piling them on to a tray and carrying that over to the serving table. Finally, when the table was completely clear, she returned to her place directly opposite me. At first her hands were clasped in front of her, but under the onslaught of our silent scrutiny, she reached up to clasp her shoulders, inadequate slender arms covering terrified slender breasts.

'Are you going to do it now?' She was biting at her lower lip and shifting from one foot to the other.

'Yes, I think so. Would you fetch the cane, please, and then get up on the table? Just like Anne Markham.' It was cruel to make her walk naked round the room again where everybody could see her; to make her come right round the table to collect the cane, make her hand it to me and then return to her chair and climb up to sit on the table.

'How do you want me?' Her voice was so low it was almost a whisper, yet she would not let her fear defeat her determination – not now, not after waiting so long.

'Kneeling on all fours, please. Your head up this end and your bottom down here.' I tapped the appropriate spots on the table with the tip of the cane.

Lucy turned round and crawled along to the position I had indicated and placed her hands, carefully spaced towards the edges of the table. After a moment she shuffled her knees apart as well and then waited.

I stood up and moved my chair away before speaking to the others. 'Kathy, I must ask you to move back, but the rest of you may stay where you are or move to whichever end most interests you. Personally, I believe there is much to be said for either view on these occasions. I should explain that although Lucy has been spanked before and even strapped, she has never received the cane, so she does not yet fully appreciate how much it is going to hurt. I have told her that it is for her to signal the end when she cannot take any more so we will see how long she lasts. She is a brave little thing and I will be disappointed if she stops before six, but I intend to lay them down pretty hard so I do not expect to reach twelve.'

It could perhaps form part of some psychometric test, seeing which position any given person takes up to watch a girl being caned. Mark, as might be expected, immediately moved down to stand at her feet, treated to a clear view of her bottom, and her open sex freely exposed between her parted thighs. Graham, having to my certain knowledge, seen and participated in the caning of any number of girls' bottoms, went to the other end where he could witness the expression on her face as the first few strokes fell. Doubtless he realised he would have ample opportunity to examine her buttocks and her stripes when I was finished, but while the ordeal was actually in progress, her face would be the more telling indicator of her suffering.

Interestingly, the two wives took opposite positions from their respective husbands. Judith Worthing had already shown a taste for her own sex which, whether she acknowledged and indulged it or not, led her to seek the same view as Mark. Kathy, on the other hand, appeared to have formed some kind of bond with Lucy, founded perhaps on their similar ages, and the shared experience of stripping away Lucy's last covering. In any case, she took one of the empty seats at Lucy's shoulder, reaching out to hold her hand in a warm gesture of support.

I took up my position and measured the cane across the neat round bottom that was presented for me. At first I couldn't quite bring myself to begin, and paused to brush my hand slowly down the smooth skin, damp with the light sweat of fear, and felt it tremble at my touch. This would be so much more cruel an assault than when I had spread her over my knee and spanked her by hand. That had been quiet and private and of course nobody has ever come to any great harm from a spanking with the bare hand. This was to be entirely different. Here she knelt, exposed not just to me but now to four other people as well, her firm little breasts hanging beneath her in a way which exaggerated their shape, enhanced their fullness and left them begging to be cradled in an open palm.

Her bottom was stretched taut and all the more vulnerable for that, so that every stroke would be that much more painful. Her legs, admittedly at her own instigation, were parted to give me as well as the guests beside me a clear view of the separated cheeks of her bottom, of the precious dark star of her anus and even the lips nestling terrified between. The whole was so available and accessible, with no defence and no comprehension at all of the ordeal to come.

And as if the exposure were not enough, I held in my hand a long firm cane, an instrument utterly insensitive to feeling, designed purely to concentrate misery along a single narrow band. It could be brought down on her exposed bottom as hard as I liked as often as I liked without my feeling any discomfort, no matter how intense the suffering I might cause her. She turned her head round to see why I was waiting, and I tapped the tip of the cane on the full round curve of the nearer cheek then traced a small circle round the area of my target. She closed her eyes and turned away.

I tapped again. 'Count these out, Lucy. I will do them in groups of three.' I pulled the cane back and whipped it down through the air so that she automatically recoiled to escape the agonising blow that she had expected but which had not landed. The instant she had returned to her proper position, I brought the first stroke down on her tender skin.

The effect was immediate. An agonised gasp was torn from Lucy and instantaneously a thin white line appeared straight across her skin and faded almost as quickly into a livid pink. Yet even as that was happening, Lucy sat back on her heels and turned round to glare at me with such pained accusation across her face, her mouth open in speechless horror, her eyes blinking in uncomprehending agony, and both Kathy and Mark were sucking in their breath in shock at the strength of the stroke.

195

I ignored the ring of horrified observers; I may have known most of them for longer than I had known Lucy, but she was the one who I knew best and whose feelings weighed in the scale. She knelt there for a couple of seconds, her eyes staring wide, watering already, and I began to wonder whether she would manage even six, even two, but as she gingerly stroked some comfort back into that anguished patch of skin, her expression was melting from outrage into determination and finally she took another deep breath and leant forward again, placing her hands back on the polished surface of the table, and muttered a single word.

'One.'

In the expectant silence from the onlookers, I tapped the cane just above the rapidly rising weal. A rapid staccato of raps, hard enough to echo off the ancient panelling and impress on every ear that the strokes were genuine. The horror on the faces of the younger couple, matched by the excitement on the faces of the older, betrayed how fully they were all imagining themselves into the respective positions of master and victim.

I whipped down the second stroke.

Lucy cried out again, but this time managed to stay down even though her little bottom, meagre and inadequately padded in any case, puckered up in a contraction of fear and pain as the second red stripe appeared across the smooth round surface.

'Two.' I didn't torment her for long before the third.

As I had promised, I paused briefly after the first three and stroked her tortured cheek, running my fingertips as lightly as I possibly could across the thickening ridges that were swelling and darkening as we watched. I cannot explain the appeal of the change from the utterly pure unblemished picture she had presented so recently, but maybe that inexplicability is the essence of the allure. No matter how fine the cake, it still needs icing; no matter how pure the bottom, it still needs striping.

I could have continued there for ever but I owed Lucy more than that and I was not convinced that a long delay was any great kindness. Quickly I returned to my position and she settled back to hers, her elbows now resting on the table in front of her and her forehead resting on her forearms. She reached for the comfort of Kathy's hand.

The 'four' was a brave attempt at normality; the 'five' a strangled sob; the 'six' no more than a whisper accompanied by a sniff that gave better indication than any of the effect. She was not moving, but struggling to hold herself proudly still for each stroke. She never protested or objected, although I saw that her grip on Kathy's hand was growing stronger with every blow that fell. But Kathy's scowls, directed fiercely straight at me with the intensity of a tigress protecting her cub, fed off Lucy's reaction and illustrated best of all the level of her pain.

I paused again at six. When Lucy released her hand, Kathy came down to my end of the table and gasped at the sight she found. The cheeks were still mostly quite pale, but six pairs of angry ridges were scribed across them, the last ones still red, the first few already purple, each neatly crossing the centre of the smooth round buttocks.

Kathy stared, then carefully dipped the edge of her napkin into the water jug and stroked lightly, so lightly that she was barely touching at all, along the worst of the stripes. Delicate though she was, Lucy still trembled at the touch, so as soon as Kathy lifted her hand away, I landed one ringing slap down on to each quivering cheek. Kathy's squeal of outrage was almost as piercing as Lucy's cry of pain.

'How can you do that to her?' Kathy clearly had no comprehension whatever of the powers and balances at work and I knew of only one way she could learn. I took hold of her wrist, pulled Lucy's knees further apart and pressed Kathy's hand in against the open crease. When I pulled it away, she stared at the rich dew that now glistened along her own fingers and turned incomprehendingly to consider the injured bottom that faced us.

'Do you see?' I asked. 'Lucy will tell me when she wants me to stop.' Kathy fell into silence.

We all returned to our positions again and I tapped the cane on a clear area of unmarked skin. 'Next three?'

Kathy might have accepted the logic but her heart still didn't understand the emotion. She scowled at me as Lucy lay her head back down on her forearms. 'All right.'

Having dropped her head down lower and lifted her bottom up higher, a new expanse was now available for me to aim at which would avoid landing across any of the swollen weals that already crossed my target. I tapped on the clear new area and in the still silence, feeling the eyes of Anne Markham burning down on me, I started again.

'Seven' came through gritted teeth. 'Eight' the same but several seconds had passed before she could find the breath to whisper 'nine'. I paused again at that. Kathy nursed her again, comforted her again and tended the new collection of swollen stripes. When we started again after that, little unmarked skin remained.

'Ten' was all right. Even 'eleven' she managed. At 'twelve' she simply burst into tears. Kathy immediately reached up and hugged her, cradling the little sobbing figure in her arms and stroking her hair, her shoulders and her back. She glared across at me.

'That's enough. For heaven's sake, Alex, she can't take any more.' I could not blame her for her concern – I felt the same myself – yet Lucy knew how easily she could make it stop.

'It's enough when she says it is.'

The tears continued and I gave her ample time to stop me. I delayed over the little taps that told her the next batch was coming but she kept silent. Her pride and determination seemed to have overcome her common sense and I felt it would be a kindness now to break it. I laid the next stroke on with full strength. And the next, and as I prepared for fifteen she rolled over on to her side and, to my relief and delight, squealed at me to stop.

She was quivering and sobbing as Kathy led her away upstairs where they stayed for over half an hour before finally reappearing, both looking shy and embarrassed with Lucy now draped in my own dressing gown.

After all the guests had left, I turned to Lucy and did something I had never done before, something I had yearned to do almost since the day that she had first arrived on my doorstep, but somehow had managed to resist for so long. I put my arms around her and I held her. Just briefly her tears came back and I waited until they had subsided before I released her again, gently removed the dressing gown and turned her round to examine her. The sight that I beheld was a fine array of prominent purple ridges, neatly spaced, neatly parallel, as fine a display as I have ever created in my life. I squatted down behind her and traced my fingertips down each line and then for the first time in our relationship, I kissed her. I leant forward and softly kissed each swollen bruise on the crest of each quivering beaten cheek.

'There.' I stood up again. 'They'll be practically gone by Monday, but I'll put some cream on to help cool them down.' Lucy went to fetch it, moving more slowly than usual, and quite subdued when she returned with the jar. I had her lie across my lap on the sofa where she settled so easily, so trustingly, that I felt the devil return to perch on my shoulder. This was such a perfect position to have her for a spanking, and with her bottom already so bruised, so striped and so tender, every additional stroke would feel like 50. I don't know how I held back.

She stretched right out; her long legs out to my right, her arms stretching out to my left. In the middle, her bottom rose up over my thighs, so cruelly pink and beaten, fourteen deep weals scattered over the fullest, roundest curve of each proud quivering cheek. I tipped a little cream on to the top and with the lightest strokes of the tips of my fingers, delicately caressed it into her skin. A thin stream trickled, as if by accident, down into the little valley between the cheeks and had to be chased and gently massaged in there, where the skin was untouched and undamaged and the tight little wrinkles firmly prevented any possible breach. I crept on beyond that.

My fingers found her lips, warm, swollen and wet, yet the wetness seemed dissipated, spread over a wider area than would have been expected if it had flowed new from the source. I pushed down beyond her lips, feeling them part to admit me and close to retain me until I was nudging against the warm softness of her clitoris. She shivered as if it were too much, but the wetness suggested it should have been just right.

'Did Kathy put some cream on your bottom for you?' Always start with the easy questions.

'Yes. She's very kind.'

'Yes, I'm quite sure she is.' I continued to run a single finger along the length of that sweetly oiled crease; up as far as the sensitive little anus; down as far as the sensitive little clitoris; along the surface of the sleek warm lips that drew and sucked at me like a little mouth. The cream for her bottom was already forgotten as she focused on the present, on the steady caress along her lips, on the pressure building for what was, I was now certain, the second time that evening.

'And did she stroke you like this?'

'No.' She knew my silence suggested disbelief and craned round to peer up at me. 'She didn't, honestly. She nearly did, though; she definitely wanted to.' She giggled and turned away again.

'Lucy! I hope you weren't seducing her.'

'Me? I couldn't do that. I'm an innocent virgin, remember?'

'This bit may be.' I tapped across the lips of her pussy. 'But this bit isn't.' I tapped her head.

She giggled again and squirmed down to enjoy the sensation as my caresses concentrated on the little nib at the end of her crease. Soon her breath was coming in ever shorter gasps and her thighs squeezed and swivelled and her little fists clutched at my ankles as I held her there, face down over my lap until she finally gave in and squealed out a welcome to the pleasure that so much attention over so long an evening had made inevitable.

She was quiet afterwards, still and dreamlike, although her fingers gently traced the patterns along the woodgrain of the polished floor, showing she was not asleep. I continued stroking around and across her bottom as lightly as I could until she suddenly spoke.

'It's funny, Mr Mortensen, because in some ways you're the cruellest man I have ever met. You have done all kinds of things which made me so embarrassed and ashamed. You have made me strip naked in front of lots of people. You've spanked me. Tonight you caned me even though you knew that it really, really hurt. You have done all that, and yet I feel safe with you.'

What answer could there be to that?

'Thank you, Lucy. I do appreciate the compliment.'

'Mr Mortensen?' The delay had been as long as she could stand but I now knew that the flattery had been to bait a trap. 'You know you said that I couldn't cane Mrs Ackworth until I had been caned myself?'

'Yes.' I had little doubt where this was leading.

'Well, now I have been, so now can I do it?'

'Why?'

'Well, she deserves it. Besides, she's got such a fat bottom, it would look really good.'

'I'm not sure, Lucy. You see, I did rather promise her that she could cane you.'

'Why?' She turned over to look at me, curious more than indignant.

'I thought she'd probably like to.'

'What about me?'

'Well? What about you? Wouldn't you like that?'

She considered this carefully for quite a while, periodically reaching back to rub at the bruises she already had. 'I suppose so; a bit. But if I let her give me six, can I give her twelve?'

What could I say?

201

13

Tuesday

Second by weary second, another two days of famine dragged by and brought with them a taste of what life would be like once Lucy's visits stopped. Already less than one week remained before her wedding, an event which I was anticipating with steadily decreasing enthusiasm, and was bitterly regretting accepting her invitation: I should have made an excuse.

Yet even the prospect of Monday's diversion now seemed less appealing than it had done. According to our timetable, agreed but never stated, this would be Lucy's last visit and I wanted her all to myself. Why should I share her with Mrs Ackworth? Why should I share her with anyone? The prospect of that woman's leering presence hung above me like a waiting reprimand for my weakness, a rich opportunity thrown away.

Then Monday morning came and with it a phone call from Lucy. She had forgotten that she was due the final fitting for her wedding dress straight after work and a rehearsal for the service after that. The little optimism I had nurtured shattered as my day spiralled away into despondency.

By Tuesday, I had been starved another 24 hours, and I spent a sultry morning in the garden achieving nothing but the raising of hopes that part of me argued were unfounded. I telephoned Mrs Ackworth early and extended the invitation but she was initially cautious and suspicious. She weakened when I gave her my word that she would be permitted to give Lucy six strokes of the cane, but even then was not committed. I tossed in another temptation.

'Is Lucy there?'

'No, not yet. She isn't due for half an hour.'

'Oh!' I pretended surprise. 'It might be better not to mention this during the day, if you do decide to come, that is.' I knew the suggestion would have the opposite effect and the prospect of having a whole day to torture the girl with reminders of what awaited her would, for a woman like Mrs Ackworth, prove irresistible. My invitation was accepted.

As three o'clock came and passed I was pacing like an expectant father until, at last, the doorbell jingled in its cheerful way and I made myself count to ten before answering it lest I should seem too eager. Honestly! I thought I had given up those games when I was a teenager.

I opened the door and there she stood: smiling, patently pleased to see me, ready for whatever the day would bring. All my worries lifted away as she bustled in and I took her through to the study to undress.

'I'm sorry, Mr Mortensen, only I couldn't get away because Mrs Ackworth kept finding things for me to do. She told me she was coming here this afternoon.'

'I see. Well, we are running rather late now, Lucy and, as you know, we don't have a great deal of time.' Her face wrinkled up in anxiety at my tone. 'Come here.'

Immediately she thought she was in trouble again and about to receive a spanking so she hastily apologised and started to work on the buttons of her blouse. I stopped her.

'No, Lucy. Come here.'

She shuffled up to me, clasping her hands together behind her back and waited. Her blouse was askew, half unbuttoned, a peep of white bra was visible on the shoulder and a fluster of shame was gathering at her cheeks. I have loved watching her taking her clothes off, seeing those dainty fingers put to so commendable a use, but there is also merit in variety, so I reached up myself to the buttons and carried on. She stared down her front as I undid them, one by one, inch by inch revealing more of her, finally pulling the blouse out of her waistband, undoing the last button and slipping it off her shoulders.

Next her jeans: first the top stud and then, fumbling in the fly and finding another row of studs, I unpopped these one by one. My hands gripped the top of her jeans and I slid them down, taking care not to disturb her knickers as the jeans crossed her hips and tumbled free down her thighs, her knees, her calves and bundled up at her ankles. I bent down to untie her trainers and slip off her socks, and at last the jeans were gone. She stood waiting in her underwear.

I turned her round once to see the vision from all sides before having her face me again so I could reach up to slide the straps of her bra down and then peel them away from her breasts, gently stroking the soft nipples as I did so. I had never touched her breasts before now and yet I knew them intimately. The smooth, warm softness was exactly as I had known it ought to be, had to be. Perfectly shaped; perfectly textured: perfect.

I swivelled the bra round, unhooked it and tossed that down on the heap. Now her knickers. These, the most private and secret of her clothing, I had removed several times before, and yet she could never get used to my habit of inhaling their scent. Heaven knows what strictures of hygiene and cleanliness had been drummed into her as a child, but she clearly had no confidence that the aroma of her femininity could ever be anything but offensive.

I tugged the knickers free, quickly slid them down and she stepped out and waited, and watched and blushed in agonies of shame as I raised them to my nose and sampled their sweet warmth and salty scent.

'Thank you, Lucy.'

She blushed, as she always did, and quickly changed the subject. 'Shall we go outside now, Mr Mortensen? Shall I make some tea?'

'Yes, if you'd like some. Personally, as it's so hot, I think I'd prefer fruit juice. There is some in the fridge. You find whatever you like and bring it out.'

She turned and trotted happily down the hall while I followed, intrigued at the little bouncing bottom, its compact slenderness still carrying the fading bruises of Friday's cane, and I returned to the terrace and Giovanni Boccaccio. She soon came tiptoeing out.

'Mr Mortensen, there's some champagne in the fridge. Shall I make bucks fizz?'

A pedant might have balked at using really rather a good vintage for this purpose, but he would have been the poorer, so Lucy turned to scamper back inside happily and a few moments later came the familiar pop followed immediately by squeals of distress as she failed to catch the flow. She emerged balancing a tray precariously.

I don't like to drink during the day and settled for orange juice but Lucy clearly had no such inhibitions. She sat on the grass in front of me, glass in hand, and tucked in with gusto. The bottle emptied steadily as she chattered away, informative about people I had never heard of, excited about her wedding and slanderous about Mrs Ackworth's tea shop. She was lying there when I heard the rattle of the gate behind me and Alan appeared. His eyes lit up at the sight of Lucy sprawling naked on the grass and although she hastily sat up, with nothing available to cover herself she had no choice but to suffer his scrutiny. His cheerful banter fell on rather stony ground.

'Anything particular for me to do today, Mr Mortensen?'

Of course there was, for I had decided to introduce Lucy to the traditional whipping horse and so I had him bring that up from the cellar. I am not an enthusiast for the highly elaborate equipment which some people seem to find necessary and this apparatus had always served me well. It is an extremely plain, thoroughly traditional solid timber frame with a padded top at hip height and the necessary anchoring points on all four legs to enable the victim's wrists and ankles to be secured firmly in place. I have had it for a great many years, and although Alan, coming across it once in the cellar, had been highly inquisitive, he had never witnessed it in use.

Lucy watched silently as it was fetched up and set in the centre of the terrace. She nervously drained her glass and poured herself another, her eyes never leaving Alan as he worked. When he was done, I sent Lucy upstairs to fetch the leather wrist and ankle cuffs and a blindfold.

On her return, I led her up to the frame and applied the blindfold first so that, unable to see her fate, she was both more amenable and more sensitive to every touch as the wrist and ankle cuffs were attached and she was bent over. I fastened the cuffs to the four feet so that her legs were held wide apart, her bottom was presented at a perfect height for caning – or for any other prescription that I might decide – and her little breasts, their nipples already starkly erect, hung down on the other side. I then settled back to my work and Alan returned to duties around the garden all of which, I noticed, kept him close to the terrace, and frequently required him to cross behind her. At every pass, he sneaked up quietly behind her and delivered a swift slap across her upturned bottom.

This is a degrading position for the victim who is deeply aware of their vulnerability, made even worse by being blindfolded, but it is not uncomfortable. A person can therefore be kept there for several hours, unless of course they have a particular need to be released. It was half an hour before Lucy called out to be freed.

'No,' I answered. 'Certainly not.'

'Please? Just for a few minutes. I need to go inside.'

'No.'

'But I need the toilet.'

'I said no.'

Fifteen minutes went by before she tried again, begging now. 'Please, Mr Mortensen. It's urgent.'

I didn't bother to answer and, some ten minutes later, it was the noise that first alerted me – not the pee itself but a sob from Lucy as she discovered that she could not hold on any more and a little dribble had already escaped. The sound of the pee followed soon afterwards, cascading on to the flagstones and splashing over her feet. The minute she realised that both Alan and I had gathered behind her to watch, she swiftly cut off the flow, although not before a huge puddle had spread all round her so that when she moved her feet they splashed noisily in the pool. Once the stream had subsided and finally stopped, the last few drops glistening on her lips and her fur, she asked if she could go and clean up. Naturally I refused although I did remove her blindfold so that she could see the mess she was now standing in.

I knew both how much she had drunk, and that there was another ordeal yet to come. Having stopped herself before her bladder was empty, she would stand there in her own pee for the next twenty minutes or so, but before long she would need to go again, and she would know both that she had no option but to do it where she stood, and also that as soon as she started, Alan and I would come over to watch her again.

As I picked up my book and found my place, I offered a little word of encouragement. 'If you've got any more to do, Lucy, you may want to do it soon.' I paused a second. 'Before Mrs Ackworth gets here.'

She did do more; in fact, she lasted less than ten minutes before the trickle started again. Alan and I exchanged smiles and watched her as her face turned crimson and her pee flooded the terrace. She knew better this time than to ask to be allowed to clean up although the smell of her urine quickly grew stronger as it started to dry out in the warm sun. Even so, being left to stand in a pool of her own making while she was ignored was more than she could stand.

'Please will you untie me now, Mr Mortensen? I don't want Mrs Ackworth to see me like this.'

'Nonsense, I'm sure she'd be very pleased.'

'But it's so shameful.'

'Well, yes, I suppose it is.'

I wandered over and ran my hand across her bottom. 'I suppose if we keep you there longer, it might get even worse. If you had to do anything more.' I trailed my finger down the crease of her bottom and pressed firmly and indicatively on the little clenched star. Lucy gasped. This had obviously not occurred to her.

The splashes on the stones evaporated quickly, but the puddle had not decreased noticeably when the sound of the front doorbell floated out to us.

207

'Ah,' I said. 'I imagine that's Mrs Ackworth.'

Lucy craned round over her shoulder. 'Please?'

Mrs Ackworth did a good impression of dismay at seeing Lucy in that position.

'I'm afraid she's wet herself,' I explained as I poured her a glass of champagne.

'How disgusting!' She sniffed, held the glass carefully up away from any nastiness and picked her way carefully across the puddle. She prodded at Lucy's buttocks with a disdainful finger. 'Girls nowadays just have no self-control whatsoever.' She bent down to peer at Lucy's bottom and, using both hands, pried open Lucy's cheeks to inspect her anus and her lips hanging damp and swollen beneath. 'Do you know, Mr Mortensen, this girl appears to be lubricating. I am appalled, utterly appalled.' She prodded again.

It was time to move on. 'Alan? Would you fetch a bucket of water, please?'

I expect Lucy envisaged a similar shameful sponge bath to that she had suffered before, but when Alan returned, sauntering happily along with a bucket slopping water at every step, I told him to sluice her down.

He came up behind her, the bucket held in both hands. 'Ready, miss?'

Yet he gave her no time to come up with a sensible reply before swinging the bucket back and throwing the whole bucketful of water over her in one go. She screamed, doubtless in part at the cold, but also at the force of it against her body, on the sensitive insides of her thighs, right in between her legs, between the cheeks of her bottom and over the undefended lips of her vulva.

It cascaded everywhere, a good amount flowing along her back to run down underneath and drip off her breasts, the little nipples hardening instantly on contact with the freezing water.

I fetched her a towel as Alan was unbuckling her. Not a big towel, so she could not wrap herself in it. She stood in front of us, twisting round to dry her back, between the cheeks of her bottom, and as far forward as she could reach. Eventually she had to sit on the grass to finish off her legs and feet while Mrs Ackworth pointed out bits she seemed to have missed and, at the end, examined her carefully to ensure she was thoroughly dry.

Finally she took the towel away and threw it on the table, leaving Lucy standing naked and shivering in front of her. 'You know what I'm here for, don't you, girl?'

'Yes, Mrs Ackworth.'

'Right, well run and get Mr Mortensen's cane, then.'

Lucy disappeared inside and Mrs Ackworth sat smugly sipping her champagne, but her eyes darted excitedly round the garden the whole while, giving the lie to her pretence of calm indifference.

On Lucy's return, she grabbed the cane and sat turning it over in her fingers, stroking along its length with the enthusiasm of a real devotee. Finally she stood up.

'Right. Let's get started. Elbows and forearms on the bench here, I think, and up on your toes.' She indicated the whipping horse, still wet and shining in the sun, and Lucy stumbled up to it and bent over, clasping her hands together and carefully laying her arms along the horse. She pulled herself up on to her toes. Alan had given up any pretence of gardening and now perched on the wall surrounding the terrace. I took up a position on the side where I could see everything that happened and Mrs Ackworth moved up close to her victim, still nursing the cane in loving fingers.

'Now, then, I want no crying or snivelling from you. The only sound I want to hear is you counting out each stroke. If you miss counting one, then obviously that doesn't count. Is that understood?'

'Yes.'

'Yes?'

'Yes, Mrs Ackworth.'

'Right. Over you go! Bottom right up! Toes together, legs straight. That's better. Now, ready?'

'Yes, Mrs Ackworth.'

She took her time preparing the first stroke, tapping the cane up and down the full expanse of Lucy's bottom before lifting it clear and whipping it back down ferociously.

Lucy gasped. This was far harder than I had been caning her on Friday and for several seconds as her legs twisted and bent and straightened, Lucy struggled to speak. Eventually her voice came out in a whisper. 'One.'

The cane tapped again, tapped repeatedly against the single red streak which was already growing out of the pale skin, and then flicked out and back. It landed in the crease right at the bottom of the round cheeks and left its trail down across her thigh. Lucy sagged down and her knees crumpled as she absorbed the shock and again it took her a moment to find her breath.

'Two.'

Mrs Ackworth brought the cane back again to scrape it over the exposed skin. 'Stay still and keep your bottom up! Up! That's it!' Lucy lifted herself up once more and her head dropped down as she prepared for the next one.

She could not hold back a cry this time. The cane landed almost exactly on top of the first rising weal, biting into skin already sensitised and suffering. 'Three.' She sniffed back her tears.

Mrs Ackworth was unmoved. She reached out to fondle the weals she had already created and the skin she intended to hurt next. 'Keep your bottom up. I've told you! Legs straight, toes together. No, not your heels, girl. Your toes. Stay like that!' Of course, maintaining the pigeon-toed position which the woman demanded contrived to open Lucy's buttocks so that the crawling hand, still examining its successes, could easily slide in to explore at will.

Mrs Ackworth returned to her position, scraped the cane across the tender weals, and then whipped it down again. As the stroke sang through the air, Lucy could not hold it. She dropped to her heels and half turned away, the cane catching only the buttock nearer to Mrs Ackworth and the cry was torn from her more in shock than consideration. 'Four.'

Mrs Ackworth almost stamped with rage. 'You moved! You moved, didn't you? I'm not going to count that one.' She grabbed hold of Lucy's hips and twisted her back round again. 'Stay there! Just stay in the position I put you in.'

Placidly, all resistance gone, Lucy stayed still for the next stroke, her mumbled 'five' almost lost in the sobs which were now unhidden.

'No, that was four. I told you the other one wouldn't count.'

Lucy didn't argue. Her thighs and bottom were quivering as she waited for the next one and when it came she dropped down almost into a squat before she could find words again. 'Five.'

She stayed there while Mrs Ackworth impatiently slapped the cane against her own leg and finally slapped it across Lucy's shoulders. 'Come along, girl. Last one. Stand up, on your toes and cock your bottom right out.'

Lucy struggled back upright, managed to lift herself up on to her toes and turn her heels out, but when the cane came tap, tap, tapping back across her skin again, she dropped away.

'Do keep still! I want to see your bottom properly presented. Lift it up to me.' But Lucy couldn't. She couldn't keep stretching up on to her toes, opening her cheeks to the prying eyes and probing hands, turning her bottom towards the flailing cane that she could hear whistling through the air towards her. As it approached, she dropped away again, this stroke catching her half across the flank. She cried out 'six!' but it sounded more in optimism than belief.

'You moved again, didn't you? Well, I'm going to give you one more for making all that ridiculous fuss, all that moving about and fidgeting. I warned you, didn't I? Now. Up on your toes, push your bottom right out towards me and this time, stay still!'

Lucy allowed herself to be pushed into position, allowed the hands to slide across her hips, down her cheeks and then, ostensibly showing how her bottom ought to be lifted up, to sneak in right between her legs and squeeze.

The cane returned, its last time, and Lucy managed to hold still as it whipped down, but her legs kicked out behind her and she crumpled on to the terrace and sobbed. Mrs Ackworth peered down at her, then laid the cane on the table and picked up her glass.

'Thank you, Mr Mortensen. Most satisfactory.' If I had retained any misgivings before, this smug indifference dispelled them. I reached out for her glass and she quickly drained it before holding it to me to be refilled. I took it and placed it on the table.

'Your turn now, Mrs Ackworth. Please get undressed and take Lucy's place.'

She glared at me and her face fell briefly before she recovered that familiar arrogance. 'Oh, no, Mr Mortensen. You will not catch me again.'

'Have you watched any of those videos that I . . . er . . . borrowed last week?'

Misgiving was starting to show in her eyes. 'No.'

'Would you like to?'

'They are locked away safely in a place not even you can steal from!' Alan's eyebrows shot up; he does love a challenge.

'No, actually, they are not. They are here in my study. Those tapes you took the other day and which, you may remember, you scarcely looked at, were in fact blank although the cases were, of course, yours.'

She glared at me in black silence for several seconds and when she finally did speak, her voice was ice. 'Are you attempting to blackmail me again, Mr Mortensen?'

'Not at all, Mrs Ackworth. I made a deal with Lucy, that is all. I agreed that if I allowed you to give her six strokes, she could give you twelve. I honour my agreements.'

'You do as you like, Mr Mortensen. I was not consulted on your so-called agreement and so have no intention of going along with it. I came here under false pretences.'

'Not exactly. Lucy came here knowing full well what she would suffer and what the reward would be. Had I told you the same, you would probably not have come. Lucy is perhaps a little more courageous.' The woman's eyes narrowed. 'The fact that you were permitted to give her six strokes and you gave her eight, we will gloss over. For the moment.'

'She wriggled about all over the place!'

'Then you will have to try to do better.' From behind her came a little gurgle of glee, the first cheerful sound that

212

Lucy had made in several minutes. She was standing up now, one hand stroking behind her, the other wiping away her tears. I smiled at her. 'There you are, Lucy. All yours.'

However, Mrs Ackworth was not yet defeated. 'No, Mr Mortensen. I refuse.' She folded her arms in front of her and glared at us both, determined that her confidence would win her through. Even so, the eyes followed closely when Lucy picked up the cane and whistled a couple of trial strokes through the still air before turning to her opponent.

'I do think you should do as you are told, you know, Mrs Ackworth. It will be very embarrassing if I have to ask Alan to strip you.'

'He wouldn't dare.' He was still sitting on the terrace wall and as she turned to glare at him, she could see immediately that her assessment had been utterly mistaken. It would be a task that he would relish.

'I refuse,' she repeated with just enough tone to sound convincing but it was sufficiently weak compared to her first refusal for me to realise that she would ultimately agree. I realised it, but Alan did not. He pushed himself off the wall and she immediately understood her mistake. 'Wait!'

Alan stopped. Lucy, proudly naked, stood tapping the cane on her palm. I sat and watched it all unfold.

'I didn't agree to this.'

'Alan!' Lucy nodded to him and in a moment Mrs Ackworth was face down over the horse with her arms pulled up behind her. Her shouts and protests were undiminished but she finally managed to get out a coherent sentence.

'All right, damn you! I agree, now let me up.'

She came up, red faced and muttering, but stood belligerently staring at all of us before rounding on me. 'Mr Mortensen, I thought we had some kind of an understanding about the correct treatment of young girls!'

'Indeed we do, Mrs Ackworth. So perhaps you will set an example.'

She stared round again, but when Alan let out a deep sigh, as if the task he now faced was too wearisome to consider, she knew she was beaten. Her hands came up to her throat and after that it was a fairly quick process. Her top, something between a shirt and a jacket, had buttons down the front which unfastened readily enough. The skirt came next, a heavy pleated affair in dark blue, which she unzipped and, together with her shoes, tugged off. The slip underneath, having an elastic waist, quickly followed, leaving her standing in her underwear.

It would have been tempting to leave her like that, for there is something wonderfully humiliating in showing off the underwear of a woman who has not dressed for being undressed. Her tights appeared to be quite ordinary mass-produced things, beneath which were visible a substantial pair of white knickers which did not match the robust black bra that cradled her ample bosom. She saw my mocking smile at the revelation and her face blackened further but such niceties were lost on the younger members, who chivied her to complete the process.

She reached round to unhook her bra and let her breasts tumble free but spent an age arranging this carefully on her pile of clothes before she picked at her tights and peeled them down her legs. After this she hesitated again. Only the gleam on Alan's face as he considered the prospect of being allowed to pull her knickers down himself persuaded her to continue, shoving them down, bundling them into a quick ball and stuffing them into the pile beside her before turning back to face us defiantly.

Lucy really is an excellent pupil. 'Give those to me, please, Mrs Ackworth.'

The woman stopped and then blushed like a schoolgirl. Lucy's face shone as the knickers were fetched out again and handed over. Lucy carefully opened them out and the reason for the embarrassment became clear: a thin, not entirely clean, sanitary pad was revealed. Lucy peeled it away, tossed the knickers back on to the pile and examined the clear white stain across the middle of the pad.

'Have you had an exciting day, Mrs Ackworth?'

Mrs Ackworth almost spat as she turned away, ashamed beyond endurance that her secret was revealed, but Lucy wasn't finished yet. The two were the same height, their similarly pale skin shining similarly naked in the afternoon sun, but where Lucy could now be confident in her nakedness, Mrs Ackworth stood blushing, resentful of her exposure in front of us all. Where Lucy was young and slender, firm and golden, Mrs Ackworth was full, verging on plump, the first tiny wrinkles showing in the soft skin. Where a bra was optional for Lucy's neat round breasts, for Mrs Ackworth's fuller maturity, it was essential. She must have been aware of the inevitability of these comparisons, as she suffered in her shame, and as they stood together one other difference was noticeable. Lucy's small round bottom was striped with a tangle of red welts; Mrs Ackworth's broad flanks were entirely clear. Lucy had received her beating; Mrs Ackworth was about to suffer hers.

Lucy was undaunted. 'I suppose you enjoyed all those little comments today. Suggesting I sit down while I still could; that I save my voice for when I might need it, and so on. Well, now it's my turn for the fun. The agreement I made was that you get twice the number I got. You gave me eight, so you get sixteen. Bend over the horse.'

At this the torrent of protest started again, threatening Lucy with all manner of retaliation. I found something bizarre about the sight as, stark naked and quivering with rage so that her breasts shook with every outcry, the woman launched into a catalogue of intimidation with such ferocity that ultimately Lucy looked to me for reassurance.

'Please be quiet, Mrs Ackworth,' I finally joined in, 'or I will have to gag you.'

Alan was enthusiastic. 'We can use her own knickers, Mr Mortensen!'

'Alan!' I was genuinely surprised at him. 'Are you developing a taste for this sort of thing? Where on earth did you get that idea?'

'I must have read it somewhere. It seems appropriate, though, doesn't it?'

'No, it does not. It is a quite disgusting idea. Lucy, please run and fetch your knickers. We will use them.'

While Lucy hurried to fetch them, Mrs Ackworth continued to argue, but she showed little confidence. When Lucy returned clutching her own little white knickers and she could see this was no idle threat, she fell silent. Even so, I had little confidence that she would stay like that, so Alan got his way and the knickers, doubtless still aromatic, were bundled into a small ball and carefully pushed into her mouth. It was a pity Lucy's puddle had been sluiced away; the gag would have been even more effective wet and the humiliation for Mrs Ackworth would have been near total.

Lucy took her arm and led her up to the horse. 'Will you stay in place, Mrs Ackworth, or would you like me to tie you?' Her eyes blazing, the woman shook her head. 'Right then, right over, so your breasts are resting on the top of the horse and you can grip the legs on that side. Legs straight and wide apart, please.'

With a scowl at the girl, Mrs Ackworth stepped up and bent over the horse, but her feet were still together and her hands were holding the horse at the top rather than the bottom of the legs. Her bottom was thus not proffered as completely as it should have been and Lucy was not satisfied. She came up close to her employer and rested her hand on her podgy round back. She reached underneath to the woman's full bosom hanging beneath her and for a few seconds she hefted up each heavy breast in turn, massaging and squeezing, pinching the thickening nipples.

'I want these –' She gave each of them a final twist '– down on here.' She patted the top of the horse. 'I want this –' She slapped her hand down across the broad bottom '– up in the air. I want these –' She slapped each plump thigh '– spread wide apart and I want this –' She reached down to feel between the thighs, pushing in right between the sloppy lips '– and this –' She ran her hand back up the crease of the woman's bottom to poke at her wide brown anus '– nice and accessible.' Lucy took her hand away and wiped it against the round cheek of the woman's bottom.

Mrs Ackworth groaned but ultimately submitted herself in the position dictated. Her breasts were flattened against the whipping horse; her bottom was offered up for its beating; her thighs were spread obscenely wide and her loose, floppy vulva and her taut, closed anus were both fully displayed to all of us. Seeing her in that position, I wished we had more time and that I had given her more to drink. It would have been an exquisite humiliation to keep her there until she too was standing in a pool of her own urine on the stone flags.

Lucy moved all round the woman, her hand sliding over the rounded back and flanks, and across the bottom. Finally, round by her head, she suddenly squatted down.

'I'll take the gag out now, because I want you to count the strokes, but if there's any trouble, it will go back, understood?'

The knickers were disentangled and laid out on the table. Lucy took up position and tapped the cane against the round cheeks. 'Ready? Count them out nice and loud.' Then she started.

Every time the cane whipped down, Mrs Ackworth's buttocks clenched up and a shiver rippled through her and by the time Lucy stopped at four to assess the marks she had made so far, the woman's thighs were trembling continuously. However, she had managed to stay in place, she had not cried out and had managed to keep the count steadily and audibly. By the second break at eight, the pattern had been established and although the wide pale cheeks were liberally printed with vivid red weals, Lucy had not the experience which was required for a bottom as well padded as this. I soon realised that Mrs Ackworth would withstand the physical ordeal with no undue difficulty although the humiliation would doubtless live with her for longer.

At twelve Lucy reached underneath to her victim's sex, and when she brought her hand out again, she showed all of us the wetness that glistened on her fingers before pushing them into Mrs Ackworth's mouth to have them licked clean.

Lucy returned to her position, tapped the cane on a white area of skin and then stopped. She went over to Alan and took him by the wrist to lead him up to the horse where Mrs Ackworth was craning round to see what was happening.

'Come up and rest your elbows on the top here, like you made me do.' Once Mrs Ackworth had obeyed and Lucy led Alan round in front of her, the rest was obvious. She unbuckled his belt, unzipped his jeans and pushed them down his legs. His pants followed and she reached in to pull out his penis, already thick and erect.

'Open your mouth, Mrs Ackworth.' Alan grinned.

'I don't do that!' she protested, but suddenly she did. Alan simply hooked his hand round the back of her head and before she had drawn breath, he had pushed between her lips and the round head of his penis was filling her mouth. Lucy picked up the cane again, paused on her way round to squeeze the swaying breasts, and then took up her position to finish the sixteen strokes.

Unable to speak now, a guttural grunt greeted each of the last four strokes; and the fifth, and the sixth, although as the seventh landed, Mrs Ackworth was clearly in real trouble. Alan was holding her head tightly. She was squealing and trying to pull away and he was wrapped in a beaming smile. He finally released her and she hung there, spitting his semen on to the ground, utterly ignorant of the last three strokes that Lucy flashed down on to her bottom while Alan reached for Mrs Ackworth's bra and used that to wipe his penis.

After Mrs Ackworth had gone, stamping off towards the cross, and Alan had gone, whistling down towards the river, we returned to the terrace and Lucy, still naked, came and curled up on my lap. I stroked her hair and her face and, because they were there, her breasts and little soft nipples. When I reached down to her soft curly bush, she opened her thighs for me, but shifted gingerly.

'Sore?' I asked.

'Not too bad. Will the marks still be there on Saturday?'

'Yes, I expect they will. Does that matter?'

'Well, I don't know what David will make of them. He's never seen me with nothing on, remember?'

Ah, yes: her wedding; her wedding night with David Palmer, not something I wanted to consider. 'You'll have to play maidenly modesty for a few days and insist on keeping the light off.'

'I don't feel very maidenly.'

'Well, you are, technically at least. You'd better be gentle with David, though, or you'll scare him off.' We stayed in silence for some while, until she took hold of my wrist to lift my hand off her breast and push it down between her legs.

'Do it once more,' she whispered.

So I slipped my fingers down the warm groove, damp already, or maybe damp still; she had come a long way. 'Do you remember your first day in this garden?'

'Yes. I was terrified.'

'You've done very well in so short a time. I just wish we'd had longer.'

'Would there be more for me to learn?'

'Oh, yes, and I believe you have quite a talent.'

'I suppose . . .' but she tailed away.

'What?'

She was still, deeply thoughtful and then gradually I felt her body tensing up beneath my fingertips, the incredible softness beneath her skin tightening in a way I hadn't known before.

'I don't know.' Her glib response was given the lie by her body. I let a few moments pass.

'What?' More circles of my fingertips. More long seconds.

'It's nice when David kisses me, strokes me. I liked it when Alan did . . . you know, those things he did. I like it now, when you're touching me.'

'But?' The question hung between us while my fingers slowly circled.

'No. Nothing.'

'Something, Lucy, and if you can't tell me, who can you tell?'

She turned awkwardly towards me, wincing when her weight was straight on her bottom but though her face was now turned upward, she didn't look at me. She grabbed my hand and pressed it hard against her soft little breast, but she couldn't quite look up, couldn't quite meet my eyes. 'But it was rather nice with Mrs Ackworth, too, so now I wonder . . .' She tailed away again.

It was more than just a guess; enough signs were showing for me to be almost certain. 'Sam?'

'I just wonder. That's all.'

'Do you think she would have come?'

'Oh, yes! She's ever so curious about you and this house and, you know, everything. She's kept asking to come.'

'You should have asked her.'

'Yes, I should. Now it's too late.' She dug her head back into my shoulder as she slid her thighs further open, and her short breaths turned to low moans.

14

Saturday

Alan had cheerfully accepted my suggestion that he act as chauffeur to collect Lucy from her home and drive round to the church. He would never have agreed to be my chauffeur – indeed, I would never have presumed to ask – but I believe he was as much in thrall to Lucy as I was. As he handed her into the car, he passed over a neat square present, beautifully wrapped and tied with a bow.

'You can open it now if you like.' His smirk gave me some misgivings that it would be coarse and tactless but I should have known better. It contained a rather grubby yellow sponge that Lucy recognised immediately. She blushed.

'Thank you, Alan.'

'You're very welcome, and if you want a hand with it at any time . . .'

'Thank you. I'll bear that in mind.'

I gave her my present then. Although I had adopted the Asian custom of giving the young couple the one thing that they most desire at that stage of their lives, money, I also had something personal for her. She unwrapped it carefully and when the last tissue paper fell away to reveal the flawless carved ivory, she blushed again at the memory of my catching her prying in my attic.

'Thank you,' she whispered.

'I hope you will treasure it always, and possibly think of me sometimes when you use it. However, if the need arises, feel free to sell it, but do so prudently. It is worth several thousand pounds if sold to the right collector.'

The wedding was magnificent. Lucy wore a traditional full-length wedding dress, pure white, as she was fully entitled to wear, and was the most glorious bride possible. The sun beamed down on us from a blue sky; the little church was packed out; the service went without a hitch; the photographers were no more banal than usual and by 3.00 p.m. the reception was in full swing. It threatened to continue the rest of the afternoon until, in the custom of modern weddings, it turned into another party to be held that evening to which many of the less intimate friends, younger work colleagues and so forth were invited. The afternoon was principally family, of which David Palmer seemed to have an unnecessarily generous supply, and Lucy a pathetic deficiency. Indeed, her mother was about all she had to offer of close family. Her father did not appear but a couple of scrawny aunts arrived, took up comfortable vantage points from where they could pour criticism on all the other guests and otherwise did not move except to send for more refreshment. The celebration was not noticeably diminished once they had dozed off.

We were in The Dolphin Hotel, a local coaching inn which had unjustified pretensions to being the grandest place in town simply on the ground of its being the only proper hotel, but it isn't a place I care for. Furthermore, I knew nobody there, except Lucy herself, the groom (with whom relations were obviously a little awkward despite his ignorance), and Sam, who was acting as bridesmaid. Sam did approach me once to offer herself in Lucy's place but seemed not entirely surprised or saddened when I declined. She quickly followed tradition and fell enthusiastically into the clutches of David's best man. Mrs Ackworth had, of necessity, been invited but had unexpectedly cancelled shortly after her visit to my house on Tuesday.

Consequently, I considered myself to be somewhat spare, and by five o'clock felt I had stayed long enough and could reasonably leave although I was unsure whether, in my capacity as father of the bride and stand-in host, I should remain. While anxious not to leave Lucy in the lurch, neither did I want to intrude in what was essentially a family occasion.

222

I was floundering in a marsh of strained small talk with her mother, a severe and unappealing woman who clearly resented my presence and influence entirely (a resentment that would have been much better warranted if she had known the work I had been putting in over the last two weeks filling out those areas of Lucy's education which she herself had left uncovered), when Lucy appeared beside us. She agreed I should leave and said she was herself going upstairs to have a short nap for an hour or so before the next stage started but would see me on my way. I said my goodbyes and it was a relief to get out into the quieter reception area. Lucy stopped there, hesitant and awkward, as was justifiable in the circumstances. Nothing in our relationship so far had prepared us for such respectable social occasions or such conventional surroundings.

'I've got a little present for you. A thank you for everything you've done for me.'

I blustered protests that it was all quite unnecessary but Lucy was not to be deterred. 'Can you come upstairs a minute? I'll give it to you up there.'

She bundled up armfuls of the flowing skirts and I followed her up the wide staircase, along the corridor to the honeymoon suite that had been arranged for the happy couple.

She held the door as I followed her in, then turned, shut it carefully and locked it. She fiddled with the key and finally drew the curtains. The light still filtered through from the setting sun and cast a muted warm glow over the room, but when she turned on the bedside lamp, a brighter circle was thrown down across the bed-head, lighting up the neatly arranged pillows, bedspreads and canopy over the bridal bed.

'This is our last day together, Mr Mortensen, but my period of repayment is over and this is my wedding day so today you have to do what I tell you. Agreed?'

I smiled and accepted her little game. I could not think what kind of present she would have bought me, only that I would treasure it whatever it turned out to be.

'Right, then. Sit in that chair.' I duly obeyed. 'And stay there.' She stepped back into the middle of the room, reached back behind her and I heard the unmistakable rasp of a zip.

Whoever designed wedding dresses knew what they were doing: so many layers of silk, of underskirts, of gauze. So many flimsy barriers, frustratingly semi-opaque and irresistibly semi-transparent. The process of their removal was so agonisingly slow, so protracted and, although I had watched her undress so often over the last two weeks, still so magical. Yet that dress carries so much symbolism, an emblem of innocence, worn only once when that innocence is to be surrendered to another person. On this, the final time that I would be treated to the sight of her nakedness, it was both exquisite and appropriate that the offering should start from so formal and elaborate a costume.

We neither of us spoke – we never had during these rituals – but I took in every fleeting glimpse of a bare arm, of her shoulders, her back and, when the dress was finally lifted over her head, her long white stockings, traditional blue garters hugging her thighs and then the short stretch of bare skin between the stocking tops and satin knickers. The garters slid down, the stockings scraped over the downy skin to reveal the elegant little feet and wriggling toes which – I immediately realised and lamented – I had all but ignored during the past two weeks and which I would never now be entitled to touch or explore or kiss.

The bra too was white, a plain satin, slightly padded in honour of the day, and this quickly joined the pile on her bed before she turned to me, dressed now in only the one remaining item. In spite of all that had happened over the last days, she was still shy and clenched her hands under her chin, leaving the little pink nipples to peer out from the crook of each elbow. For a minute she stayed still, then dropped her hands away and clasped them behind her back; completely uncovered now, she was mine to admire again.

'Come here.' She sidled up to stand in front of me and to allow me one last time to take the waistband of her knickers between forefinger and thumb and slide them down her long willowy legs, and to inhale their sweet scent.

Then she climbed up on to the bed before turning and lying back like some artist's model to offer herself quite naked to my inspection.

The purity of her skin was still breathtaking: not a blemish, not a mole, not a scar anywhere. She was as perfect as a new-born baby. Her round breasts sagged slightly to the sides, the nipples soft and sleeping, and they rose and fell with every light breath. Her legs were towards me, the thighs parted just enough to show the downy lips nestling between them. The direction of my gaze must have been clear, for as I watched, she moved her thighs steadily further open until they were spread out wide, to present my final view of the unopened treasure she had guarded so carefully until this day.

For some minutes neither of us spoke; I sat on the bed at her feet and lightly stroked her legs as I gazed down on her and she in turn stared back at me. At last, after two weeks' labour, the shy smile on her face now contained more pride in her nakedness than embarrassment.

Finally her tongue appeared and ran once round her lips. 'You know I promised I would stay a virgin until I was married, Mr Mortensen.'

'Yes, my dear, and very commendable of you.'

'Well, I am married now, so I don't need to stay one any longer. We have at least an hour before anyone will come for me, so I want you to have my present. It's the only thing I have that I can offer you.' With that, she simply lay back on the bed and opened her arms to me. I was speechless; gazed down on her eager face, her delicate breasts and there, directly in front of me, the open thighs, pink folds, slightly parted lips, softly covered nib, all waiting for me.

I was completely overwhelmed not just in surprise but by the richness of her gift. She had prized and guarded this honour for so long; today was the day that she should share it with her new husband and yet she was offering it to me. I sat and gazed at her in wonder.

'Lucy, I am honoured more that I can say, but I feel that is too valuable a present for you to give me. I really do not feel I should take that. After all, I too made a promise when you came to me: I promised not to take that from you, nor press you to surrender it nor allow anyone else to penetrate your vagina. That should be for your husband alone and today you should give it to him.'

'Rubbish!' I smiled at her bluntness. 'You will appreciate it more than he would, and besides, he can think he has had it and be perfectly happy. Where's the harm? No, Mr Mortensen, I have thought about this carefully and I am certain that I want you to have it. That was really my reason for asking you to be here to give me away today.'

So I weakened and, for the first time in our acquaintance, the tables were turned and Lucy watched while I undressed. Finally I lay down beside her and cherished the feeling of so much of her naked skin in contact with my own. Then I began to kiss her. I am sure her fiancé – now husband – had kissed her and would doubtless kiss her again, but I was not sure he had done so enough. What can any boy of his age understand of the wealth of possibilities that are to be found by those who take the time and trouble to search? Such knowledge comes only from experience and the best teachers, so if Lucy was now bound to this man for her life, she deserved as much as I could offer in the short hour we had.

I kissed her: her mouth, her cheeks, her neck, her ears, her eyes. I kissed her lightly downed arms and her damp armpits and of course her velvet stomach and soft breasts, finally using my tongue to lift up the little peaks that I had admired and that had tantalised me for so long. And in time I moved on to the neatly trimmed down of her pubic hair and kissed her there, inhaling at last her unique scent direct from its source.

I buried my face between her thighs and swept great laps along the length of those full, floppy lips, sucking them right into my mouth, pushing them round with my tongue and nipping as she sighed and squealed and giggled somewhere above me. I dug the tip of my tongue beneath the loose hood of her clitoris and she squirmed away, frightened by the intensity of so direct a contact. It too rose

226

beneath my lapping and the flavour of the region changed perceptibly from the delicious tang of a long sweaty day to the sweet intimacy of an anticipated evening. Damp turned to moist; moist turned to wet; wet turned to flowing and I was drinking of that sweet juice that, at last, in expectation of pleasures to come, was now running with unabashed confidence. I suckled like a baby at the breast, licking around the outside of her plump lips and right down the full length of her crease. At the top her clitoris pushed forward, eager for the same attention. At the bottom, the juice gathered enticingly at the entrance to her innocence. Like a gift in a doorway it beckoned passers-by.

'Do you use tampons, Lucy?' I asked.

She peered down at me, embarrassed again, blushing crimson in terrified soul-searching at what dreadful evidence I could have found to raise such a question.

'Yes.'

So she would have no trace of a hymen: I really wasn't depriving her husband of anything.

'I just wanted to be sure.' I dipped my head back down and slid my tongue as far as ever it would reach up inside the tight channel which I had never thought to enter at all. She opened to me at once, her thighs spreading wider, her fingers toying with my hair and the lightest faintest mewing whispering round the shadowy room. So full and unmistakable an invitation could not be entirely refused, for though I still hesitated to accept her gift in full, I could not refuse her entirely. Where would be the gallantry in that?

So I finally succumbed and slipped a single finger into the little place, sliding over the ridges as her muscles automatically opened to allow their first visitor and as automatically closed to hold me there. She sighed, a long deep breath rising from deep in her soul, and I glanced up to find her eyes tight shut and a smile of tranquil pleasure and confidence on her lips at this, her first penetration.

I wanted more, and had her turn over on to her hands and knees where I could pull her up and lick the whole length of her crease right from her fluffy pubic bush to her spine. The first sweeps passed lightly down the central crease, floating over the most sensitive little rose, and Lucy moaned in either shame or frustration, trying to wriggle round to present her vulva nearer to me. I could not deny her request entirely and licked her there again, once more digging into the deep folds of her vagina and further, circling the impatient nib of her clitoris, but even as I did so I was tempted again. Her vagina was gaping open in earnest need; it was untouched, would be sweet and tight and divine. Just above that her bottom was closed tight, glistening in the meagre light, but looking so small and well sealed that only a saint could have resisted. The little claws of that devil dug once more into my shoulder.

I turned her over again, spread her open on her back, and she pulled herself up to see, encountering for her first time a man with an erect penis that was about to penetrate her. She grinned at the sight and threw herself backward again, so I lifted her legs and then went down to lick her again, to wet her, relax her, open her and prepare her. She needed very little and if, as she said, she had planned this in her mind for many days, presumably her body had been preparing for this for many hours. Her sighs were starting to turn from excitement and desire to frustration, so I eased away at last, moved up her and finally lay the head of my penis at her entrance. Though she clamped up automatically, she quickly relaxed again and I slid deep inside.

She sighed and giggled, hugged me closer to her and tucked her legs up behind me, urging a steady movement whose inevitable result would finally make her a complete woman. Yet I had other plans and although I was filling her tight, I brought her hand down between us where she needed no further encouragement to toy with the little nib and gurgle in delight at the wealth of stimulation. Between her own caresses, further fondling of her eager nipples and the steady rhythm of a new sensation of being filled, she soon climaxed enthusiastically, wildly and loudly, crying out as it all became too much and she hugged me and wrapped herself into me and voiced endearments that she can't have known she knew and finally wept as the richness of the experience broke over her and embraced her. Afterwards she was delightfully embarrassed as she wiped her eyes and said she'd only been laughing so I told her I realised that. I was still buried deep inside her and when she had relaxed a little she urged me to carry on and to fill her. I did continue for a little longer, because she was clearly ready for more, but I said we still had plenty of time and then I eased out of her again, turned her over on hands and knees again and returned to lick her open crease.

Her vulva was now relaxed, loose and open, the lips still puffed and welcoming, and although I did kiss her there, drawing in her lips and suckling and chewing on them, I soon left that again. I moved my focus a fraction along the crease to concentrate once more on the crease of her bottom, licking and pressing and probing. From time to time, I drifted back to her vagina, but always kept returning to the other little puckered mouth, the one where Lucy found my attentions so mortifying so that, when I finally succeeded, despite her shrieked protests and opposition, in sliding my tongue in there too, she fell forward with a sigh of outraged delight.

She tasted bitter, naturally, but it was such a savoury enchanting bitterness that I lapped deeper and harder until, minute by minute, she relaxed and my entrance became easier until I found that the full length of my tongue was reaching in. Even so, it needed easing more yet if I was to take the prize on which I had set my sights.

I could have lost myself in that bottom; my tongue had now cleaned it as completely as it could be and the little ring was now so accustomed to my probing that when I lightly laid the ball of my thumb right on its centre and pressed, it was learning to relax readily to allow me entry. I had reached that point when I heard Lucy's worried voice, muffled by the pillow.

'Mr Mortensen?'

'Yes, my dear?'

'Are you . . . ?' She stopped. Nothing in her experience or her knowledge, nothing in her dreams or her fears had prepared her for this or even provided the words to ask about it. She tried again. 'You aren't going to do anything in my bottom, are you?'

But she knew the answer and turned to face me, scrabbling round on the bed to consider the erection that she was being asked to fit. She looked at it, her face creasing up as she took in the length, the width and the determination. Gingerly she reached out a hand and wrapped her fingers round me.

'I don't think you can. I mean, I'm sure it wouldn't fit. That's far too big.'

I stroked her hair. 'It'll fit.'

She was still holding my shaft but her hands had already taken up a slow, gentle rhythm. 'It might hurt me – you know, damage me.'

'It will hurt, certainly, but no damage, I promise you.'

She looked up at me, uncertain, but desperate to trust me and to please me, then back at the danger she was still nursing in her small fist.

'Shall I wet it, then?'

She didn't wait for my answer but her head bobbed down and her lips encircled me, only a very slight suction but the tongue working round with as delicate a touch as I have ever known. Eventually she released me and turned round again, silently presenting herself for whatever I chose to do.

I leant forward to press my tongue inside again; the defence was half-hearted. I tried a finger, but the resistance to this was more determined and it took some working before, with a little cry from the other end of the bed, I was through the initial ring and able to feel the deep corrugations surrounding me within. I withdrew the finger entirely, waited a moment and pressed in again. It was easier this time.

So now the real thing. I pressed the point of my penis against the centre of the little wrinkles and pressed. I got in no more than half an inch before, with a sudden yelp from Lucy, her muscles automatically clamped up and expelled me. A second try made a little more progress, and although it produced an even louder cry, I was able to keep the ground made and press in a little further before pulling

230

out again. After this she turned round to me again, the tears already running down her cheeks.

'I'll try wetting you again.' She took the head of my erection back in her mouth and licked one great circuit before taking it out and staring up with exhilaration shining through the tears. 'I can taste my bottom!'

'How does it taste?' But she didn't answer me, just grinned broadly and plopped it back in her mouth before continuing to lick with as much enthusiasm as ever she had.

When she turned round to let me try again, I knew that further gentleness would not be kind. I started her briefly with a finger but when that entered without undue resistance, I lay the head against the centre of her puckered wrinkles, felt her relax a little and with one push entered deep inside. She screamed out and collapsed on to her stomach with me lying on top of her, not moving at first, just holding her there as she became accustomed to the novelty, to the stretching and to the pain. She whimpered, squirming a little and then lying still because moving hurt, but then squirming again because staying still hurt just as much. Each time she wriggled, I struggled to stay inside her; each time she lay still, I pushed a little further in. She felt unbearably hot, impossibly tight and gloriously alive. Every push produced another cry and another moan that was beginning to turn from resistance to welcome, from pain to pleasure.

At last I was so deep inside that my stomach was pressed against the straining cheeks of her bottom, and I was there. The struggle was over and occupation was glorious, but invasion had been better, and would be almost as memorable in repetition. Gently I withdrew, inch by inch, feeling her bottom contract around me as I pulled until finally, with a sigh of frustration or desire, I reached the mouth and the tight little ring closed behind me. She had been unprepared for this, and looking down, my penis bore the marks of its passage so I pulled her round again, took her hair in my hands and offered myself up to her mouth again.

For a moment she hesitated, repulsed by the presentation and the knowledge of where it had just been, but I drew her closer and pressed it to her lips until finally she allowed me in and her tongue, at first slowly but with growing enthusiasm, lapped me round, circling the head, sweeping the shaft in steady strokes until I was impatient to return.

She swivelled round once more, dropped down on to her elbows and lifted up the neat round cheeks of her bottom and the taut little rose of her anus.

The entrance was a little easier this time. She relaxed as far as she could and I was wetter so that I was able to press in, fraction by fraction, until I was again tight against her. She sighed, but it turned to a giggle.

'This is the rudest thing I can imagine. Just wait till I tell Sam.'

'Lucy, it isn't usual for a woman to discuss with her friends the discoveries and experiences of her wedding night. Especially if they have not been made with her husband.'

She giggled again, sending a tightening ripple running through her whole body that squeezed me dangerously. 'She'll be ever so jealous.'

I gave up and reached round to fondle her round breasts, nursing each of the compact little handfuls and pulling the pale nipples up into peaks. When I moved on down to ruffle through her pubic hair, I found her fingers already in place, so I lightly covered her hand with my own as she continued working herself onward.

'Are you getting used to this now, Lucy?'

'What? Having you in my bottom? No!'

'No, I meant playing with yourself.'

'It's very nice. Anyway, I've got a lot of time to make up.'

I let her continue, working gently in and out of her bottom while she steadily relaxed, becoming more slippery, more accommodating and more vocal. She was also becoming a great deal more lively, squirming and writhing as her thighs clamped greedily on her hands and she pressed her bottom back against my hips and pressed her breasts forward into my hands. Soon she was twisting and turning so much, I could no longer stay inside her. When her twisting pushed me out a third time, she was as frustrated as I was. She reached up for the pillow, and jammed it under her stomach, then she lay face down on that, spread wide her legs and buried her face in the mattress.

Her words were muffled. 'Do it now, and do it hard.'

Entry was easy now, and she even lifted up her hips to welcome me except that in this position penetration was deeper than ever and she squealed as I pushed right in. Her hands had worked back underneath her and from time to time I felt her fingers brushing against me as they stroked long sweeps of joy along her lips. Through the thin separation I even felt her own fingers reaching deep inside herself when her exploration became still bolder.

Yet I had a succession of past days to pay for. Days of seeing her, watching her, hearing her, even smelling her. Once or twice touching her, but never like this, never experiencing everything that her enthusiastic inexperience had to offer, and now it was all available to me, all offered, all given and accepted. She had spread herself down and open, and when I could no longer keep my self-control, and I knew that my determination was causing her pain so that every thrust ended with a scream spilled out into the mattress, it was too late to stop. I ploughed on and emptied myself as deep into her as I could, a glorious culmination of years of experience, months of celibacy and days of frustration. She screamed again, but this time the scream turned to a gurgle of delight as her own fingers finally produced the release that every bride deserves and normally expects to receive in the arms of her husband.

I didn't stay with her. I washed and dressed then tucked her in, pausing only to drop one last kiss on each sleeping nipple, on her hidden clitoris and succulent vagina, on the centre of each smooth round cheek of her bottom and, of course, on the damp little star that I had desired for so long and whose potential she had never considered. Then

233

I pulled the sheets round her shoulders and crept out. She was not asleep, but it suited us both to pretend she was.

Downstairs, I slid past the dining room where the disco was just starting, slipped out into the fading evening light and turned for home. A light drizzle was starting to fall.

Epilogue

November

The nights are darker now, and longer too, while the days are shorter, colder and bleaker through my house and sorrowful garden. Winter seems to have descended this year with an announced intention to stay for a long time, if not forever. I rattle around here on my own and wonder whether the glorious energy of that early summer can ever be resurrected or whether it is really time that I sold this place and moved on. At first I continued taking coffee in the Castlegate Tearooms from time to time, but Lucy had stopped working there on the day she was married; Sam was embarrassed and barely acknowledged me and I began to suspect that even Mrs Ackworth was avoiding me. Eventually I found the visits becoming more of a frustration than a pleasure so I gave up going. In all the months since Lucy's last visit here, I have only once caught a glimpse of her: just the top of her head bobbing about on the other side of the street as she hurried along with all that young determination and enthusiasm which I had so much enjoyed.

Only this morning, I happened to be in the area, visiting my old friend Duncan McQuillan, who is in full flow with his investigation of the Markham diaries. When I stepped out from the castle gate, the north wind was pushing in down the collar of my coat, the air was sharp and unforgiving and I felt in deep need of some comfort. Next to the gate-house stood the familiar ramshackle Tudor building, its lights glowing warm and beckoning through the gloom of a miserable dank day. So, just for old time's sake, and for the friendly cheer of a cup of coffee and a toasted tea-cake, I thought I would look in and see who might be there.

I ducked in through the low door and quickly scanned the room; only one table was taken by customers, a trio of earnest women locked in earnest conversation, but at the tinkling of the bell a little figure pushed through from the kitchen and suddenly there she was again: Lucy was peering at me over the counter. She looked as startled to see me as I was to see her and although she blushed as prettily as ever she had, I swear that her little face brightened just a touch.

She hurried over to show me to a comfortable little table in the corner by the open fire, and she fussed around me and took my coat and hung it to dry and smiled and asked how I was and what was my news and I felt warmed again.

It was excellent, the coffee, as was the tea-cake and I was working my way through *The Times* crossword when she sidled up to my table.

'I'm very sorry to trouble you, Mr Mortensen, only I remember you don't like the paper napkins, so I've brought you one of our special ones.' Here she paused, and pushed a small bundle of white nylon into my hand, a warm, fragrant and slightly damp bundle. She blushed again, hesitated and then her words tumbled out in a great rush.

'The thing is, David and I have separated. I know it's wrong and we weren't together for very long, but it just wasn't working. He's just such a baby, and he didn't want me to do any of the things I wanted. Maybe it was like you said – I scared him off. Anyway, that is all over, but I want a new life now. I'm going to go to university next year. I've already been accepted but I need to get a proper job, not just messing about in this place, and my mother says I can't stay living with her because she's so ashamed of me leaving David and everyone at the church says I should have stayed with him. So . . .'

She paused before the final rush. 'So I wondered if you knew of anywhere I could live or work or anything. I mean, I know I have been neglecting you recently, and I really am very sorry, but you know so many people and I wondered if you would help me.' She stopped for another breath. 'Perhaps I could come round to your house this afternoon and I could make you some tea, you know like we used to have, and you would consider it? Please?'

I agreed, of course I agreed, and I even managed to put up something like a show of careful consideration as if these were not the sweetest words I could possibly hear, but still she didn't leave me even though the three women at the other table were calling for their bill.

'Is there something else, Lucy?'

She glanced round. 'Do you remember Sam, who used to work here? Well, I wondered if she could come too, because she's always been ever so curious about you. Would that be all right?'

I have made up the fire in the sitting room, a roaring blaze of all those logs she so laboriously restacked for me at the start of the summer, and I've shaken out the thick-pile Persian rug that looks so inviting spread in front of the fire. She should be here any moment. Ah, I do believe that is the doorbell now.

Historical Notes

Chapter 5

The carvings were not in fact destroyed but have recently been rediscovered. It appears that Sir Samuel Baldwyn moved them to his home in Shropshire around the middle of the seventeenth century where they have remained since. Now in the care of English Heritage, the panels depicting Anne standing naked in her harness and her sister beside her are on view to this day.

Chapter 10

The tawse remains in the author's private collection and is not accessible to public view. The inscription is *'Al Mio Signore Tuono. Sempre Il Mio Maestro. Natale 1799'* which may be translated as 'To My Lord Thunder. My Master Ever. Christmas 1799'. Charles Greville's papers have never been published and remain in the family. Greville first met Emma (then calling herself Emma Hart although she was born Emily Lyon) when she was staying at the country house of a friend of his, Sir Harry Fetherstonehaugh, but Emma became pregnant, possibly by Greville, and she was thrown out, attaching herself to Greville. When he subsequently wanted to get married, he tried to get rid of her and the letters between him and his uncle, Sir William Hamilton, then envoy to the Court of Naples, discuss their plan to transfer the girl's affections from the nephew to the uncle. Greville's recommendation to his uncle was based, in part, on the fact that 'she takes the strap more willingly than any girl I have known'.

After her marriage to Sir William, Emma became notorious for her 'attitudes' which, with the enthusiastic encouragement of her husband and later also of Horatio Nelson, she presented at many gatherings and dinners. These 'attitudes' entailed her adopting a sequence of poses, many based on Greek or Roman mythology, in which she was either partially or entirely naked, or sometimes draped in muslin. She would remain entirely motionless for several minutes while the other guests were invited to view, as closely as they wished, and to marvel, but on several occasions guests reported that her poses revealed signs of severe whippings.

NEW BOOKS

Coming up from Nexus and Black Lace

Captive by Aishling Moran

4 January 2001   £5.99   ISBN 0 352 33585 8

Set in the same world of nubile girls, cruel men and rampant goblins as its prequel, *Maiden*, *Captive* follows the tribulations of the maid, Aisla, as she endeavours to free her mistress Sulitea from a life of drudgery and punishment, only to find her less than grateful. As she struggles to return home with Sulitea, they must overcome numerous men, trolls and yet worse beasts, and when Aisla is taken prisoner in foreign lands, it is her turn to escape, or else face a humiliating public execution.

Soldier Girls by Yolanda Celbridge

4 January 2001   £5.99   ISBN 0 352 33586 6

Stripped of her uniform for 'sexual outrage', soldier-nurse Lise Gallard is forced to endure corporal punishment in the Foreign legion women's prison. But she is spotted there by dominatrix Dr Crevasse, who engineers Lise's release for her own flagellant purposes. Can Lise hope to escape her cruel mistress? Or will she in turn learn to wield the cane?

Eroticon 1 ed. J-P Spencer

4 January 2001   £5.99   ISBN 0 352 33593 9

A Nexus Classic unavailable for some time; a selection of a dozen of the most exhilerating excerpts from rare and once-forbidden works of erotic literature. They range from the work of the French poet Guillaume Apollinaire to the most explicit sexual confession of the Edwardian era – Walter's *My Secret Life*.

Angel by Lindsay Gordon

8 February 2001   £5.99   0 352 33590 4

Angel is a Companion. He has sold his freedom for access to a world inhabited by the most ambitious, beautiful – and sometimes cruel – women imaginable: an executive who demands to be handled by a stranger in uniform; a celebrity who adores rope and wet under-things; a doctor who lives her secret life inside tight rubber skins. And it's not Angel's place to refuse.

Tie and Tease by Penny Birch

8 February 2001   £5.99   0 352 33591 2

Caught by a total stranger, Beth, while playing the fox in a bizarre hunting game, Penny finds herself compromised by Beth's failure to understand her submissive sexuality. Penny is determined to seduce the girl, but her efforts get her into more and more difficulty, involving ever more frequent punishments and humiliations until, turned on a roasting spit, she is unsure how much more even she can take.

Eroticon 2 ed. J-P Spencer

8 February 2001   £5.99   0 352 33594 7

Like its companion volumes, a sample of excerpts from rare and once-forbidden works of erotic literature. Spanning three centuries, it ranges from Andrea de Nericat's eighteenth century *The Pleasures of Lolotte* to the Edwardian tale *Maudie*.

Man Hunt by Cathleen Ross   £5.99

4 January 2001   £5.99   ISBN 0 352 33583 1

Angie's a driven woman when it comes to her career in hotel
management, but also when it comes to the men she chooses to
pursue – for Angie's on a man hunt. For sexy, challenging men. For
men like devilishly attractive but manipulative James Steele, who
runs the hotel training course. When she turns her attention to one
of her fellow students, Steele's determined to assume the dominant
position and get her interest back. This time it's Steele who's the
predator and Angie the prey.

Dreaming Spires by Juliet Hastings

4 January 2001   £5.99   ISBN 0 352 33584 X

Catherine de la Tour has been awarded an assignment as writer-in-
residence at a Cambridge college but her lover James is a thousand
miles away and she misses him badly. Although her position promises
peace and quiet, she becomes immersed in a sea of sexual hedonism,
as the rarefield hothouse of academia proves to be a fertile
environment for passion and raunchy lust.

Ménage by Emma Holly

4 January 2001   £5.99   ISBN 0 352 33231 X

Bookstore owner Kate comes home from work one day to find her
two flatmates in bed together. Joe – a sensitive composer – is
mortified. Sean – an irrepressible bad boy – asks her to join in. As
they embark on a polysexual ménage à trois, Kate wants nothing
more than to keep both her admirers happy. However, things become
complicated. Kate has told everyone that Sean is gay, but now he and
Kate are acting like lovers. Can the three of them live happily ever
after – together? This is a Black Lace special reprint.

Stella Does Hollywood by Stella Black
8 February 2001   £5.99   0 352 33588 2
Stella, fur-clad heroine of *Shameless*, returns to romp through the wilder reaches of California. On meeting an old acquaintance and finding he's now the chief of the largest adult entertainment empire in the USA, Stella plunges head-first into a career as a porn star, only to cause more trouble than even she bargained for. Settling down with cowgirl girlfriend Kitten to a life on the range seems like a good idea. But, for a girl like Stella, maybe in trouble's the place to be after all.

Up to No Good by Karen S. Smith
8 February 2001   £5.99   0 352 33589 0
Emma is resigned to attending her cousin's wedding, expecting the usual round of relatives and bad dancing. Instead she meets Kit: it's a passionate encounter, the kind that don't usually get repeated. But her current flame Geoff is not the jealous type, as she discovers when she bumps into Kit again unexpectedly. Over the course of one turbulent year, and two further weddings, she learns that they don't have to be such dull affairs after all.

Darker Than Love by Kristina Lloyd
8 February 2001   £5.99   0 352 33279 4
It's 1875 and the morals of Queen Victoria mean nothing to London's wayward elite. Young, beautiful Clarissa Longleigh is visiting London for the first time. Eager to meet Lord Marldon, the man to whom she is promised, she knows only that he is tall, dark and sophisticated. He is in fact depraved and louche, with a taste for sexual excess. Can Clarissa escape him, and the desires he wakes within her? A Black Lace special reprint.

Nexus

NEXUS BACKLIST

All books are priced £5.99 unless another price is given. If a date is supplied, the book in question will not be available until that month in 2000.

CONTEMPORARY EROTICA

THE BLACK MASQUE	Lisette Ashton	
THE BLACK WIDOW	Lisette Ashton	
THE BOND	Lindsay Gordon	
BRAT	Penny Birch	
BROUGHT TO HEEL	Arabella Knight	July
DANCE OF SUBMISSION	Lisette Ashton	
DISCIPLES OF SHAME	Stephanie Calvin	
DISCIPLINE OF THE PRIVATE HOUSE	Esme Ombreux	
DISCIPLINED SKIN	Wendy Swanscombe	Nov
DISPLAYS OF EXPERIENCE	Lucy Golden	
AN EDUCATION IN THE PRIVATE HOUSE	Esme Ombreux	Aug
EMMA'S SECRET DOMINATION	Hilary James	
GISELLE	Jean Aveline	
GROOMING LUCY	Yvonne Marshall	Sept
HEART OF DESIRE	Maria del Rey	
HOUSE RULES	G.C. Scott	
IN FOR A PENNY	Penny Birch	
LESSONS OF OBEDIENCE	Lucy Golden	Dec
ONE WEEK IN THE PRIVATE HOUSE	Esme Ombreux	
THE ORDER	Nadine Somers	
THE PALACE OF EROS	Delver Maddingley	
PEEPING AT PAMELA	Yolanda Celbridge	Oct
PLAYTHING	Penny Birch	

SAMPLERS & COLLECTIONS

NEW EROTICA 3		
NEW EROTICA 5		Nov
A DOZEN STROKES	Various	

NEXUS CLASSICS
A new imprint dedicated to putting the finest works of erotic fiction back in print

AGONY AUNT	G. C. Scott	
THE HANDMAIDENS	Aran Ashe	
OBSESSION	Maria del Rey	
HIS MISTRESS'S VOICE	G.C. Scott	
CITADEL OF SERVITUDE	Aran Ashe	
BOUND TO SERVE	Amanda Ware	
SISTERHOOD OF THE INSTITUTE	Maria del Rey	
A MATTER OF POSSESSION	G.C. Scott	
THE PLEASURE PRINCIPLE	Maria del Rey	
CONDUCT UNBECOMING	Arabella Knight	
CANDY IN CAPTIVITY	Arabella Knight	
THE SLAVE OF LIDIR	Aran Ashe	
THE DUNGEONS OF LIDIR	Aran Ashe	
SERVING TIME	Sarah Veitch	July
THE TRAINING GROUNDS	Sarah Veitch	Aug
DIFFERENT STROKES	Sarah Veitch	Sept
LINGERING LESSONS	Sarah Veitch	Oct
EDEN UNVEILED	Maria del Rey	Nov
UNDERWORLD	Maria del Rey	Dec

Please send me the books I have ticked above.

Name   ....

Address   ....

          ....

          ....

          .... Post code........................

Send to: Cash Sales, Nexus Books, Thames Wharf Studios, Rainville Road, London W6 9HA

US customers: for prices and details of how to order books for delivery by mail, call 1-800-805-1083.

Please enclose a cheque or postal order, made payable to **Nexus Books**, to the value of the books you have ordered plus postage and packing costs as follows:

UK and BFPO – £1.00 for the first book, 50p for the second book and 30p for each subsequent book to a maximum of £3.00;

Overseas (including Republic of Ireland) – £2.00 for the first book, £1.00 for the second book and 50p for each subsequent book.

We accept all major credit cards, including VISA, ACCESS/ MASTERCARD, AMEX, DINERS CLUB, SWITCH, SOLO, and DELTA. Please write your card number and expiry date here:

....

Please allow up to 28 days for delivery.

Signature ....